In all her life, Catherine had never seen such a beautiful man.

Luke's body was hard, his muscles taut and long, but it was the look in his eyes that she would never forget. She held up her arms, welcoming him to her bed.

"I don't expect you to promise me something you can't give," she said. "Just know that for now...for me...this is enough."

He stood above her, imprinting her image in his mind. Her flat belly and slender waist that flared into the woman-shape of her hips. Black hair fanning out on the pillow beneath her head. She watched him from under heavy lashes, her lips slack with desire.

"No, Catherine, this will never be enough."

DINAH MCCALL

THE
RETURN

ISBN 1-55166-584-0

THE RETURN

Copyright © 2000 by Sharon Sala.

All rights reserved. Except for use in any review, the reproduction or
utilization of this work in whole or in part in any form by any electronic,
mechanical or other means, now known or hereafter invented, including
xerography, photocopying and recording, or in any information storage or
retrieval system, is forbidden without the written permission of the publisher,
MIRA Books, 225 Duncan Mill Road, Don Mills, Ontario, Canada M3B 3K9.

All characters in this book have no existence outside the imagination of the
author and have no relation whatsoever to anyone bearing the same name
or names. They are not even distantly inspired by any individual known or
unknown to the author, and all incidents are pure invention.

MIRA and the Star Colophon are trademarks used under license and registered
in Australia, New Zealand, Philippines, United States Patent and Trademark
Office and in other countries.

Visit us at www.mirabooks.com

Printed In U.S.A.

Home is supposed to be a place of comfort, and of safety—and of peace. But for some, that's not always the case. Home is sometimes a place that you need to escape.

Home is the place that builds our character and the place that tears it down. And sometimes, even in leaving, you will be drawn to it in your dreams.

The yearning that leads us back to our roots is inherent. Because it was the first way of life that we knew, it is the place that shapes our hearts.

The inevitable parting that comes as we each "leave the nest" can be bittersweet or a matter of sanity. Torn between the excitement of life on our own and the pain of leaving loved ones behind, we often hurt those we love best.

Regret can cripple your life, leaving you with nothing on which to focus but the past. It's only when you find the strength to return and face your errors that the healing begins.

This book is dedicated to the brave ones— the ones who aren't afraid to go home.

1

Rural Kentucky, 1973

The night was cold—the moon full. A faint hint of wood smoke stirred in the air, while tortured shadows lay upon the decaying forest floor like puddles of spilled ink.

On a nearby hill, a cougar slipped between an outcropping of rocks on his way to his lair, dragging his prey as he went. Tomorrow, a farmer would find his best goat had gone missing, while down in the valley below, animals of the dark abounded. The night seemed no different from any other as they scurried about, intent upon the simplistic routine of their existence. Then, without warning, everything stilled.

A raccoon paused at a creek bank, tilting his head toward the forest behind him before dropping the minnow he had been about to eat and shinnying up a nearby tree. A fox, who had been lying outside her burrow letting her kits nurse, suddenly bolted to her feet and hustled them back inside. An owl abruptly took to the air from a nearby tree, moving through the forest on silent wings. On the heels of his flight, a primordial shriek shattered the silence, hanging on the air like mist, then echoing within the valley.

Over a mile away, and on another mountain, a woman up tending to her sick child heard the faint cry and shuddered as she glanced toward the partially opened window. Even though she knew it was most likely a cougar, the similarity between that sound and a woman's scream was all too eerie— especially at this time of night. She pulled the covers back over her child, then walked to the window and pushed it the rest of the way shut.

Back down in the valley, another cry followed the first, weaker in intensity, but more distinct in sound. There was no mistaking it for that of an animal. It was the cry of a newborn baby, shocked by the abruptness of its entry into the world.

Flames from the campfire burning at the back of the cave flickered weakly, shedding little light on the drama playing out within the cavernous depths. A thin column of smoke spiraled upward, escaping through a small hole in the high domed ceiling, forming a natural chimney. It dissipated without notice in the outside air.

Nineteen-year-old Fancy Joslin lay only a few

feet from the fire on a makeshift cot. The last spasms of childbirth had passed, leaving her weak and weary. Cradling her newborn child upon her belly, she cleaned the babe and herself as best she could. She wouldn't let herself think of the lack of sanitation in which her child had been born. For now it was enough that they had both survived.

A suitcase near the mouth of the cave held all of her worldly goods. It wasn't what she'd planned to take to her home as a bride, but it would have to do. All of the Joslin heirlooms that should have been hers had burned up over a month ago in the fire that destroyed their home. She couldn't prove it, any more than her family had been able to prove any of their losses over the past one hundred years, but in her heart, she blamed Jubal Blair.

Uncle Frank was dead because of him. They'd called it an accident, but everyone knew it was just part of the ongoing feud between the Joslins and the Blairs. And, truth be told, over the years, the Joslins had done their fair share of keeping the hate between the two families alive. There were plenty of Blairs resting six feet below the rich Kentucky earth who could attribute their passing to an angry Joslin.

Even in Fancy's lifetime, she'd heard the men in her family talking about things that they'd done in the name of justice, but there wasn't anything fair about a feud. It was revenge, pure and simple.

She rolled her baby up into a blanket, then set her jaw. It did no good thinking about the hate that had destroyed her family and, ultimately, her home. As long as Joslins and Blairs still lived on the mountain, it would continue.

And that was the reason she was in hiding. She was the last of the Joslins, but she would not risk her life or her child's by staying in this place any longer.

With a weary sigh, she lay back on the pillow. In a way, she'd already fallen victim to a Blair. Turner. But not in the way Jubal would have imagined. She couldn't remember a time when she hadn't loved Turner Blair. But it was only after she got pregnant that panic set in. This was a secret she wouldn't be able to hide forever. Turner's joy in the news had lessened her fears, and when he'd insisted on a moonlight wedding ceremony beneath the overhang of Pulpit Rock, Fancy's anxiety had lessened even more. The fact that it had been less than proper hadn't mattered to either of them. In their hearts, they were man and wife.

And they'd made plans to run.

But then Turner's mother had taken sick. Running away in the midst of her last days had been more than he could do. So they'd waited. And they'd waited. It had taken Esther Blair six months to die, and with each passing month, Fancy Joslin's condition had become more and more apparent. Her uncle Frank had been shocked and then incensed, demanding each day for her to name the man who'd wronged her. But giving up Turner's name would have been the end of them both, so she'd remained silent, suffering Uncle Frank's condemnation instead.

And then came the fire. After that, she'd been certain that Turner would come and take her away. He'd come, all right, but not as she'd expected. He'd hidden her in this cave, asking her to trust him for a few days. He had some money coming to him from a job he'd just finished and they would need it when they left. Telling him no was impossible, which was most of the reason she was in the shape she was in. So, two months from delivery, she hid. But the days had turned into weeks, and now it was too late.

Weak and aching from the trauma of the birth, Fancy raised up on one elbow, looking at her baby through a blur of angry tears, then fell back onto the makeshift cot, clutching the child against her belly. Damn Jubal Blair. She and Turner should have been in Memphis by now.

The baby's weak cry stopped her thoughts. She raised herself up again in sudden panic. But the baby had stopped crying and her eyes were fixed upon the dancing shadows of the dwindling fire. Fancy stroked the tiny head and the cap of thick black hair, marveling at the sheer perfection of her and Turner's love. Her sweet Kentucky drawl broke the silence in the cave.

"You listen to me, baby girl. Your daddy and I are going to get you out of here. I swear on my life that you will not be raised in this hate."

The baby turned toward the sound of her mother's voice, as she must have done many times within the womb. Fancy's heart contracted with a sweet ache she wouldn't have believed. With shaking hands, she traced the shape of the baby's face and knew the power of a mother's love. And, in that moment, she also knew a great shame. She closed her eyes against tears, wondering how she'd come to this—married in secret, hiding in an abandoned cave like some animal, instead of living in a home like normal people.

And therein lay her problem. Normalcy had no place in her life—not as long as she stayed in Camarune.

Something moved beyond the shadow of the firelight. She clutched the baby in fright, staring fearfully into the shadows. Suddenly a small possum waddled past on its way toward the mouth of the cave. She dropped back onto the pillow with a shudder and clasped the baby close to her breasts.

"My God, little girl, what have we done to you?"

Then she rolled the baby more tightly into the

blanket and snuggled her close. With a pain-racked sigh, she stretched out upon the cot.

"I need to rest," she said, more to herself than to the baby. "Daddy will come, and then we'll get you out of this awful place."

The dark and absence of sound within the cave where mother and baby lay must have been reminiscent of the womb that the baby had just exited. With hardly more than a squeak, the tiny girl turned toward the steady beat of her mother's heart and slept.

Turner's suitcase was under his bed. His money was in his pocket. On a normal day, Jubal Blair wouldn't have been anywhere close to the house, but for some reason, today had been different. Turner felt less than the man he should have been for not standing up to his father. But he'd been raised too many years under the looming shadow of Jubal's wrath to break free from it so easily now. To make matters worse, he was worried sick about Fancy. Keeping her hidden in the cave like an animal shamed him. God had decreed that man should protect the woman who was his wife. He should feed her and care for her. Stand by her side in the day and lie by her side in the night. But Turner didn't just have a wife to consider. There was the feud.

He'd been raised on hate. Hate for anyone with

the name Joslin. Only the first time he'd seen Fancy Joslin, he'd fallen in love. As he remembered, she'd been nine years old to his eleven. Even then, they'd known to keep their friendship to themselves. By the time Fancy was sixteen, Turner had known she was the woman for him. But sneaking the occasional meeting in the woods was dangerous. Their love had stayed true, but their meetings had been sporadic. Until Fancy told him about the baby.

Anger at their situation had spurred him to a daring he might never have achieved otherwise. One night, long after midnight had come and gone, they met on the mountain beneath the overhang of Pulpit Rock and pledged their lives and love. After that, leaving was a foregone conclusion.

He shivered with excitement, thinking about their child. By this time next month, they would have a whole new life. He imagined himself bathing her, watching her learn to walk and talk, hearing her laughter, protecting her as he would protect her mother.

A raucous shout startled him, and he quickly moved to the window. It was his brother John. John's hounds were in the back of the truck. That explained why Jubal had stayed close to the house today. They were going to run the dogs.

He turned, staring nervously at his bed and picturing the packed suitcase hidden beneath, then smoothed sweaty palms down the front of his jeans.

Coon hunts were nothing new. Just a part of family tradition in the mountains. And it wasn't so much the kill that Jubal Blair craved as it was the camaraderie of the event.

Turner's belly drew tight as he glanced out the window again. Another delay in getting to Fancy. Then a new thought occurred. Maybe he wouldn't go on the damned hunt. He would make some excuse and when they were gone, he would slip away, get Fancy, and they would be off this mountain before sunup.

But what to tell Jubal Blair was another problem. What could he say that would get him out of the hunt? He saw his father shaking John's hand and then helping him get the dogs out of the truck bed. The hounds were antsy and swarmed around the men's legs like blowflies on a dung heap. Turner watched his father turn toward the house and thought to himself that if he lived to be one hundred, he would never be the force his father was. The man radiated power, from the thick shock of gray hair, to his broad, weathered stature.

"Turner, your brother is here!"

Turner winced at the underlying demand in his father's voice. Jubal still treated him like a boy. Why didn't his father realize he was a grown man, too? Turner sighed. He'd lived through many nights like the one that was being set up. Before long, his other two brothers, Hank and Charles, would surely

arrive. Hank with Old Blue, and Charles with his
Little Lou. All three brothers swore their hounds
were the best, and each time they were together, it
was a battle of whose dog struck trail first, rather
than the thrill of a hunt. Turner knew that Jubal
liked the underlying discord. It fed the anger that
lived in his heart.

"Turner! Damn it, boy, I'm talkin' to you!" Jubal yelled again.

Turner sighed. He was twenty-one years old. His
daddy shouldn't be talking to him like that anymore. Even as he was thinking it, he caught himself
moving quickly through the small frame house as
he headed for the door.

"There you are, boy!" Jubal said. "Get these
dogs some water." Then he patted John on the
back. "Come on inside, son. I've got a little something in the cupboard you might like to taste."

Turner's sense of injustice grew. His daddy never
offered him a drink of whiskey. As he headed for
the well house to get a pan to water the dogs, he
kept telling himself that he would never treat a child
of his own the way Jubal treated him.

Before he was through, his other two brothers
had arrived with their dogs. The congregation of
four-legged hunters began baying and howling at
each other in what could only be described as a
welcome. Turner sighed. Even they had a bond. His
brothers smiled at him and waved as they walked

on into the house, but they didn't stop to talk. Turner's indignation grew. *What the hell do they think I am, hired help?*

He slammed the pan of water down on the ground, then scooted it toward the dogs with the toe of his boot. His forehead was furrowed, his posture stiff, as he stalked into the house. But his anger soon changed to fear as he overheard the conversation in progress.

"...about the fire."

Turner froze. The only fire on the mountain had been the one in which Frank Joslin had died.

"Yeah," Jubal growled. "There ain't nothing they can prove. The chimney was cracked. The house caught on fire. Case closed."

One of Turner's brothers laughed. The sound was harsh and ugly. How could men rejoice in another man's death? He listened as another round of whiskey was poured into glasses.

"Here's to the Blairs. Right's on our side, and it's over. God is good," Jubal growled.

Turner listened as the light clink of glasses drifted into the hall where he was standing. His belly clenched. God couldn't possibly have anything to do with the hate that had entrapped them all.

"Well now, Pa, it ain't *exactly* over," Charles said. "Don't forget, there's still a Joslin somewhere on the mountain."

"Hell, Charles, she's only a woman. Women don't count," Hank added.

Jubal's words came out of his throat in a growl. "That's where you're wrong, boys. Women are the worst. They're the breeders."

"I heard tell she ain't been seen since the cabin burned," John added. "Maybe she's gone."

"And maybe she's not," Jubal said. "All I can say is, if I see her..."

The implied threat was left hanging as the men downed the rest of their drinks, while Turner's fear for Fancy increased. This was worse than he'd imagined. He had to get her out of these mountains tonight. He straightened his shoulders and jutted his chin forward in a manner not unlike that of the old man himself, then strode into the room.

"The dogs are watered."

Jubal turned and lifted a glass in Turner's direction. "Help yourself, boy. I reckon you're way past old enough."

Turner's heart twisted. The first time his father had offered him a step into the family circle, and he was going to have to refuse it.

"Not in the mood for drink," he said shortly. "I'm going down into Camarune shortly. Is there anything you'd be needing?"

Jubal frowned.

"We're goin' huntin', boy!"

"That's fine by me," Turner said. "But I got other things to do."

Jubal's frown deepened. "Like what?"

Turner's gut knotted, but he thought of Fancy and stood firm.

"Daddy, I'm twenty-one years old. I don't suppose I need your permission to go into town."

John laughed and slapped his little brother on the back.

"He's right, Daddy. Besides, Turner never did have the stomach for blood."

Any other time, the jeer would have cut Turner to the quick, but not this evening.

"You're right, John. I don't savor killin' just for the sake of the sport."

Jubal snorted beneath his breath. He was more than a little surprised by his youngest son's refusal and didn't know whether to push the issue or not. But the whiskey was warm in his belly, and his other sons were more than willing to pick up the slack.

"Good enough," Jubal said, and set down his glass. "It'll be dark in less than an hour, and I'm hankerin' to hear Little Lou's bugle."

Turner exhaled softly as the men filed out of the house, leaving him alone. He bolted toward his room and dragged his suitcase from under the bed. Now all he had to do was wait until they were gone. He felt better than he had in months.

But time passed, and Turner's father and brothers had yet to leave. He kept glancing at the clock and then out the window, wondering when they would leave. Nightfall had long since come and gone, and they were still outside, laughing and talking. The dogs were wired, knowing that a hunt was imminent. They kept weaving themselves and their leashes into knots. Turner's gut was in a knot of its own, thinking of Fancy, alone in that damned cave. Then he took a deep breath, making himself relax. This time tomorrow they would be in Memphis, and she would be safe in his arms and sleeping between clean white sheets.

He looked around his room, conscious of the comfort of his bed and the warmth within the walls. Then he thought of where she was and felt shame. As a man, he should have been able to stand up to Jubal and tell him what was in his heart, but his fear for them both kept him silent.

He paced within the room, growing more anxious by the minute, until, suddenly, the sounds outside began to fade. He ran to the window. The bobbing lights of the lanterns and flashlights the men were carrying were disappearing in the trees.

With a great sigh of relief, he grabbed his suitcase and a flashlight, started out the door, then stopped. He couldn't just up and disappear without telling his father something. Knowing Jubal Blair, he would take it in his head to come and find him unless he gave him a reason not to. He needed to leave Jubal a note.

Turner kept it brief. No need volunteering any information that his father didn't need to know—just that he was leaving to work in Memphis and he would be in touch. He propped the note in the center of the kitchen table between the salt and pepper shakers and then paused on his way out the door, giving the old house one last look.

He'd been born here, and except for a very few times, had spent every night of his life under this roof. But it hadn't been a home for more years than he could count, especially after his mother had died. He glanced toward the fireplace to the picture of his mother on the mantel. He remembered vividly the day it had been taken—an Easter Sunday when he was sixteen years old. She was wearing a pale green dress and standing beside the lilac bush near the back door. Momma had loved that lilac bush. Oddly enough, after her death, it hadn't come out. Jubal had cursed it, blamed it on the hard winter they'd had, then dug it up and tossed it in the hog pen. With that gesture, his father had destroyed the last remnants of her presence in this house.

He took the picture from the mantel and put it in his suitcase. As he turned to go, he saw his rifle hanging on the wall above the hall table. He would have little use for such a thing in Memphis, but his grandfather had given it to him for Christmas when he was twelve. He didn't want to leave it behind. He lifted it down, absently noting it was loaded. With one quick motion, he flipped on the safety, then slung the strap over his shoulder. Moments later, he was in the yard and heading toward the woods. The flashlight bumped the side of his leg as he walked, but it would be a while before he would need it. The moon was bright, and he knew these woods well. In the distance, he could hear the intermittent yips of his brothers' hounds as they scattered through the trees in search of prey. Somewhere farther along, his father and brothers would set up camp, build themselves a fire, and then trade lies and whiskey until the pack struck a trail. After that, the thrill of the chase would be on. There was a small part of him that regretted the fact that he would never know the camaraderie of such a gathering again, but his love for Fancy was far too strong for the regret to be anything more than fleeting. Fancy was his life. He didn't need anything more than her—and their child. So he walked, confident of his plans and anxious to feel the brush of Fancy's breath against his face.

The fire in the cave was little more than glowing embers when Fancy roused. Disoriented, she looked into the darkness above her head and panicked. Almost instantly, the baby at her side wiggled, then gave a soft squeak, and she remembered.

It was late, so late. Turner should have been here long ago. What could possibly be keeping him? She threw back the blanket and scooted to the edge of the bed before trying to sit. Almost at once, her head began to spin, and she closed her eyes and took a slow deep breath, willing herself to a calm she didn't feel. With tender movements, she laid the baby in the middle of the cot and then made herself stand, using the back of a chair for a crutch. She needed water and food, and she needed to get to a doctor. God only knew what horrible infections she had exposed herself and her baby to by giving birth in such circumstances.

With trembling hands, she laid a couple of small sticks on the fire. She wouldn't build it high enough to cause a large flame, just enough to keep curious wildlife away. Satisfied she had it just right, she moved toward the water jug on a makeshift table.

The water tasted stale, but she swallowed it just the same, then splashed a couple of handfuls on her face. There were things to be done, like burying the afterbirth and the bloody clothes that she'd been forced to use for cleaning. She didn't want any wild animals to be led toward them by the scent.

By the time she'd finished, she was weak and shaking, and the baby was beginning to fuss. After washing her hands once more, she staggered back to the cot, bared her breast to the night and took the baby in her arms. Unaware of her Madonnalike pose, she pushed a nipple into the baby's tiny mouth. It took several tries, but finally, the baby caught. Fancy's eyes widened in wonder at the beauty of the tiny mouth working so diligently against her flesh.

"Turner, I need you," she whispered. A tear rolled down her cheek.

Time passed—enough that the baby had gone back to sleep and Fancy was about to do the same. Her head bobbed, lurching sideways like a rubber-necked doll. The movement woke her, and she groaned, then glanced toward the baby and smiled. In spite of everything, the child seemed to be thriving. A little of her panic lifted. Surely this was a sign. Everything was going to be all right.

It occurred to her then that the child was not named. She and Turner had discussed many names, but almost all for a boy. Somehow, they hadn't seriously considered the possibility that a Blair would father a girl.

She traced the tip of her finger along the side of the baby's cheek and thought of her own mother, who had long since passed away.

"Catherine," Fancy whispered, and then repeated the name, familiarizing herself with the feel of the syllables against her tongue. They felt good. They felt right. "Catherine you'll be," she said softly, then kissed the side of her baby's cheek.

Time passed. The fire ate its way into the sticks

she'd put on earlier, until it was time to feed it again. She stretched gingerly, reaching for a small log. Her fingers curled around the rough, dry bark as she lifted it from the pile. Inches away from the flame, she stopped, listening to a sound that struck fear in her heart.

Hounds!

Someone was hunting on this side of the mountain.

She dropped the log back onto the pile, unwilling to add even the smallest bit of fuel to a fire that could give her away. In a panic, she reached for the baby, clasping her close against her breast. The soft in and out of the child's breath was calming. Fancy took a deep breath, too, reminding herself that this wasn't the first time since she'd gone into hiding that she'd heard hunters on the mountain. Still, she sat with her eyes wide and fixed upon the mouth of the cave.

Minutes passed. The baby slept on, unaware of the growing danger, but Fancy couldn't relax. The hounds sounded closer now. She thought of Jubal Blair. She knew from her years with Turner that the Blairs often hunted on this side of the mountain. What if it was him? What if he found her here alone?

Turner…Turner…where are you?

The baby began to squirm, and Fancy groaned

with regret, only then realizing she'd been holding her too tightly.

"Sorry, baby girl, Momma's sorry," she whispered, and laid her down on the cot.

Almost instantly, the baby ceased fussing. Quiet enveloped them. Everything became magnified, from the sound of water dripping far back in the cave, to the intermittent pop of a twig on the fire—increasing her growing fear of being found.

Finally, she couldn't sit anymore. Awkwardly, she stood and made her way to the mouth of the cave, stepping out into the darkness and staring down the hillside into the trees. Even in full moonlight, the trees were so thick it was difficult to see more than a few feet ahead, but sound still carried, and she could tell that the dogs were moving in her direction.

Nervously, she looked around for something to pull in front of the cave, but there was nothing but brush, and a few uprooted bushes wouldn't throw a pack of hunting dogs off the scent of blood.

She looked up at the sky, trying to judge the time by the position of the moon, and guessed it was probably near midnight. Accepting that fact pushed her to accept another. What if Turner didn't come?

Suddenly one hound's shrill bugle made her flinch. In that moment she believed her safety had been compromised. She looked back into the cave and then into the trees. What should she do? If she went down the mountain, she would run straight into the hunters. She looked upward toward Pulpit Rock, where she and Turner had secretly married, and as she did, her heart skipped a beat. There was a place up there that no hunters would go—not even Jubal Blair.

The witch's house.

She'd never seen it, but she knew it was there. At one time or another, everyone around Camarune had seen the fires late at night. Stories abounded about human sacrifices made in the light of a full moon, but Fancy didn't really believe that. To her knowledge, no one in the whole of this mountain had ever gone missing, so if the witch was making sacrifices, it was more likely animal than human.

The hounds bugled again. She shuddered. Her decision was made. She darted back inside the cave, returning moments later with the baby wrapped warm against the night, and started up the mountain toward the shadow of Pulpit Rock.

She was wearing her last clean dress, an old blue denim, and had pulled a shawl around her shoulders, wrapping herself and the baby within. Despite her pain and weakness, she would rather face a witch than the likes of Jubal Blair.

She moved through the trees like a small blue ghost, her movements stiff and awkward. The pain in her belly and the one between her legs was great, but they were nothing compared to her fear. Tree limbs grabbed at her hair and clothing, but she continued constantly upward. Brush often caught in her clothing, leaving tiny tears in the fabric and stinging scratches on her face. The baby was starting to squirm. Fancy knew she must be hungry. But there was no time to stop.

A short while later, the hounds set up a terrible howl. It was then she knew they'd found the cave. If it was only hunters, they would be curious, but little else. But if it was Jubal...

Unwilling to contemplate the consequences, she increased her pace, but it was taking a toll. The muscles in her body began to spasm, and each step she took was more torturous than the last. Just when she thought things couldn't get worse, something popped inside her belly. She paused, gasping for breath, then moaned as something warm began running down the insides of her legs.

In a panic, she tried to get a fix on her location. To her relief, the silhouette of Pulpit Rock was just ahead, jutting out over the landscape like the point of an anvil. It wasn't much farther. Fancy gritted her teeth and kept walking, but the pain and weakness were winning. Her head was beginning to swim, and there was a constant buzzing in her ears. Faintly she could hear the baby starting to cry, and she wanted to cry with her, but sound carried on the mountain. After the blood in the cave, the dogs would be crazy. Even if the hunters were innocent in their pursuit, they would be too far behind their own dogs to stop the carnage she knew would ensue.

A long, loud bugle from one of the dogs suddenly sounded in the night. Fancy groaned. She knew, as well as she knew her own name, what that meant. The hounds had struck trail. They were on the move again. And they were coming after her.

"God help me," she whispered, and started to run.

2

The campfire was small but hearty, the flames eating hungrily into the deadwood that Jubal had piled into a teepee shape before setting it ablaze. Now, minute bits of burning bark drifted up into the air along with a thin spiral of smoke, marking their place in the woods. The forest was fairly dry for this time of year, but the men had been woodsmen too long to be careless. The ground around the campfire was spacious and barren, and added to that, a heavy dew was falling. Hank passed the jug to his brother John just as one of the dogs sent up a howl that echoed throughout the forest.

"That's Little Lou!" John cried. "She's struck trail."

Charles laughed. "So she did," he said. "Now pass me the jug."

Jubal grinned. "Easy on the whiskey, boys. You don't want to be runnin' into any trees like Hank did last time."

Hank frowned. "Damn near put my eye out," he muttered, as his father and brothers laughed, remembering the chaos that had erupted from the accident.

They sat for a while longer, enjoying the heat from the fire and the warmth of whiskey in their bellies. It was Little Lou's howl, followed by an answering chorus from the other hounds, that changed their perspective.

Jubal stood abruptly. "Sounds promisin', boys. Let's go see what we've got."

Hank reached for his gun as John doused their fire. "Maybe it's a painter, Pa."

The mountain term for panther was familiar to them all, and, to a man, they shivered as they followed their father's lead.

The pack was moving upward. Five minutes into the run, the muscles in Jubal's legs began to burn, but he refused to acknowledge his pain. This would be his last winter to hunt. Age was doing something that his wife never could. It was slowing him down. But he kept on moving, refusing to show weakness in front of the men whom he'd sired. It wasn't until Hank suddenly stopped that they all realized the howls of the dogs sounded fainter.

"What the hell?" Charles muttered. "Where did they go?"

Jubal stood with his head cocked to one side, trying to identify the familiarity of the sound. Suddenly he knew.

"They've gone underground!" he yelled. "Hell's fire, boys, they must be in a cave."

"It *is* a painter," Hank cried.

Jubal grinned. "Then let's go kill us a cat."

They started off at a jog, still following the faint, but distinct, sounds of the pack.

It was John who first saw the opening.

"There!" he shouted, and they turned, holding their lanterns high and their guns at the ready as they moved inside.

The dogs were everywhere, noses to the ground, running over the makeshift bed, digging in a dimly lit corner. The cacophony of their baying and howls was painful to the ear within the confines of the enclosure.

"What the hell?" Jubal muttered, as he held his lantern high. "This ain't no animal's lair."

John shouted, calling down his dogs. Hank and Charles quickly did the same. The noise trickled down to a series of soft whines and yips, but it was enough that the men could make themselves heard.

"Look here, Pa," Hank said, pointing toward a satchel of clothes. Surprise colored his expression when he pulled out a woman's dress. "Well, I'll be danged. Women's clothes."

Jubal's expression darkened as he poked into the jumble of boxes with the barrel of his gun. Then he looked at Old Blue and Little Lou, who were digging frantically in a darkened area of the cave.

"What the hell are those dogs digging at?" he muttered.

John moved toward them, holding his lantern high, then suddenly cursed and took a step back.

"There's something buried here," he yelled, pushing the dogs away from the hole.

They all converged on the place, holding their lanterns and flashlights aloft. Charles knelt for a closer look, then turned away suddenly, gagging.

"Shit," he muttered, as he staggered to his feet. "There's something bloody in there."

Jubal shoved them aside for a closer look. His nose twitched, but his belly stayed steady.

"It ain't nothing but some innards or somethin'," he said. "Most likely whoever is stayin' here just buried the guts of some game."

"That ain't like no guts I ever saw," John said. "There's some bloody clothes here, too," he said, and lifted them out with the barrel of his gun. "Hell. It's another dress." He dropped it back in the hole with a shudder and moved away, poking through a book that was lying on a block of wood that had obviously been used as a table. Moments later, he spun, his face slack with shock. "Pa! Look here."

Jubal took the book, read the name inscribed and dropped it into the dirt.

"Fancy Joslin."

Then he spat, as if the name alone had poisoned his tongue.

Hank and Charles cursed, while John remained silent.

"So this is where she got off to," Jubal muttered.

"Now, Pa. I don't imagine no woman has been living in here," John said, trying to add a bit of sanity to the moment.

"Where the hell else would she be living, then?" Jubal asked. "Frank's house is gone. Burned to the foundation...remember?"

John looked away. The feud was a bone of contention between father and son, and had been for some time now. John was loyal to his blood, but of the opinion that a feud was something that belonged with the old ways, not the twentieth century.

"Well, wherever she went is no concern of ours," John said. "Come on, let's go."

Jubal turned on his son, and in that moment the hate that burned in his heart was focused on John Blair's face.

"What do you mean, it's no concern of ours?"

John held his ground. "Just what I said. It's over, Pa. Let it and her be."

Before Jubal could answer, Charles interrupted. "Well, I'll be damned. Look at this."

They turned. Charles was holding up a baby blanket and a newborn-size gown.

Jubal cursed, then spat again. His voice was

shaking as he yanked the items out of Charles's hand, then threw them in the dirt and ground them beneath the sole of his boot.

"See there?" he yelled, pointing at John. "That's what happens when you leave them alone. Females are the worst of the lot. Just when you think you've gotten rid of a pest, they'll breed up another batch."

He grabbed the dress Hank had found and pushed his way past his sons toward the mouth of the cave.

"Come on," he yelled. "Bring the dogs!"

John blanched. "Pa! What do you think you're doing?"

Jubal turned, and the smile on his face chilled John's heart. "I'm goin' huntin', boy!"

"No!" John yelled, then looked to his brothers. "Hank! Charles! Tell him!" he begged. "We don't wage war on women."

Hank shrugged. Charles shook his head. "Pa's right," he said. "It ain't over till it's over." Jubal whistled up the dogs, then thrust the dress into their midst.

"Go get her, boys. Go get her."

Still antsy from being called off the hunt, the dogs took the scent of the dress and then burst out of the cave into the night like bullets out of a gun, with the hunters right behind them.

John ran, too, with his heart in his throat, hoping

that they'd been wrong, that it wasn't Fancy Joslin after all.

Fancy's legs were numb. She couldn't feel anything but the child in her arms and the thunder of her heartbeat slapping against her chest. One step, then another, then another, and suddenly she was on her back in the leaves and looking up at the sky.

"No," she wailed, and curled onto her side, sheltering the child in her arms in the only way that she could. Her heart was hammering against her eardrums, her breath coming in jerks and gasps. If only Turner could have seen their daughter. He would have been so proud.

Suddenly someone was pulling at her shoulders and whispering in her ear. She screamed faintly, thinking they'd found her already, when she realized it was a woman's voice she was hearing. She rolled over, then looked up, at first seeing only the silhouette of Pulpit Rock above her. And then she focused and sighed. It would seem that she'd found the witch after all.

The woman's hair was dark and long, braided into a single plait that hung over her shoulder as she knelt at Fancy's side. Her hands were gentle, her voice soft as she urged Fancy to her feet.

"Get up, girl, get up."

"I can't," Fancy whispered. "Something broke inside me. I'm bleeding."

The woman's hands were swift and sure as she made a quick assessment of Fancy's wounds. The shadows hid her shock at the pool of blood beneath the girl.

"I can help you," she whispered. "Just try to stand. My cabin isn't far."

But Fancy's world was already diminishing, and moving even an inch was beyond her.

"Don't let them get my baby," Fancy begged, and thrust the child into the witch's arms.

The woman rocked back on her heels, shocked by the choice the young mother had just made.

"I'll stay. We'll fight off the dogs together until the hunters get here," she said. "I can't leave you."

Fancy shook her head. "If it's Jubal Blair, he'll kill you, too, just to get to me."

"What do you mean?"

"My name is Fancy Joslin. Turner Blair is my husband and the baby's father, only Jubal doesn't know."

The woman was shocked. Even in her isolation, she'd known of the families' feud.

"Surely he wouldn't…"

Fancy grabbed the witch's arm. "I'm dying, woman, and please God, you've got to grant my last request. Save my child from this hell. Take her away from these mountains and love her as you would your own.'' Fancy's voice faded, then caught on a weak sob. ''Her name is Catherine, and when it matters, tell her how much her mother loved her.''

The woman bowed her head as she cradled the now crying baby close to her breasts.

''I just can't leave you here,'' the woman cried. ''Don't ask me to do this.''

With her last bit of strength, Fancy grabbed the woman by the wrist and raised herself up on one elbow to stare directly into her eyes.

''Your name, witch...'' Fancy gasped. ''What is your name?''

The woman hesitated, then touched the side of Fancy's face in a comforting gesture.

''My name is Annie Fane.''

''Then go, Annie Fane. If you do nothing else on this earth in your time, for God's sake, save my child.''

The dogs were closer now, too close. By best estimates, less than a quarter of a mile away and closing fast. Fancy stared into the woman's face until she was satisfied with what she saw; then she dropped back onto the forest floor.

Suddenly the woman stood. Fancy blinked. One moment she was there. The next she was gone. At that point, Fancy shuddered with relief. It didn't matter anymore. Nothing mattered now. She closed her eyes, giving herself up to the inevitable.

* * *

Turner was in tears by the time he reached the cave. From the fading sounds ahead, he guessed he was a good five minutes behind. And from the appearance of the interior, he knew that she'd been found. The place was in a shambles, but what frightened him most was the bloody dress on the floor and the fact that everyone was gone. Had they taken Fancy hostage, or had she, by some miracle, escaped ahead of them? And why the blood? Had they killed her already and were trying to hide the body? And the baby—what about the baby? Fear threatened to swallow him whole, but there was no time to panic. His only option was to follow the pack and pray that he got there in time to stop a tragedy before it happened. He dashed out of the cave, saying a prayer as he went.

He ran with his flashlight in one hand and his rifle in the other, dodging low-hanging limbs and jumping over exposed roots that might cause him to fall. Once he thought he saw a light a few hundred yards ahead and yelled out his father's name, but no one answered. He kept on moving, running until the stitch in his side had spread to his belly, and his lungs were weak and burning, refusing to admit that his legs felt like rubber and his boots felt as if they were made of lead.

Just when he thought he could go no farther, he got a second wind. Desperately, he increased his speed, ignoring the stinging slaps of tree limbs

against his face and body, unaware that his clothes
were being ripped into shreds by the tentacles of
dry limbs and brush. Nothing mattered except
Fancy.

It seemed the sound of the dogs and the run
would never end when, up ahead, he saw a trio of
lights. It was them! Wanting to yell for them to
wait, he found he had no breath left to speak.
Spurred on by the fact that they were so near, he
flipped the safety off the gun and fired, praying that
they would hear the shot and stop.

Fancy jerked, coming back to consciousness as a
shot rang out. She moaned and opened her eyes,
only to realize she could no longer see the stars—
only a spreading darkness that was coming closer
and closer to where she lay. In the distance, she
could hear the flurry of rustling leaves as the
hounds traversed the forest floor. Their barking had
turned into bays and howls, but it no longer mattered. The darkness was closer than the hounds.
Within it would be shelter and salvation. She wel-
comed it with her last breath.

She never knew when the hounds burst into the
clearing and raced toward Pulpit Rock. What they
did to her earthbound body no longer mattered. She
was soaring toward the light.

As the sound of Turner's gunshot was still echoing within the trees, he saw a hesitation in the lights

and almost cried with relief. But the relief was short-lived. The growls and yips of snarling dogs struck fear in his heart—it was the sound they made as they fell upon their prey. All he could think was, *No, Daddy, no.*

Seconds later, he ran into the circle of lights, shouting at Jubal Blair like a man gone mad.

"Where is she?" he screamed. "What have you done with Fancy?"

Taken aback by his behavior and appearance, their hesitation in answering was to become their last mistake.

Turner groaned, then pushed past them, following the sound of the pack. Seconds later, he burst out of the trees into the clearing to find himself below Pulpit Rock—the moonlight casting harsh, ugly shadows onto the carnage below it. In the blue-silver glow, he could see a bit of leg and the fabric of a woman's dress beneath the pack, and he began to come undone, shooting dogs as he ran.

The silence that came after was as horrifying as the hounds had been. With choking sobs, he dragged the carcass of a dog off of her body, then dropped his gun, frantically gathering her up in his arms.

At first the wounds upon her body didn't register. He kept stroking her arms and her face, begging her to move, to call out his name. But she was too still—too silent. He laid a hand on her stomach, trying to shake her awake. As he did, it hit him that her belly was almost flat. The baby! My God...the baby!

A new fear shafted through him as he looked around the clearing and saw nothing but dogs. The coppery scent of blood was everywhere, but he wouldn't give in to the truth. Choking back sobs, he laid his cheek against her face, cradling her close.

"Fancy...honey...it's me, Turner. Wake up now, sweetheart, I've come to take you home."

She didn't answer. Instead, her head rolled to one side, revealing pale, sightless eyes. He exhaled on a moan. Too late. He'd come too late.

A sense of loss washed over him, so profound that it took the breath from his body. At that moment, he didn't think his next breath would come. Yet when it did, it was a roar of such grief that the echo of it spilled out in the night, then filtered down into the valley below.

It stopped his brothers in their tracks, but not his father.

"What the hell are you doin'?" Jubal yelled, and yanked Turner roughly to his feet. "Have you gone crazy—comin' in here and killin' your brothers' dogs like some madman?"

For once the ugly accusations in his father's voice passed through his mind without connecting.

He picked up his gun, then pointed it directly into his father's face. The quiet, noncommittal tone in his voice was deadly deceptive.

"You killed her."

Jubal hid his shock as he struggled to answer. "We didn't touch her, but even if we had, she's just a damn Joslin. What the hell would it matter?"

Turner shifted his aim until the barrel was pointing straight at his father's belly.

"Fancy was my wife. You set the dogs on my wife."

His brothers were stunned into silence, but not Jubal. "What the hell did you say?"

Turner took a step forward. Now the barrel of the gun was firmly against his father's belly.

"Where's the baby?" he asked, his gaze slowly shifting from Hank, to Charles, to John. "What did you do with my child? Did you feed it to the dogs, too?"

"Jesus Christ," John whispered, and took a step forward. "We didn't know, Turner, we didn't know."

Turner shifted the barrel of the gun from Jubal to John. His voice was flat, completely devoid of emotion.

"Don't touch me," he warned them. "You're all evil to the core. Now where's my child?"

Hank was getting scared. They'd crossed a line that not even he could excuse.

"We didn't know," he said. "But you can't blame us...after all, she *was* a Joslin."

Turner's finger twitched as the gun swung sideways. The shock on Hank's face spread as swiftly as the blood in the middle of his chest. Seconds later, he dropped to the ground without uttering a sound.

Jubal lunged toward Turner. "God almighty!" he roared. "You shot your brother, your own flesh and blood, over a piece of filth."

Turner fired again, this time at his father. Jubal dropped to the ground, screaming in pain, his kneecap gone.

Within seconds, Charles was taking aim. John held up his hand, begging for the killing to stop, and stepped in front of the bullet meant for Turner.

Turner watched the look of disbelief on John's face as he fell forward. Instinctively, he caught him, lowering him to the ground as Jubal fired off a round. But Jubal's bullet hit Charles beneath his right eye. Now he, too, was gone.

Turner rocked back on his heels and stood. His clothes were covered in blood. Fancy's blood. John's blood. The smell of death was everywhere. He turned, looking upon the area without registering the sight. He was out of his mind with grief and at the point of turning his gun on himself when it clicked on an empty chamber. He dropped the rifle with a painful grunt.

The pain—the pain.

He wanted it to go away.

Without looking at Fancy, he reached for John's gun with every intention of using it on himself, when a different sound penetrated the horror in his mind. It was the weak but unmistakable cry of a newborn baby. He spun around, frantically searching the tree line as if he expected the baby to miraculously appear.

"Baby... is that you?"

The sound persisted, faint but clear. His body and his voice were beginning to shake as he took a step forward.

"Don't cry, baby.... Daddy will find you."

He dropped the gun and started walking like a man in a trance. He didn't feel the shot that hit him in the back, but the one that tore through his leg sent him tumbling to the ground. He rolled as he fell, then looked back. Jubal was up on one elbow, with a rifle in his hand.

Turner looked past his father to the woman on the ground. He kept waiting for the pain, but everything felt numb. He looked at Fancy again. It would be so easy to let go.

"Finish the job, old man," he screamed, shaking his fist in the air.

Hate spilled across Jubal Blair's face as he raised the rifle, taking shaky aim.

Turner braced himself for the shot that never came.

Instead, the features on Jubal Blair's face began to melt. The gun fell from his fingers as they curled into a fist. Instead of curses, nothing came from Jubal's lips except a series of grunts as he fell to the ground with a thump.

Turner dropped backward with a groan. Now pain was spilling through his body with every breath. He turned his head. In the distance, he could see the outline of Fancy's body.

"I'm so sorry," he whispered, and closed his eyes, willing himself to die.

Then it came again, the faint but unmistakable cry of a tiny baby, mewling in the night, and he rolled onto his side. Moments later, he began crawling toward the trees—and the sound.

Some time later, a silent figure of a woman slipped out of the woods and knelt beneath the shadow of Pulpit Rock. Her shoulders were shaking, her hands fluttering helplessly. Finally she stood and, with a burst of great strength, lifted Fancy Joslin's lifeless body into her arms.

Sometime during the night it started to rain. Softly at first, then harder and harder, until the raindrops sounded like bullets against the leaves, splattering upon the bodies of men and dogs alike and washing them clean of blood. Thunder ripped through the heavens, shaking Jubal Blair from the darkness. The raindrops felt like ice against his cheeks, and there were rivulets of water running beneath his body. He tried to scream for help, but nothing came out of his throat. He was alive, but trapped within a body that had already died.

Meanwhile, higher up on the mountain, Annie Fane was frantically packing. She'd buried the young mother beneath a tree in her backyard, then burned her own bloody clothes. It was only a matter of time before the bodies would be found, and she was the only one within hearing distance of the site. Already distrusted by the people of Camarune, she knew someone would be blamed for the deaths. As superstitious as they were, it stood to reason it would be her. So using the light of the moon as a guide, she began to cover her tracks. She planted the bare earth above Fancy's grave with some of the herbs growing on her porch, then ringed it with a circle of stones. By the time she was through, it was impossible to tell it from her other flower beds.

The baby was crying again, and she hurried into the house, quickly washing her hands, then cuddling it to her chest. Fashioning a diaper from one of her dish towels, she gave the baby a change. The momentary comfort was enough so that after a few minutes of rocking, the baby drifted back to sleep.

Annie gazed longingly at the little cabin that had been her home and salvation, then looked at the baby asleep on her bed. It had been a long time since she'd had a responsibility to anyone other than herself. But she'd made a promise—and Annie Fane was a woman of her word. She ran to a closet and pulled out an old suitcase. It was time to move on.

It was morning before the county sheriff, acting on an anonymous tip, found the bodies beneath Pulpit Rock. Shock reverberated within the community of Camarune as the pastor of the local church raced to Jubal's home to give young Turner the bad news. But there was no sign of Turner Blair. Only the note that he'd stuck between the salt and pepper shakers telling his father he would be in touch. Another great shock moved through the town when it was discovered that the men had seemingly died at their own hands. Bullets found in the dogs and the bodies matched the guns that they carried. There was an extra gun, but it bore the name of Henry Blair, Jubal's father, so they assumed that one of the men had been carrying two. It made no sense to the people, and even less to the sheriff, but Jubal wasn't in any shape to explain. It was also common knowledge that when the sheriff had gone up the mountain to question the witch, he'd found nothing but an abandoned cabin.

Days later, as his sons were laid to rest, Jubal Blair lay motionless in a hospital bed in a nearby town, suffering from the gunshot wound to his leg, as well as the stroke that had struck him dumb. The town grieved, and then grief moved on, leaving only the brothers' families to suffer the loss. Soon they, too, moved on, unwilling to stay in a place with such memories.

There were those who claimed that the witch had put a curse on the Blairs and that they'd killed each other while under her spell. Then days turned to weeks, and weeks to months, then to years. Only now and then would someone mention the mystery at Pulpit Rock, and when they did, they would follow it with a prayer.

It was part of their past, and that was exactly where they wanted it to stay. And stay it did—until Annie Fane returned.

3

Nellie Cauthorn, the preacher's wife at the Church of the Firstborn, had been saying all day that things didn't feel right. She'd told Preacher so during breakfast. Then she went to the store to tell her best friend, Lovie Cleese, who owned Camarune's only grocery. Lovie had heard Nellie's predictions before and never put much stock in them. But in the midst of cleaning out the produce section, she heard a commotion out in the street, then heard Nellie screeching.

Lovie darted toward the front of the store to see what was wrong. When she got to the window, her heart skipped a beat. A long black hearse from the Lexington Funeral Home had just run over a dog. The dog was past help, and from the looks of the casket just visible inside the hearse, so was the person residing inside.

To Lovie's dismay, at the sight of the dead dog,

Nellie fell to the floor in a faint. By the time Lovie had revived her friend, the dog's carcass had been removed from the street and the driver of the hearse was reimbursing the owner for the loss of his pet.

Nellie was mumbling something about premonitions and wiping her face with the cloth Lovie pressed in her hand when another vehicle pulled up behind the hearse. The woman getting out of the dusty black Jeep was a stranger. Lovie judged her to be in her mid-twenties, and from the cut of her clothes, probably a city dweller, a bit above average height, and erring on the side of slender. But it was the blue-black hair brushing the tops of her shoulders that made Lovie take a step forward for a closer look. She squinted through the streaks in the windows, absently thinking they needed a wash, and kept staring.

Who was she? She looked so familiar. But the thought wouldn't connect.

If only she'd turn her head a little bit to the...

The woman turned, and for the first time, Lovie got a good look at her face.

"Have mercy," Lovie muttered. "Who is she?"

"What? What is it now?" Nellie cried, gawking around Lovie's shoulder toward the street.

"That woman," Lovie said.

"What about her?"

Lovie inhaled sharply. "She looks familiar."

"Looks like who?" Nellie urged, her curiosity piqued.

"I don't know...probably no one," Lovie muttered. "I guess I was mistaken."

"She's coming inside!" Nellie said.

Lovie turned.

The bell over the door jangled. The woman was standing in the doorway with a hesitant look upon her face. Her jeans were clean but travel-worn, as were her shirt and jacket.

"Can I help you?" Lovie snapped.

Nellie stared at Lovie as if she'd just lost her mind. Never in her life had she heard Lovie use that tone of voice with a customer.

The young woman tugged at the lapels of her jacket, then took a couple of steps farther, letting the door close behind her.

"I need to hire someone with a truck."

When Lovie remained silent, Nellie felt it her duty as the pastor's wife to answer the stranger's request.

"Maynard Phillips down at the service station has a—"

"Maynard's probably busy," Lovie snapped, interrupting Nellie before she could finish.

The young woman's gaze centered on Lovie's face, silently acknowledging her rudeness, but she stood her ground.

"Maybe there's someone else?" she asked.

Lovie shuddered. The way the stranger pursed her lips before speaking seemed familiar, although she knew good and well she'd never seen the woman before.

"Doubt it," Lovie said. "People are pretty busy around here."

The woman's chin jutted mutinously, and for the first time since she'd entered the store, her voice took on an edge.

"Does that come naturally, or do you have to work at it?" she asked.

Lovie frowned. "Work at what?"

"Being rude."

Nellie gasped. She hated confrontation. Her hands fluttered around her chest like butterflies caught in a cage as she gave Lovie a nervous glance before speaking.

"I'm sure Lovie didn't mean to be—"

"Is there anything else you'd be needing?" Lovie snapped.

This time, even Nellie was shocked at Lovie's rudeness. "Lovie! What on earth is wrong with you?"

Lovie didn't answer. But it wasn't because she wouldn't. Truth be told, she didn't know what was wrong. But every time she looked at that woman's face, she got a sick feeling in the pit of her stomach. And Lovie Cleese hadn't lived to be seventy-five without paying attention to her instincts.

"Never mind," the woman said. "I'll be asking elsewhere. Surely there's someone in this town who's interested in making some extra money."

Nellie took a step forward. A pastor's pay was far from generous. Maybe Preacher could borrow a truck.

"What was it you were needing hauled?" she asked, ignoring Lovie's indrawn hiss of disapproval.

The young woman pointed over her shoulder. "My grannie's casket."

Nellie's eyes widened in sympathy. "Oh, my dear, I'm so sorry for your loss."

All the stiffness of the young woman's demeanor deflated as her voice softened.

"Thank you," she said.

Nellie felt better. Condolences were part of her job as a pastor's wife. She was on firm ground again, but curious. "The hearse is already here. Why can't the driver take the casket to the cemetery for burial? It's just at the edge of town."

The woman's eyes disappeared behind a sudden pool of tears. Nellie sighed. Had it not been for Lovie, she would have put her arms around the girl and held her close.

"Because Grannie wanted to be buried behind her old home," the woman said. "I've already seen to the grave being dug, but I've been told that a hearse won't be able to traverse the road up the mountain."

"That's certainly true," Nellie said, and then added, "exactly where are you headed?"

The woman began digging through her jacket pockets. "Somewhere up the mountain above a place called Pulpit Rock. I'm sure I have the directions right here." But when she couldn't find them, she shrugged. "They're probably in my car."

To Nellie's disbelief, Lovie Cleese actually cursed. Fearing another confrontation, Nellie felt obligated to point out what she felt sure was a misdirection.

"I'm sorry, my dear," Nellie said. "I fear you've been misled. There's nothing up there but the old witch's cabin."

The woman jerked as if she'd been slapped. "I didn't believe her," she muttered, more to herself than to the two women, then she turned sharply and started toward the door, and as she did, something in the way she moved sent another shudder up Lovie Cleese's spine. In spite of her fear, curiosity won.

"Wait!"

The woman paused, then turned.

"What's your name, girl?" Lovie asked.

The woman's chin tilted, and in that moment, both Nellie and Lovie felt the fire of her glare.

"Catherine Fane."

Lovie paled. "Even in death," she muttered cryptically, then sank into a nearby chair.

Nellie gasped. "The witch's kin!"

Catherine was so angry she was shaking. "You people are a bunch of superstitious fools. If you'd known Annie Fane, you wouldn't be accusing her of such a thing." Then she pointed straight at Lovie's face. "And with or without your help, Annie Fane's last wishes are going to be fulfilled."

The door slammed behind her, leaving the two women alone.

"We're doomed," Nellie muttered. "The witch has come back to Camarune."

"Just shut up," Lovie said. "The woman's dead."

"And so is Henry's dog," Nellie said. "God only knows who'll be next. I told you something wasn't right today. I told you, didn't I?" she said.

Lovie had more things on her mind than Nellie's predilection for prophecies. But Nellie wasn't about to be silenced. Not when she'd just been proven right.

"Yessiree, I knew something bad was going to happen today."

As if the last few minutes had not been enough to prove her right, a loud crack of thunder rattled the grocery store windows, and then it started to rain.

* * *

After a few brief words to the driver of the hearse, Catherine slid behind the wheel of her car and then sat, trying to regain her composure. The last few days had been nothing short of hell. Facing her grandmother's death had been inevitable. The cancer had been eating at her body for over a year. But the deathbed confession of the woman she loved had destroyed what was left of her world.

She closed her eyes, picturing her grandmother's face and then remembering the words that had shattered her soul.

She was no relation to Annie Fane. After that, she'd absorbed only bits and pieces of what Annie had been trying to say.

Feuding families.

Forbidden love.

Lies.

Murder.

She took a deep, shuddering breath. Alone. She was so alone. Her past was a lie. No, she thought, not everything she'd been told was a lie. Her parents *were* dead, after all, just not in the romantic fashion she'd been led to believe. So they hadn't died in a train crash in each other's arms. So in reality her grandfather had caused her mother's death, as well as his own son's. The urge to scream was overwhelming. Dear God, if all that was true, then what did that make her? What sort of monster's blood ran through her veins?

A loud crack of thunder made her jump. Seconds later, the heavens opened, diluting her view of the store and the two women staring at her from behind the dusty windows. Well, she thought, wryly, at least one side of the glass was about to come clean.

She started the car, then turned on the windshield wipers before pulling away from the curb. The intensity of her anger was making her sick to her stomach. She needed to cry, but she was afraid if she started, all she would do was throw up. And, she reminded herself, she wasn't taking the word of anybody who dared to call her grannie a witch. Maybe the man named Maynard would help her, after all.

She found the place easily and parked, noting several large pickup trucks parked about the station. Surely one of these men would be willing to earn a little extra money. Without giving herself time to think, she got out on the run, dashing through the rain to the door.

Luke DePriest was downing the last of his Coke when the door to Maynard's Gas and Guzzle suddenly flew open and a young woman rushed in. He had a brief glimpse of her face—enough to know she was a stranger—and then she was past him, heading toward the counter and the other three men lounging there. He set the empty Coke can on the windowsill and waited, curious as to her intent.

"I need to hire someone with a truck to carry something up the mountain for me," she said.

Luke watched all three men come to attention. Extra money was hard to come by in these parts. He took a step closer, curiosity overcoming manners.

Maynard Phillips figured since this was his store, it was his right to get first dibs. He braced himself against the counter and offered her a grin.

"Well now, Missy, I've got the newest and best truck in these parts. I reckon I can help you out. Exactly what is it you're needing hauled?"

The woman's answer startled everyone, including Luke.

"A casket," she said. "I'm taking my grandmother's body up the mountain to her home place to be buried, and the hearse can't make the trip."

The smile on Maynard's face slipped a bit, but Luke had to give him credit for maintaining it.

"I can't say as how I've ever hauled me a dead body before," Maynard said, then peered out the window, his eyes widening as he saw the long black hearse parked down the street. "However, I don't suppose it'd do no harm."

Luke saw her shoulders sag with relief.

"That's wonderful," she said softly. "I'll go tell the driver."

As she started to turn, Luke caught a glimpse of her profile. Raindrops clung to the tips of her eyelashes, shimmering like tears, and her lower lip was on the verge of quivering, too. She looked as if she was running on guts alone, and he wondered how far she'd traveled to get to Camarune.

"Say, Missy," Maynard called. "I reckon I should ask exactly how far up the mountain you're needing to go? The roads get slick pretty fast in a rain."

She paused, and Luke saw her worry her lower lip before answering.

"About a quarter of a mile above a place called Pulpit Rock."

Maynard frowned. "I think you've got your directions confused. There ain't nothing up there."

Then one of the other men interrupted. "Just the old witch's cabin."

The woman's posture stiffened, and Luke could tell by the tone of her voice she'd been offended by what they'd said.

"I'm offering one hundred dollars to drive less than four miles. Are you going to help me?"

"Are you saying that's where you're going?" Maynard asked.

"Yes."

Maynard's eyes narrowed. "I don't recall your mention of the deceased's name."

This time there was no mistaking the tension in the woman's shoulders.

"My grandmother, Annie Fane."

Luke winced. He hadn't grown up here, but he knew the name, and he knew damned good and well that none of these men would go up that mountain with Annie Fane's body in the back of their truck.

Maynard took off his cap and swiped a hand through his hair, then jammed it back on his head.

"I'm sorry, Missy, but I can't help you after all."

When the young woman's chin began to quiver, Luke sighed. Damn. He never could stand to see a woman cry.

"I have to get my grandmother's casket up the mountain to be buried. Are you saying you don't want the job?"

"Yes, ma'am, I reckon I am," Maynard said.

Before she could ask any of the other men present, they bolted out the door to their trucks and drove away.

Luke was torn between sympathy for the woman and understanding for the men. Superstition was as much a part of these people as the air they breathed. Although he didn't believe in such gossip, he'd heard plenty of stories about the witch, and the curse she'd put on Jubal Blair and his sons. He watched the woman, wondering what she would do next.

"Is there anyone in this place you could recommend to me?" she asked.

At that point Luke knew she wasn't going to quit.

A part of him admired her persistence, while the rest of him worried what kind of hornet's nest she was bound to stir up. With the rash of thievery that had been going on in the mountains above Camarune, he already had more trouble than he cared to cope with, but he had always been a sucker for a woman in need.

"Hey, Maynard, can I borrow your truck for about an hour?"

Maynard looked startled, but not as much as the woman, who pivoted suddenly, unaware there had been another man at the back of the room.

"Well, sure, I reckon so," Maynard said, and started digging out his keys. "But Pete will be through changing the oil in your Blazer pretty soon."

"Yeah, I know," Luke said softly, staring intently at the fear on the young woman's face. "But the patrol car isn't long enough to hold a casket."

Maynard cursed beneath his breath as he handed Luke the keys.

"You wash it out before you bring it back," he muttered. "I don't want no death marks on it."

Luke pointed out the window. "You haven't washed it since the day you bought it. Thanks to the rain, I can guarantee it'll come back cleaner than when we started." Then he tipped his Stetson to the woman. "Ma'am, my name is Luke DePriest, sheriff of Taney County. I'll be glad to help you."

He felt her relief as her expression softened. "I'll pay you after we're there."

"No charge, ma'am. Consider it part of my job."

"My name is Catherine Fane," she said quietly, then took a shuddering breath. "I don't know how to thank you."

"No need, and I'm sorry for your loss." Then he put his hand under her elbow and guided her out the door. Within minutes, the transfer had been made from hearse to truck.

"I'll follow you," Catherine said, and started to get in her car.

"I'm not sure you'll be able to drive all the way up," Luke warned.

"I'll take it as far as it will go," she said. "I'll need a way to get off the mountain when I'm done."

For the first time since he'd made the offer, Luke wondered how he would get the casket out of the truck. It had been fairly simple to get it from the hearse to the truck bed. He'd just backed the truck up the open door of the hearse and slid it from one to the other, but there was no way he and this slender young woman could lift it out on their own.

"We're going to need some help unloading," he said. "And there's the grave. What about digging the grave?"

Her gaze was steady, her voice confident. "Help will be waiting."

His eyes rounded. "Are you sure you know what—"

"Just get me and my grannie there and leave the rest up to me."

He shook his head at the foolhardiness of it all, gave his cargo one last check to make sure it was safely in place, then crawled into the cab of Maynard's truck. Moments later, he was on the way out of town with the woman not far behind.

As they passed by the city limit sign, the rain began to lessen, and by the time they were out of sight of Camarune, it had stopped.

The relief Catherine felt was overwhelming, but she was starting to shake. She couldn't remember the last time she'd eaten, and sleep had been scarce this past week. But she'd made her grannie a promise, and she wasn't about to quit on her now. She'd come this far. She could hold out a little while longer.

And there was another thing—something that had happened to her when she'd seen the man's face. It had been a true but quiet knowing that he would matter.

"Grannie, do you believe in love at first sight?"

Annie tried not to laugh. It was a pretty serious question from a girl who'd just turned ten.

"Well, now, I suppose that I do," she said.

Catherine giggled. "Did you know you were in love with Grandpa Billy when you saw him?"

"Lord, no, girl," Annie said. "But you have to remember that I knew Billy Fane all my life. You don't fall in love with a boy who puts frogs down your shirt. That comes after he becomes a man."

Lord, where had that come from? Catherine thought, and then caught herself staring at the breadth of the sheriff's shoulders in the truck in front of her. Nerves tightened, knotting her belly and bringing tears to her eyes. *Oh, Grannie,* she thought. *I would like to believe in such things as destiny, but I don't think I do.*

It was only after they drove out of town and started up the mountain that she began to take note of her surroundings. The trees over the road were tall and dense, often forming heavy canopies that prevented both rain and sun from getting through. The bare ground that was the road was heavily rutted and in places quite rocky, making her thankful for the durability of her Jeep. The pain between her shoulder blades was moving toward her neck. She took a deep breath, rolling her head to loosen the muscles and hoping it went no farther. She'd had a few migraines before. This wasn't a day to have one.

The truck ahead slowed down for a pothole. She hit the brakes, waiting while he negotiated the obstacle, and again caught herself focusing on the back of his head and the set of his shoulders. She squinted her eyes, trying to remember what he looked like.

His eyes had been dark, probably brown. And what she'd seen of his hair was thick and short, but she couldn't remember if it was brown or black. His face was something of a blur, but she had an impression of strong features. What she did remember was his voice. It had been kind. So kind.

Tears spiked, but she blinked them away. She was so tired of crying. But after what Annie had told her, would she ever be able to let go of the pain?

Suddenly, she realized that he'd made it on through. She straightened her shoulders and followed. Gradually, the incline began to steepen. She downshifted once, then again, until she was driving in first gear, bouncing in and out of rock-laden ruts and often just missing being stuck on high center. The forest around her now was so thick it was impossible to see more than a few feet past the trees at the edge of the road. It was daunting to realize how far away from civilization a mere four miles could be. But before she could panic, the truck ahead of her pulled over. She followed suit, wondering if they were already there.

Catherine got out. "What's wrong?"

Luke was already out and shuffling through the jumble of objects in the truck bed.

"There's a tree down in the road. Surely Maynard has a...oh, good...here it is."

Catherine stepped backward, her eyes widening as he hauled a chain saw over the rim of the truck bed.

"What are you going to do?"

He paused, giving her a slow, curious look, then pointed past the truck with his chin.

"Move the tree, ma'am," he said.

Catherine nodded. As he started to walk away, she hesitated, then spoke.

"Call me Catherine."

He stopped then turned, giving her the full force of a dark, silent stare. Then he smiled, and she caught a quick flash of white teeth and what looked like a small dimple to the right of his mouth.

"Catherine it is."

She clasped her hands in front of her stomach to keep them from shaking as he disappeared around the front of the truck.

Grannie, do you believe in love at first sight?

Ignoring her flight of fancy, she stood out of the way, watching as he bent to the task. Moments later, the chain saw roared to life. She leaned against the hood of the Jeep and thrust her hands through her hair, massaging the muscles at the back of her neck. After a bit, the pressure eased. Curious now, she surveyed the area, trying to picture her grandmother traipsing about these woods gathering her herbs.

To her right, a large projection of rock was visible above the tops of the trees, and in the same moment she saw it, she knew it had to be Pulpit Rock. The skin at the back of her neck suddenly crawled. She needed to see—to stand in the place where it had all ended.

But how?

She couldn't just walk away without telling the sheriff where she was going, yet she needed to do this alone. She stood for a moment, trying to decide what to do, then tilted her chin and headed toward Luke DePriest.

The chain saw vibrated the length of Luke's arms as the saw blade ate through the wood. The tree was large and would have to be cut in several pieces for him to be able to move it aside. The roots were gnarled and dry. The tree had been here for some time.

The piece he was cutting off suddenly dropped to one side. He grunted with satisfaction and was setting the chain saw aside when Catherine Fane walked into his line of vision.

"Something wrong?" he asked.

She pointed toward Pulpit Rock. "I'm going over there to take a look."

He frowned. The idea of her wandering off in

any direction bothered him, never mind that she was pointing toward Pulpit Rock.

"If you don't mind waiting a few minutes, I'll go with you," he said, then wondered at the way her expression blanked.

"No. This is something I'd rather do alone." Without waiting for him to agree, she walked away.

Luke watched her go, taking careful note of her direction—just in case. The last thing he needed was to have to instigate a search party, especially up here, and especially for her. He doubted if he could round up a half dozen people who would be willing to set foot on this side of the mountain to look for the lost granddaughter of Annie Fane.

Then he remembered what he'd been doing and turned back to the tree. The quicker he got it out of the road, the quicker he could deliver her to the cabin.

The trees were alive with sounds, from the insistent squawk of a blue jay to the chatter of squirrels as they leaped through the leafy branches, using them like a highway as they moved from tree to tree. On another day, this would have been charming, but everything inside her was in knots. Even now, she could hear the echo of her grandmother's shaky voice, relating the events that had led to her being orphaned.

A couple of minutes passed as she continued to

move toward the looming promontory. The closer she got, the denser the trees became. Tension knotted in her belly, and her legs began to shake. Less sunlight filtered through the canopy, which in turn meant less undergrowth beneath the trees. In places she could see bare rock showing through the earth, and the forest was silent, absent of life.

Suddenly she was standing in the clearing and looking up, trying to imagine what freak of nature had created this natural pulpit. It stretched out from the face of the mountain, as if defying gravity, to overlook a spacious meadow. The natural resonance of sound must be amazing in this place. Then her gaze fell to the shadow below the rock, to the place where Grannie had seen her mother die. Sorrow moved through her like a wave.

She walked closer, needing to see—to touch—to be in the place where her parents had died, and as she did, she saw that what she'd taken for shadow was actually barren ground. She knelt, fingering the thick, dark earth and then stood, letting it filter through her fingers, and wondered why nothing grew in earth this rich.

Then she spun, suddenly aware of faint whispers, but there was no one there. In spite of the heat, she shivered as she searched the area for signs of life, but it was as empty as her heart. In the distance, she could see leaves moving in the tops of the trees, and convinced herself that was the source of the sounds. Yet as she turned away, a powerful urge to run overwhelmed her. She didn't believe in ghosts, but there was a miasma here that had no earthly roots.

"Cath...rine."

The faint sound of someone calling her name made her jump. She spun, subconsciously expecting to see the specter of Fancy Joslin, but when the sheriff walked out of the trees instead, she silently scolded herself for the fantasy.

"I'm here," she called back, and as she started toward him, she realized she was glad to see him.

He met her at the edge of the clearing.

"Are you all right?" he asked. "I've been calling you for several minutes."

"Sorry," she said. "I suppose I was lost in thought."

He hesitated, then touched her shoulder. "Do you know about this place?"

She hesitated, unwilling to reveal her identity to anyone. "Just what my grannie told me," she said. "Something about some people dying up here because of a feud." Then she turned, pointing toward the pulpit. "Isn't that odd?"

He looked in the direction in which she was pointing, trying to decide what she meant. "Isn't what odd?"

"That bare spot beneath the pulpit. It's not rocky

like some of the other places up here, and yet nothing grows.''

Luke sighed. What he was going to tell her would only add to the legend, yet the truth of it was there for the world to see.

"It didn't used to be," he said. "Story goes that after they carried away all of the bodies, the grass began to die. Supposedly, nothing has taken root there for almost thirty years.''

Catherine blanched as she spun around, looking at the place with new meaning. Unwilling for him to see how the news had upset her, she took a deep breath and turned, and for the first time since she'd walked into the woods, realized that her grandmother's casket had been left unattended.

"We should be going. I apologize for the delay. Please lead the way. I'll be right behind you.''

A short while later they were back at the truck. Relieved that her grandmother's casket was still intact, she ran her fingers along the fine finish on the cherry-wood casket.

"Sorry, Grannie. I didn't mean to leave you alone.''

"I'm the one who should apologize," Luke said. "I didn't think.''

Catherine shrugged. "We can both take the blame." Then she looked—really looked—at him, appreciating the quiet grace of the man, as well as his strength. It wasn't until she focused on his face that she found herself caught in a dark, silent gaze.

"You okay?" he asked.

Brown. His eyes are brown, just like his hair. Then she nodded. "Yes."

He glanced at his watch. It was just after two-thirty. "You want to ride the rest of the way with me?" he asked.

The urge to do so was great, but she didn't want to think of being isolated without convenient means of getting off the mountain.

"How much farther?"

"About a quarter of a mile."

"I can make it."

He didn't bother to hide his admiration. "You're not a quitter, are you, Catherine Fane?"

"I am the way my grandmother raised me."

"I'm thinking she did a fine job," he said quietly, then settled his Stetson a little more firmly on his head. "Let's go. If you get into trouble, just honk."

Then he got into the truck, leaving Catherine to scramble back to her vehicle, as well. Minutes later, they were in motion.

Annie Fane's journey was almost over.

4

Luke wasn't a believer in the supernatural, yet when he came out of a sharp curve and saw a small, two-story cabin at the end of the road, the hair on the backs of his arms suddenly rose. It wasn't like anything he'd ever seen in these hills. Fashioned more in the style of a miniature Swiss chalet, it reminded him of a cuckoo clock his aunty had owned. It looked as if the owner had just left for the day, instead of the twenty-odd years he knew she'd been gone. To add to the aura of timelessness, four men seemingly materialized from the deep shadows of the porch and came down the steps to meet them as he parked.

They were tall and spare, with solemn expressions. He didn't know whether it was in deference to the occasion, or if it was their normal manner. Their faces were shaded by matching weather-stained hats with wide, shapeless brims and their clothes were simple—faded denims and cotton. Catherine pulled up beside him and killed the engine. He glanced over, curious as to what her reaction would be. She looked relieved. It would seem she'd been expecting them.

Still, when she emerged from her Jeep, he got out and moved to her side, approaching the men with caution. Mountain people didn't like strangers, so even if they knew Catherine, they were going to be wary of him. As they neared the porch, something began to dawn on Luke. He'd been sheriff of Taney County for more than eight years and knew everyone in the area—and these men were strangers to him, too. He thought of the thefts that had been going on up here for years. It would be too easy to believe that in a random act of kindness to Catherine Fane, he'd found the people he'd been trying to catch. But his musing ended when the eldest of the men suddenly took off his hat and reached for Catherine's hand.

"You'd be Annie's girl," he said, without question or hesitation.

"Call me Catherine," she said. "And you're Abram Hollis?"

"At your service, Miss Fane. These are my boys, Jefferson, Dancy and Cleveland." Then he turned to the boys. "Boys, this here is your cousin Annie's granddaughter."

The "boys" were all thirty-something in age and well over six feet.

Catherine smiled to herself at the term. Their gentle manners and soft words went a long way in washing away the hurt from the earlier incidents in Camarune.

"Grannie used to read me your letters, so I feel like I already know you. I just wish we could be meeting under different circumstances."

"No one ever said life was fair," Abram said. "Annie lived a long life. It's time she came home to be with Billy."

Belatedly, Catherine remembered the sheriff.

"I'm sorry. I forgot my manners. Abram, this is Sheriff Luke DePriest. He volunteered to help me get my..." Transient pain moved across her features as she corrected herself. "Helped me get the casket here. And, I might add, he was the *only* person who was willing to help."

Her fingers brushed the fabric of Luke's shirt as she directed his attention to the older man. "Sheriff, this is Abram Hollis. He and my grandmother were cousins, and they've worked together for as long as I can remember."

Luke's eye widened. Working? At what? As a fence for stolen goods? But undue curiosity was a breech of mountain etiquette. Instead of questions, he touched the edge of his hat in recognition of the introduction. The men nodded back, but they, too, remained silent.

Catherine sighed. Grannie had warned her that mountain people would be reserved, but she hadn't expected mute. Then she saw the shovels leaning against the porch—a painful reminder of why she'd come. She looked at Abram.

"The grave...?"

"Right next to Billy, where Annie wanted it to be."

Refusing to cry, Catherine set her jaw and looked away, letting herself take in the simple beauty of the place and imagining a young Annie Fane traversing these mountains, wrapped in the solitude she'd so badly needed after losing her young husband in the Second World War.

Oh, Grannie, you gave up so very much for me. Then she glanced toward the truck. It was time to lay Annie to rest.

"May we begin?" she asked.

Abram motioned to his sons. Immediately, they moved toward the casket. Luke felt like the odd man out as they lowered the tailgate of the truck. Impulsively, he touched Catherine's shoulder.

"Miss Fane?"

She looked up, her eyes shimmering with unshed tears.

"I'd be honored to help," he said, pointing toward the casket the men were about to lift out.

She hesitated, but only briefly. "I think Grannie would like that."

Luke stepped into place between Abram and Dancy as they pulled the casket from the truck.

He'd served as a pallbearer more than once in his life, but never in such humble surroundings.

A few moments later, they began to walk, moving toward some unseen destination behind the cabin, with Catherine leading the way. When they passed a tall oak, a small brown bird dropped from a limb above their heads, landing on a nearby bush, as if vying for a seat to watch the passing procession.

Although it had been muggy down in Camarune, the air was cooler up here. The ground was rocky and almost grassless in the front, but as they passed the side of the cabin, the ground cover changed from sparse to ankle-high grass mixed with wild-flowers and plants he didn't recognize. The fact that it had a cultivated look surprised him. If Annie Fane had been gone all these many years, who'd been taking care of her home? Within seconds of his thought, Catherine made a remark that gave him an answer.

"You've done a fine job taking care of Grannie's home."

"She was kin," Abram said. "She would have done the same for me."

Luke frowned but kept silent. Another bit of information to add to the pot, but one thing kept bothering him. If this place was so special to Annie Fane, why had she left it?

And then they stopped, bending in unison as the

casket was lowered to the ground. The pile of fresh earth and the pit beside it were harsh reminders of why they'd come. He looked up in time to see Catherine reach for a nearby tree to steady herself. The urge to hold her was strong, but without asking, he knew she would not welcome it.

He took a deep breath, feeling a sense of reverence for what was about to occur. The men gathered a series of ropes with which to lower the casket into the grave, and then time seemed to stand still. Later he would remember it in a series of brief images.

The scent of freshly dug earth as a shovelful of dirt hit the top of Annie's casket.

The soft sound of Catherine's sobs.

The trill of a robin's call from somewhere high.

The perfect unison with which the Hollis men worked as they fulfilled their kinswoman's last request.

The sonorous tone of Abram Hollis's voice piercing the silence as he recited the Twenty-third Psalm.

The wilting blooms from the bouquet of wildflowers that Catherine laid upon the grave.

And then it was over. The fresh pile of dirt lay like a wound upon the landscape. With time, it would settle, and the ivy that lay over Billy Fane's grave would blanket his Annie's, as well.

Catherine stood staring down at the grave. It was done. She looked up, her eyes brimming with tears.

"There aren't enough words to thank you men for what you've done for me today."

The Hollis men took off their hats in unison, slight flushes coloring their faces as Abram nodded.

"Like I said before, she would have done the same for me." Then he reset his hat, shifting it slightly from side to side until it fell into some invisible slot. "If you're of a mind to stay on for a while, you're welcome to stay with us over in Crocker. It's in the next county, but I'd be happy to draw you a map."

"Thank you, but no," Catherine said. "I'll only be here for a few days until I can go through Grannie's things."

Luke had remained silent through most of the proceedings, but the thought of her staying up here alone bothered him.

"I don't think that's wise," he said abruptly.

Catherine turned. Her voice took on a sharp, angry edge. "Why? Because the people of Camarune might not like it?"

He flushed. "No, ma'am. That's not what I meant at all. There has been a rash of thefts in the area, and this place is too isolated to be safe for a woman alone."

"No one is going to bother the witch's cabin or anyone in it, remember?"

The sarcastic tone of her voice was impossible to miss, but before Luke could respond, Abram Hollis intervened.

"She'll be safe," he said shortly. "Me and mine will see to it."

"I don't need baby-sitters," Catherine said, including the Hollis men in her answer. "And just so you understand, city living is far more dangerous than this place is, and I've been taking care of myself there just fine. I appreciate your concerns, but I'm staying, and that's that."

Abram accepted her decision far better than Luke. Once again, he touched Catherine's arm as he had when they met.

"As you know, we've been staying in the house a couple of times a year during hunting season, so it's not too run-down. But me and the boys touched the place up a bit while we were waiting for you, and my Polly sent you some supper. And I had the power turned on in the cabin, so the necessary is working."

Catherine's smile was bittersweet. The necessary, meaning the bathroom, was a word Grannie had used all her life. Now she knew where it came from.

"Again, Abram Hollis, I thank you."

He nodded. "We'll be going now. Boys, go get your sacks. We've got a ways to go before dark."

The three men headed toward the front of the

house, returning moments later with large, bulging gunnysacks thrown over their shoulders.

Again Luke thought of the thefts, and even though it might be bad manners to ask, he had a duty he couldn't ignore.

"What's in the sacks?" Beside him, he heard Catherine take a deep breath.

Abram Hollis turned, fixing him with a cool, blank stare.

"That would be our harvest."

Luke's thoughts slipped right into illegal drugs as his hand moved toward the pistol he wore on his hip.

"What kind of harvest would that be?"

Abram stiffened as his sons stopped in mid-step. It was Catherine's intervention that eased the moment.

"Abram, I'm sure the sheriff isn't interested in poaching on your territory."

Luke frowned. "Poaching?"

Catherine sighed. This had all been too easy. She should have expected something like this.

"Grannie was a herbalist," she said softly. "Not a witch. Abram has been harvesting Grannie's crops and sharing in the profits for as long as I can remember."

"What kind of crops?" Luke asked, still thinking along the lines of illegal drugs.

Abram took one of the sacks and dropped it at

the sheriff's feet. The top fell open, revealing a jumble of brown, tangled roots. Luke knelt, lifting one out into the light.

At first glance it looked something like a sweet potato, but then he picked up another, then another, and the humanlike shapes of miniature arms and legs began to dawn.

Ginseng.

The crop was worth big money on the Asian markets, even in the raw.

He dropped the roots back in the sack and then stood and offered his hand to Abram Hollis.

"Sorry," he said. "But in my line of work, a man can't overlook the obvious."

Abram hesitated, then shook Luke's hand. "No offense taken," he said shortly.

Within minutes, they were gone.

Now Luke and Catherine were alone, and from the expression on her face, she was impatiently waiting for him to take his leave, too.

"Is there anything I can carry into the cabin for you?"

She hesitated, then nodded. "Yes, I suppose so," she said. "I have a couple of boxes of groceries and my suitcase."

"Just show me where you want them," he said, and let her lead the way.

As they entered the cabin, once again he was struck by the fairy-tale quality of the place. It consisted of only two large rooms. One up. One down. But the inventiveness of the builder was evident. Minute nooks and crannies were filled with everything from jars of dried herbs to stacks and stacks of books. There wasn't an inch of wasted space. The furniture was sturdy, but simple, and the quiet hum of an old refrigerator was the only sound within the room.

Although Catherine was grateful for his help, she was anxious for him to leave. This was the place where Grannie had lived. She wanted to explore it in private.

"Just put the stuff down anywhere," she said quietly, then walked to the door, holding it ajar for him to exit so that there would be no misunderstanding as to her intent.

Luke did as she asked, then turned, hesitating beside the table.

"I wish you'd reconsider and—"

"Thank you again for all you've done for me today."

Luke frowned. He was being dismissed, and there was little he could do. She was a grown woman, and it wasn't against the law to be a fool.

"You're welcome, but if you don't mind, I'll stop in sometime tomorrow and make sure you're all right."

An expression of relief came and went on Catherine's face so quickly that Luke thought he'd imagined it.

"There's really no need," she said, holding the door back a little further.

He settled his Stetson a little more firmly. "On the contrary, Miss Fane. There is a need. Mine. I won't rest easy tonight, thinking of you up here by yourself. At least do me the favor of shoving a chair underneath the damned doorknob before you go to bed."

Then he was gone, moving across the porch and then the yard in long, angry strides. He got into the borrowed truck, backed up and then drove away without looking back. Catherine had the feeling that he was angrier with himself for leaving her there than at her for insisting on staying.

Then she forgot about the kindness of strangers as she turned around, for the first time letting herself into what was left of Annie Fane's world.

Catherine stared into the fire that she'd built in the fireplace, watching the voracious appetite of the flames as they consumed the dry logs that had been left on the hearth. Even though the night wasn't all that cool, the fire lent a fake cheeriness to the room. But cheer was lacking in Catherine's heart. Here, in the place where Annie had begun her life with the man she'd loved, Catherine had expected to find peace. Instead, she felt empty. The legacy of Annie's love had not been enough to assuage the horror of Catherine's birth.

A log suddenly rolled against the back of the firewall, sending a shower of sparks up the chimney. Outside, a wind had come up, whining and moaning through the trees and shifting the walls in the old cabin just enough to give an occasional creak. But she wasn't afraid of the dark, or of what lay beyond these walls. It was what festered inside her heart that she feared the most. The rage she felt at an entire community who'd let a senseless feud play on was making her sick. And the fact that they'd ignored it while shunning Annie was an evil too preposterous to accept. On her deathbed, her grandmother had warned her about their prejudice, but she hadn't believed—not until she'd seen their faces and heard the accusations and whispers.

Witch.

The notion was so absurd that it was all she could do not to scream. How could ignorance such as this still exist? They were in the twenty-first century, and these people chose to accept an eye for an eye as justice, and believed in curses and spells?

In the midst of her musing, something thudded out on the porch, then rattled across the old wooden planks.

Catherine jumped to her feet, pivoting sharply to face the door, too late remembering Luke's final warning. With racing heart, she grabbed a chair from beside the kitchen table and shoved it up under the doorknob, jamming it so tightly that she inadvertently pinched her finger.

At the moment of pain, sanity returned.

"Lord," she muttered, then she took a deep breath, silently berating her panic.

She listened again. The sound was gone. All she could hear was the wind. She made herself calm. More than likely it had been something blowing across the porch. There wasn't anything—or anyone—out there.

To prove to herself she was right, she kicked the chair away from the doorknob and yanked the door open wide, striding out onto the porch to face the night. Immediately, strands of hair whipped across her face and into her eyes, clouding her vision with stinging tears.

"There's no one out here but me," she muttered, then took a deep breath and walked to the edge of the porch. "There's no one out here but me," she said louder, letting the wind rip the words out of her throat.

She looked up at the sky. Straggly clouds scudded across the face of a quarter moon, leaving wispy bits of themselves behind as they flew. Something took flight from a nearby tree, cutting briefly across the periphery of her vision. For the first time in her life she was, quite literally, alone. No neighbors down the block. No cars. No lights.

No telephones. No sounds of civilization except the sound of her own voice. Her fingers curled into fists as she gazed into the blackness of the tree line. Again she spoke, and this time, it came out in a defiant shout.

"There's no one out here but me!"

She waited, challenging the darkness for an answer that never came. Shaken in both body and spirit, she spun around and strode into the cabin, slamming the door shut behind her.

A short while later, she climbed the stairs to the loft. When she reached the top, she took a last look down at the big room below, then at the meager lock and the chair beneath the doorknob. Hating herself for being afraid, she crawled into bed, certain she would never be able to close her eyes. Within minutes, she was asleep.

Less than a hundred yards from the house, the hunter crouched among the trees, his expression wary. Someone was in the cabin. It couldn't be the ghosts that he'd seen there before, because ghosts didn't need lights. And whoever was in there had not only turned on the power, but had also built a fire. Even though the wind was blowing in the opposite direction, there were brief moments when he could smell the smoke.

Curiosity was a powerful emotion, and the urge to move closer was upon him. But years of solitude and caution kept him hidden from sight. As he continued to watch, the door to the cabin was suddenly flung open. Instinctively, he shrank back into the trees, although he knew it was impossible for her to see him from where he was standing. Her slender form was nothing but a silhouette as the light from within spilled out around her.

When she started to speak, he stared into the darkness, believing that she was talking to someone out in the yard. But the longer he stood, the more certain he became that she was talking to herself, which made him relax. He'd been talking to himself for years.

At first he caught only a word or two of what she was saying, but when she shouted, "There is no one out here but me," he froze. Even though he didn't want to know her, at that moment, he knew how she felt.

The wind began to rise, wailing through the trees in a high, mournful sound. His stance became motionless. He tilted his head to listen, as he had done so many times before. Would this be the time? Would his search finally come to an end? His breathing became shallow, his pulse all but nonexistent, as he willed himself to an unnatural quiet.

There! He heard it again—the high-pitched cry of a newborn child. His eyes narrowed, his jaw setting as he disappeared into the night.

* * *

Luke tossed aside the latest file on the thefts and then stood up from his desk, stretching wearily as he strode to the window to look outside. Moths and other night bugs made kamikaze runs at the street-light outside his office as he stared into the dark. But his mind wasn't on what lay before him. Instead, he kept thinking of the thief, who, like a pack rat, stole one thing, only to leave another in its place. Added to that were the oddities of what he stole—anything from foodstuffs to a pair of overalls drying on a clothesline, as well as odds and ends of small tools. If memory served, the thief had once taken a handsaw rather than the more expensive chainsaw hanging beside it, and left a hand-carved bowl in its place. Another time he'd obviously watched a farmer cutting firewood, waited until the man went inside to eat a meal, then took the ax he'd left in the stump, leaving behind a small, wooden stool. Dogs never barked a warning of his arrival, and to date, no one had even gathered a glimpse of his face. Rumors were starting to spread that it was a ghost. Only Luke knew better. Ghosts had no need of earthly things, and ghosts didn't wear shoes, especially shoes with a notch in one heel.

The muscles ached in the back of his neck, and he rolled his head, thinking of a warm bath and a soft bed, and the moment he did, his thoughts slid to Catherine Fane. The fact that he'd left her on that damned mountain was still eating at him. Even though he'd been honoring her wishes, he couldn't help but think she was out of her element. Then he frowned. He couldn't save the world, even though he often tried. With a weary sigh, he grabbed his hat from the rack and switched off the lights. It was time to go home.

Much later, after a meal and the much-longed-for-bath, he crawled naked between the sheets. The cool feel of smooth cotton against his body was a sensual feast. As was his habit, he kicked at the bedclothes until his feet were uncovered, and then he stretched his legs, feeling the round, wooden bed rail against the balls of his feet. When he closed his eyes, the image of Catherine Fane's face came to him as he'd seen her first—standing in Maynard Phillips's station with raindrops running down her face.

And he slept.

5

Nellie Cauthorn was fixing Preacher's breakfast and reached for a couple of eggs. The first one she broke into the skillet was a double yolk. She smiled. She liked bargains, and this was two for the price of one. Absently, she cracked the second egg into the pan. It was already mixing with the first when she glanced down in horror. The albumen that should have been clear was, instead, a dark, bloody mass.

"Save me, Jesus!" she gasped, and yanked the skillet from the fire, dumping the mess into the garbage disposal before she thought.

Hot grease popped and spattered as it connected with the swiftly running water, but Nellie was too shocked to worry about getting burned. All she could think about was the black hearse, the dead dog and the woman who'd been buried above Pulpit Rock. In her mind, this was another sign of the discord that had come to Camarune.

Moments later, Preacher came into the kitchen for his food, at which point, Nellie burst into tears, demanding they pray, both for their safety as well as their immortal souls.

But Nellie wasn't the only citizen of the area that morning to get a rude surprise. When Virgil Kemp went outside to do morning chores, he saw Old Susie, his favorite milk cow, had delivered a new calf. But then the calf raised its head. One large brown eye stared back at Virgil from the middle of its forehead. Virgil grunted as if he'd been punched, absorbing the baby's anomaly. Within the blink of the calf's one eye, he remembered the woman they'd taken up the mountain to bury. Yesterday he'd run from Maynard's station like a coward, unwilling to come in contact with a witch—either living or dead.

Now this.

The way he looked at it, the witch's kin had paid him back for his refusal to help.

The calf bawled, then staggered to its feet. Old Susie nudged at her baby, trying to push it in the direction of her burgeoning udders, but the single eye didn't focus in the way that nature had intended. Instead of latching on to the teats, the calf took two unsteady steps sideways, then fell face down in the straw. Virgil shuddered, then turned and headed for the house to get his gun.

In the cabin above Pulpit Rock, Catherine was waking to a surprise of her own. The watch she'd laid on the bedside table last night was missing, and in its place was a piece of blue glass. She sat up with a start, looking wildly about the loft, but there was no one there. She peered over the railing to the room below and could see that the front door was still locked.

She began searching anew, believing that she must have laid the watch someplace else and that the glass had been there all along. But after a good five minutes, she gave up and got dressed. The mystery of the missing watch was secondary to what lay ahead. By the time she got downstairs, her stomach was growling with hunger.

A quick prowl through the refrigerator yielded a wrapped piece of cheese that she'd overlooked last night. Bread and cheese wasn't her normal breakfast fare, but right now she was in no mood to be picky. Digging through her grannie's old utensils in search of a knife brought a moment of sadness. If only Grannie had told her about this place sooner, they could have come back years ago. It would have been wonderful to see it through her grandmother's eyes. Then she sighed, remembering one of Annie's favorite sayings. If wishes were horses, then beggars would ride, which technically speaking meant, Get over it, Catherine. Deal with the facts, not daydreams.

Thankful for the kindness of the Hollis women for their food, as well as for making the cabin habitable, she took out a knife with an old wooden handle and used it to cut off a thick chunk of cheese. With bread in one hand and cheese in the other, she wandered out onto the porch to greet the day.

A crow that had been perched on the hood of her Jeep took to the air with a loud, raucous caw.

"Same to you," Catherine yelled, and then grinned to herself at the childishness of the taunt.

She strolled to the edge of the porch, considering having her meal in the backyard, then turned away. She wasn't ready to face that mound of fresh earth. She sat down on the front steps and began making a crude sandwich of the bread and cheese. As she ate, an odd sort of solace began to sink in. The woods were alive with all manner of sounds. Some she could identify. Some she could not. Yet unlike last night, she had no sense of fear. She took another bite, savoring the tangy bite of Cheddar with the crusty bit of sourdough bread she had left, and wished for a hot cup of coffee to wash it all down. But that would mean moving, and right now, she was in no mood to ruin the first moments of peace she'd known in weeks.

A flash of color caught her eye, and she turned in time to see a pair of cardinals light on the ground. The male, a deep, crimson red with a bright orange beak, pecked quickly, then flew to a nearby bush, while the female, a smaller, browner version of the male, continued to feed. It took a few minutes for

Catherine to realize that the male had taken a guardian position so that his mate could safely eat. Witnessing the trust one had in the other was impossible to ignore. She sighed, wishing she could claim the same thing in her life. But unlike the small brown cardinal, she had no one watching her back, nor was she likely to. She was as alone in this world as a person could be.

A sudden need to talk to Grannie had her scrambling to her feet, and even though she knew the conversation would be strictly one-sided, she tossed the last of her bread and cheese on the ground and started toward the back of the cabin.

The trees were thicker there—hiding all but the smallest bits of blue sky. The grass was damp, still bearing remnants of an early morning dew. A squirrel scolded as she passed beneath a stately spruce, unwilling to share its space with the intruder below. But Catherine's focus wasn't on what loomed above her; it was what lay before her that drew her on. Then she was standing at the foot of Annie's grave. She knelt, leaning forward and touching the fresh earth with the palms of both hands. The pain of loss was sharp, but there was also a sense of accomplishment at fulfilling her grandmother's last wish.

"We're here, Grannie Annie, just like I promised." She glanced to her right, reading the name just visible through the ivy twining around the old stone marker. "You and your Billy are together again."

Then she rocked back on her heels and closed her eyes, letting the day and the scents assail her. There was a hint of thyme in the air, and the familiar bite of dill. Sweet mingled with sharp, bitter with clean—so like the garden they'd had back home. She thought of the countless hours Annie must have spent in this place and the joy it had brought her. It made her recall so many childhood memories—of the days spent trailing at Grannie's heels as she traversed through the Texas fields, gathering the herbs that she had cultivated, as well as those she'd found growing wild. Annie Fane had been a woman ahead of her time. Catherine thought of her grandmother's health-food store back in Wichita Falls, Texas, as well as the home she'd been brought up in. The store she would keep open, but she wasn't so sure about living in that big old house all alone.

Then she opened her eyes and stood, looking back at the cabin. According to Annie's will, everything that had been hers was now Catherine's, including this.

She rubbed at an achy spot between her eyebrows. There was too much to digest in such a short time. Annie didn't have to tell Catherine the truth about her birth. She could have taken the secret to her grave, and no one would have been the wiser, which made Catherine certain that there was more to Annie's reasoning than unburdening herself of secrets before she met her Maker. She could have told Catherine the truth at any time of her life and it wouldn't have changed the facts. Annie Fane had been Catherine's world.

But there were other things to be factored into what Catherine had been told. If her grandmother's story was to be believed, everyone who might have mattered in her life was dead. The widows and children of the men who had been her uncles would want nothing to do with her—especially when they knew the circumstances of her birth. And Catherine had no idea if there were any Blairs or Joslins still living in the area. What if revealing her identity might, in some way, resurrect the feud? Annie had to have considered all that before she told Catherine the truth, which made Catherine suspect that her grannie had another reason. But what?

Annie had to have known that, in bringing her grandmother's body to Kentucky to bury it, Catherine would be thrown into the midst of whatever it was that had made the people of Camarune fear her to begin with. If that was so, then what was it that Annie expected her to do? What could she possibly do that Annie had not been able to accomplish? In the midst of her dilemma, the unmistakable sound of an approaching vehicle sent her hurrying around to the front of the cabin, her worries momentarily forgotten.

The white four-wheel-drive Blazer that pulled up was unfamiliar, but the driver who got out was not. The moment she saw Luke DePriest, she realized she'd been expecting him. He had promised he would be back, and he'd struck her as a man who made good on his promises. It gave her a small sense of satisfaction to realize she'd been right. She watched his approach, absently appreciating the way he filled out his clothes—wide shoulders, long legs and what appeared to be a hard, flat belly. He was muscular, but without all the bulk, and while his features were unremarkably even, it was the strength in his jaw and the gleam in his eye that made him a man to remember. Then he stopped before her, touched the tip of his finger to the brim of his Stetson.

"Miss Fane."

"Sheriff."

He almost smiled at her formality. "You make it all right last night?"

Catherine nodded, thinking as she did that his voice sounded like good whiskey tasted—smooth, but with just enough bite to warm your belly. A little startled at herself for letting her thoughts run in such a personal direction, she looked away and, in doing so, missed the look of appreciation on his face.

Luke sighed. The anxiety to know she was okay had been eating at him all night. As if that wasn't enough, stopping at Maynard's this morning for gas had only added to his worry. Rumors were spreading all over town that the witch's kin had come back to Camarune to pay them back for shunning Annie Fane all those years ago. Despite Luke's best efforts, he hadn't been able to change anyone's thinking. Nellie Cauthorn had sworn her breakfast had turned to blood before her eyes, which was bad enough; then Virgil Kemp had produced Old Susie's latest effort at reproduction for the town to see. One look at the deformed calf and it had been all over. All Luke could see to do was get up the mountain as fast as he could and make sure she was still all right. And while he was relieved to see her alive and well, he felt slightly rejected by her lack of enthusiasm. He found himself searching for reasons to continue the tenuous connection.

"Is there anything you need?"

"No, I'm fine," Catherine said, and brushed at a gnat that landed on her arm.

Luke frowned, resisting the urge to fidget. He felt like he had the time he'd gone to his first party, then spent the entire evening trying to get up the nerve to ask someone to dance. This shouldn't be such a big deal. So why was he making it one?

"Look, Miss Fane, I'll be in the area most of the

morning, so if you don't mind, I'll be stopping by again before I leave.''

Catherine found herself caught in an enigmatic stare. It took her a moment to respond.

''Catherine. Please, call me Catherine.''

''If you'll call me Luke, it's a deal, Catherine Fane.''

''Sheriff...'' She quickly corrected herself. ''Luke, may I ask you something?''

He nodded.

''Why the big concern? I told you I'm fine, and I'm not stranded here. And even if I were, it's not all that far into Camarune. If I had to, I could walk it in a couple of hours.''

''Don't do that!'' he said abruptly, then silently cursed himself for overreacting. She didn't know what was going on down in town, and Lord only knew what would happen if she showed up—especially on foot and unable to get away quickly. ''What I'm trying to say is, there's still a thief roaming the mountain, and I'm not going to feel good about it until he's caught.''

''I have a cell phone,'' Catherine said.

He shook his head. ''Won't work up here.''

She looked startled. ''But...''

He waved his hand toward the forest. ''The mountains are too high, the trees are too dense. They never work up here. Trust me, I know.''

The knowledge wasn't devastating, but it did take away an edge Catherine had thought she had.

"Okay," she said. "I'll be careful, and thank you."

He nodded, then stood for a moment, trying to think of another way to continue the conversation.

The silence between them lengthened.

The pair of cardinals that had been feeding earlier was nowhere in sight, nor was the crow that had been perched on her Jeep. Catherine couldn't think of another thing to discuss, but she was oddly reluctant for him to leave. When her stomach suddenly growled, she blushed. To her relief, he didn't seem to notice.

"Want some coffee?" she asked, and then gave herself a mental kick. Why had she done that? She wanted to be left alone to go through Grannie's things—didn't she?

A sense of relief settled on Luke's shoulders. "Yes, thank you."

"We might have to settle for instant."

He took off his hat. "If it's got caffeine in it, I'm game."

She led the way into the cabin.

"Can I help?" Luke asked, as Catherine began rummaging through the cabinets.

Surprised by his offer, she paused. "Well...yes, actually, you can. See if you can find a coffeepot.

I'll check out the stove. It's gas, but I have no idea if it even works.''

"There's a propane tank on the west side of the house. If Abram Hollis saw to having the power turned on, I'd lay odds he also had the tank refilled.''

To Catherine's relief, he was right. A bright blue flame flared almost immediately.

"Well, now,'' she muttered to herself, "we've got heat.''

Luke turned, giving her an enigmatic stare and wondered if she knew what she'd just said. The way he was feeling, there was every possibility that they could generate all kinds of heat. But his conscience pricked, and he shoved the thought aside.

"And I found the coffeepot,'' he said, holding up an old tin percolator.

Catherine laughed. "I can't remember the last time I saw one this old. Look, even the little glass knob on top is still there.''

"Got some coffee?''

"In that box on the table.''

Together they got the process started; then Catherine began digging through the food she'd brought. When she turned to put up some cans, she noticed that the heel of sourdough bread she'd cut earlier was gone. In its place was an old rusty bottle cap. Frowning, she picked it up and tossed it in a sack she was using for a trash can.

"Did you eat the bread that was here?"

Slightly taken aback by her question, he managed to stammer, "What bread?"

Catherine frowned. "It was right here by the cheese. I could have sworn there was a piece left when I went outside."

Luke's focus sharpened. This complaint was similar to those of the people who'd been visited by the thief.

"What did you just throw in the trash?" he asked.

She shrugged. "An old bottle cap. I don't know where it came from."

Luke dug through the sack until he found it. His concern lifted when he realized this was not the quality of item the thief left in trade. He turned to Catherine.

"You're sure this wasn't on the cabinet earlier?"

"Yes, why?"

He shook his head; then he began moving slowly around the room staring at the floor. Suddenly he paused, then dropped to his knees. There was a door missing on a small cabinet, and he could see daylight through the back wall.

"What is it?" Catherine asked, as she peered over his shoulder.

"I'm not sure, but I'll bet you've got a pack rat. They'll take just about anything, but they always leave something in its place."

Catherine suddenly moaned. "My watch."

Luke stood. "Are you missing something else?"

"I put my watch on the table upstairs by the bed last night. When I woke up, the only thing there was a piece of blue glass."

Luke smiled ruefully. "Hope it wasn't expensive."

"It was a gift from Grannie."

His smile slipped. "Sorry." Then he added. "Maybe we can find the nest."

"Really? You can do that?"

"If we're lucky, but that means I'll have to come back."

Catherine's attention suddenly focused on what he'd just said. "Are you fishing for an invitation?"

Luke took a deep breath, surprised by his reluctance to admit how much he liked her company.

"Yes, ma'am, I suppose that I am."

"If you'll remember to call me Catherine, consider yourself invited."

"Catherine...Catherine...Catherine," Luke said softly.

A shiver ran up the back of Catherine's spine as her name rolled off his tongue.

"Once was enough," she mumbled, unwilling to let him know that the sound of his voice made her heart skip a beat.

Luke glanced toward the stove, searching, like

her, for something to break the tension that kept
springing up between them.

"Looks like that coffee is done."

Catherine bolted toward the stove, thankful for
the distraction. A short while later, they were out
on the porch, sipping coffee and talking about in-
consequential things. But it wasn't until Catherine
realized she'd been carrying the conversation for
some time that she paused.

"Am I boring you?"

Luke jerked. "Sorry, what was it you were saying?"

She grinned wryly. "It's a good thing I'm a secure woman. It's not very flattering to know you
can put a man to sleep by talking."

He frowned. "It wasn't you," he said. "I've
been debating with myself about whether I should
tell you what's going on in Camarune."

"I'm not crazy about surprises, so if it concerns
me, I think I have a right to know."

He knew she was right, and gauging her state of
mind by the set of her jaw, she could probably handle whatever he told her.

"People have gotten all stirred up about Annie
Fane being brought back to the mountain, and
then…you staying here in Annie's cabin…" He
hesitated for a moment. How in the hell did you
tell someone she'd been branded a witch?

"Look, Catherine, somehow they've gotten it in

their heads that you've come to pay them back for
the way they treated your grandmother. They think
you're putting hexes on them, and they're all running scared.''

Her eyes widened. Her mouth went slack. It took
her a couple of minutes to absorb what he'd said.
Finally she shook her head in disbelief.

''You're kidding...aren't you?''

''No, and I'm serious when I tell you that I don't
think you're safe up here. The town has gotten itself
into a panic, and truthfully, I'm afraid of what they
might do.''

She stood abruptly. He followed suit. A faint
shudder seized her as she finally looked up. Her
eyes were wide with shock, her lips slack and trembling.

''To me? You think they would hurt me?''

''I don't know,'' he said softly. ''But I had to
warn you. One of the men who refused to help you
yesterday had a calf born this morning that was
disfigured. He's decided it was your doing. That
you were getting back at him for refusing to help
you.'' He thought of the preacher's wife claiming
her food had turned to blood, but decided not to go
into details. ''And there have been other things, not
quite so dramatic, but just as troubling.''

''My God,'' Catherine whispered, and turned
away, unwilling to let him see her fear.

She thought of her grannie and the years of torment these people must have put her through. Suddenly it was all too much. Tears welled, rolling quietly down her cheeks.

Luke silently cursed the fools of the world, then walked up behind her and took her in his arms.

Instinctively, she tried to move away, but he shook his head and held her that much firmer.

"Don't fight me," he said gruffly. "I'm on your side."

She hesitated, but only for a moment before going limp against him. She was tired of having to be the strong one. And he was there. What harm could it do? A sob choked back any words she might have said.

"I'm sorry, Catherine, more than I can say."

She leaned against him and felt his chin resting against the top of her head. His arms were strong, his breath steady and even against the side of her cheek. She closed her eyes.

"God...so am I."

Luke hated himself for being the bearer of bad news, but in good conscience, he'd had no other choice. When she went limp against him, he wanted to turn her in his arms and kiss away the tears he knew she was shedding. But those thoughts were as foolish as the mind-set of the residents of Camarune. Even though she felt right in his arms—even though her tears hurt his heart—she was still a stranger.

"Is there anything I can do for you?" he asked. "Anyone from back home you would like to call?"

"There's no one," she said, and then stopped. "I take that back. There *is* something you can do for me."

He thought of the investigation he was supposed to be conducting and shoved it to the back of his mind. The damned thief had been in business for years. A couple of hours devoted to something else wasn't going to change the world.

"Name it."

"Take me down to Camarune. I have a sudden need to go shopping."

Her request startled him, but it was obvious she was serious. Her jaw was set, her blue eyes flashing.

"Are you sure?" he asked.

"I don't run, and I don't hide," Catherine stated. "And I'll be damned if I'll let a bunch of superstitious fools force me into doing either."

A slight smile broke the solemness of his face as he took a handkerchief from his pocket and handed it to her.

"Then you better wipe your face," he said gently. "My daddy told me to never let your enemies see your fear."

His thoughtfulness touched her in a way she wouldn't have believed. She swiped at the tears, resisting the urge to blow her nose, then handed back the handkerchief.

"Again I find myself in your debt."

He shrugged. "One of these days I'll collect." Then he stuffed the handkerchief back in his pocket and settled his Stetson a little more firmly on his head. "Get what you need. I'll be in the car."

She'd gotten all the way into the cabin before she focused on what he'd said. One of these days he would collect? Her heart skipped a beat. Collect what?

A gnat buzzed up the hunter's nose as he watched the lawman's vehicle moving down the mountain, but he made no attempt to remove it. He'd learned long ago that the trick to perfect concealment was immobility. As they passed, his eyes narrowed. The woman from the cabin was with him. Only after the sound of the engine had faded away did he move. He walked from rock to rock, taking care not to leave any tracks as he headed uphill. Curiosity, as well as a sense of self-preservation, drove him to investigate the intrusion into his world.

A short while later, he walked into Annie Fane's cabin as if he owned it, sniffing the air like the animal he'd become and making sure he was alone. Only after he was certain there was no one else there did he begin to move about the room.

An assortment of jars and books lined the shelves on one wall. He poked among them, fingering the fragile old pages without reading the text. He had no use for words or the people who uttered them, but food was another matter. He went through the canned goods, settled on a couple of cans of meat and a can of fruit, and dropped them into a bag he slung on one shoulder, then put a small wooden carving of a horse on the windowsill above the sink.

The stairs to the second floor beckoned, but he could tell that there was only one way up and one way down—a sure trap. He moved on, unwilling to take a chance.

As he passed a window looking out into the backyard, he saw the mound of freshly turned earth and stopped. For a long, silent moment he stared. Death. He knew about death. He'd been waiting for it to catch him for far too long. Then he shrugged and turned away. This didn't concern him, and it was time to go.

As he moved toward the door, he caught a glimpse of someone from the corner of his eye and froze. It took a moment for him to realize it was himself that he was seeing. Still tense, he turned to face the image, eyes widening as he stared at the unruly shock of long, dark hair. Then his gaze slid downward, past dark, troubled eyes, to the bottom half of his face and the thick, bushy beard. The man was a stranger. He took a step closer, eyes locking with the wild, angry glare of the man looking back. Somewhere within, recognition dawned. His nostrils flared, and his head jerked back as if he'd been hit on the chin. Within seconds he was out of the cabin and running into the woods, needing to put as much distance as he could between himself and the ghost he'd just seen.

Luke drove into the outskirts of Camarune, wondering what kind of a Pandora's box this visit was going to open, then stifled his worry. It didn't matter. Catherine was right. The people in this town needed a wake-up call, and if he wasn't mistaken, she was just the woman to give them one.

"Where to first?" he asked.

"What time is it?" she asked.

"Almost twelve."

"I seem to remember there's a small café somewhere on Main Street."

"It doesn't amount to much, but their hamburgers are good," Luke said. "Are you hungry?"

She shook her head. "Your news pretty much ruined my appetite, however, I'm thinking I might ruin a few appetites of my own. Are you game?"

He gave her a nervous look. "You sure you want to do this?"

"Have they given me a choice?"

He pulled to the curb right in front of Lucy's Eats. "All right, Catherine. Do your thing. Just be careful what you say."

She arched an eyebrow. "Oh, honey," she drawled. "Trust me. Butter won't melt in my mouth."

6

Lucy's Eats smelled of old grease and bitter coffee. Green and red vinyl booths lined two walls, while the floor was filled with an assortment of tables and chairs, none of which matched. Despite the lack of cars out front, the room was more than half full with patrons in all stages of eating a meal—from a couple just giving an order to a booth full of men in a corner having their cigarettes. Catherine's nose wrinkled in objection to the conglomeration of scents, but then she reminded herself that food wasn't the reason she was here. As she moved farther into the room, she saw the waitress behind the counter look up. She only glanced at Catherine, but her smile widened as she obviously recognized the sheriff.

"Hey, good-lookin'. You caught that thief yet?"

Luke grinned and slid his hand beneath Catherine's elbow.

"Nope, just a pretty girl."

The waitress managed to snicker, but it was obvious she didn't think it was funny. A couple of older men slapped their legs and guffawed at his joke while giving Catherine appreciative stares.

"Sit anywhere," the waitress said. "I'll be right with you."

Luke was angling her toward a booth at the back of the room when Catherine stopped at table in the middle instead and gave Luke a fake smile.

"How about here?"

It was obvious she was going all out on this and had just taken center stage.

"Looks good to me," he said, and seated her before taking the chair to her right.

A few moments later, the waitress plopped two glasses of water and a couple of menus before them.

"You need a couple of minutes?" she asked.

"I'll just have the special," Luke said.

Catherine's fake smile widened as she looked at the waitress. "I'm new to the area. What *is* the special today?"

"That would be meat loaf, mashed potatoes and gravy and your choice of green beans or corn," she said.

Catherine nodded. "Make that two, and I'll have the green beans."

Luke nodded in the affirmative, and the waitress winked at him, popped her gum a couple of times, then went to turn in the order.

"So far, so good," Luke muttered.

Catherine's smile was still in place.

The door behind them opened. Catherine heard Luke groan beneath his breath and turned to look. She frowned, trying to remember where she'd seen the woman before, and then it dawned. Yesterday at the grocery store. She looked back at Luke. His jaw was clenched, and the expression on his face would have wilted a lesser woman. She had no idea that this was one of the people who had started all the fuss, and, if she had, would not have cared. The Fane name had been maligned by a bunch of fools, and restraint was not in her vocabulary.

She turned around again, giving the woman at the cash register the full force of her stare as the waitress moved to the counter to help the newcomer.

"Hey there, Nellie, don't see you in here very often. Do you need a menu?" the waitress asked.

Nellie Cauthorn dabbed at a bead of sweat running from her hairline and shook her head.

"No, dear, just give me two specials to go, if you don't mind." She dabbed at her face again with the handkerchief, then used it as a limp fan as she fluttered it toward her neck. "I don't usually have to buy Preacher's meals, you know. But I'm so rattled right now, I can't go into my kitchen. After this morning, why, there's no telling what might happen if I tried to prepare another meal."

The waitress frowned. "What happened, did you set somethin' on fire?"

Nellie's pale eyes widened in anticipation. The opportunity to tell her story again had just been presented. She lowered her voice to a theatrical whisper.

"You haven't heard?"

The waitress shook her head.

Nellie glanced over her shoulder, checking to see who else might be listening. She saw the couple at the table in the middle of the room and started to smile, and then recognition dawned. She tried to gasp, but all that came out was a small squeak. She took a staggering step backward, pointing her finger toward the middle of the room.

"It's her! Save me, Jesus, it's the witch's kin."

Catherine flinched but didn't waver. There was an audible gasp behind her as she pushed back her chair and stood. She sensed Luke was right behind her, but she was too angry to be bothered about what he might do. Right now, her attention was on the fool at the door.

"Excuse me," Catherine said, "but were you referring to me?"

Nellie reached behind her, fumbling for the doorknob, but she couldn't find it. Her eyes were wild, and there was a thread of drool sliding from the corner of her mouth as she began repeating the Lord's Prayer beneath her breath.

Catherine started toward the door.

"Stay back!" Nellie screamed, and dropped to her knees.

Catherine wanted to throttle her, but she made herself laugh instead, and the sound was as startling as Nellie's accusation had been. Suddenly everyone's focus turned from Nellie to the stranger.

"Lady, you've either got the worst case of PMS I've ever seen or you need a keeper."

Nellie gaped. "How dare you!"

Catherine's smile froze. "No, lady, how dare *you?* You don't even know me, and yet you've maligned my good name, and the name of my deceased grandmother. You've just given me grounds to sue you for slander."

Nellie rocked back on her heels and then sat down with a thump, her legs spraddling out in a most unbecoming manner.

"Sue?" she squeaked.

Catherine turned, eyeing the shocked expressions of the people in the café, then waved her hand toward them.

"You heard her. You will all be my witnesses."

Two men stood and tossed some money down on their table.

"We didn't hear nothin', lady." They strode out of the café, stepping over Nellie to get to the door.

"Two more brave souls," Catherine muttered, then refocused her attention on the preacher's wife.

"Until yesterday, we'd never met, right?"

Nellie nodded.

"And yet you have spread horrible rumors about my grandmother and me."

Nellie began to sputter. "You cursed us. The eggs...Preacher's food...it was bloody."

Catherine rolled her eyes. "Good Lord, is that what this is all about?"

Nellie nodded again.

Catherine leaned forward. "Do you mean to tell me that you've never before—in your whole adult life—seen an egg with streaks of blood in it?"

Nellie flushed. "Well, maybe, but that's not the point."

"Oh yes, ma'am, that is the point. Not only that, but you made a foolish and hurtful accusation about a gentle woman."

She took another step forward, then leaned down until she and Nellie were almost eye to eye.

"Did you know Annie Fane?"

"No, but I heard..."

Catherine inhaled sharply. "Didn't I hear you say your husband was a preacher?"

Nellie nodded.

"Then how can you justify spreading gossip about a woman you never met?"

Nellie's mouth went slack as a dark flush began spreading up her neck and face. "Um...I..."

"Did you know that she had the prettiest blue eyes I've ever seen, and that she could cure a cough and a fever with one of her special herbal remedies faster than any doctor's antibiotics, or that she loved chocolate pie with pecans in the pudding?''

''No,'' Nellie whispered. ''I don't suppose that I did.''

Catherine straightened, her voice shaking with anger. ''I'm only going to say this once, so you better be listening. Annie Fane was not a witch, she was a simple, honest woman, trying to support herself by raising and selling herbs. It wasn't enough that she lost her husband fighting a war to keep you people safe, she was forced out of her home here by superstition and prejudice, and if I was a resident of Camarune, I'd be afraid to die and meet my Maker with something like that on my conscience.''

The thought of meeting her Maker in any way, shape or form was too much for Nellie.

''Save me, Jesus,'' she moaned, and fell backward in a faint.

The woman's head hit with a thump, but Catherine couldn't have cared less. A headache was going to be the least of that woman's troubles. She turned around, giving the people in the café a long, pointed stare.

''I don't know how many of you share her opinion of Annie Fane, but I will tell you now, you better get over it. I brought her back, and here she's going to stay.'' Tears blurred the people's faces, but she didn't need to see them to finish what she had to say. "It's just a damned shame she had to die to get here."

Then she turned and found herself facing the wall of Luke's chest.

"Get me out of here," she whispered, unwilling to let them see her cry.

He took her by the hand and guided her toward the door.

Fresh air hit Catherine's face first, and she inhaled deeply, trying to rid the scent of that place from her nostrils.

"Oh, Lord," she muttered, and covered her face.

"Heads up," he said softly. "I'd lay odds they're all watching."

She straightened, blinking back tears. "Well, I think that went well."

Luke laughed aloud and then impulsively hugged her in front of God and everyone in Lucy's Eats.

"Lady, you are something, and that's a fact," he said, still chuckling as he helped her to the car. "Is there any place else you feel like leveling before I take you home?"

"I want to buy some milk."

He thought of the gossip that Lovie Cleese slung on a daily basis and just shook his head. After what he'd just witnessed, Lovie might be about to meet her match.

"Coming right up," he said, and backed away from the curb.

A couple of minutes later he parked in front of the store.

"Leave it running," Catherine said, as she reached for her purse. "This won't take long."

Luke's grin widened. "Why do I suddenly feel like the driver of a getaway car?"

Catherine glared.

"Just kidding," he said. As she opened the door, he grabbed her arm.

"What?" Catherine asked.

"Be gentle. Lovie's older than Nellie."

Catherine's glare darkened. "Then she should damn well know better, shouldn't she?"

The door slammed behind her, and then she was gone. Luke leaned back in the seat, curiously watching her enter the store. It was obvious by the determined set of her shoulders and forceful stride that she was out for vengeance. And while he understood the years and years of superstition under which these people had lived, he also understood Catherine's anger. He couldn't imagine what it would be like to be shunned and cursed by an entire community, but he knew he wouldn't like it. His admiration for this woman had been there from the start, but after what he'd just witnessed in the café, he'd come to the conclusion that Catherine Fane would be a good partner to have at his back in a fight.

* * *

Lovie was shelving canned peas when the bell over the door jingled. She glanced up and squinted, trying to identify the customer, but all she could see was a woman's silhouette in the doorway of the store. She set the two cans on the shelf and then dusted her hands as she started toward the front.

"Can I help you?" she asked, and then Catherine Fane walked into her line of vision.

"Milk."

Lovie was a bit taken aback by the woman's assertive demeanor and pointed toward a refrigerator case at the back of the store before she thought. Catherine sailed past her without further comment, her head held high, her dark hair swinging in rhythm to her stride. Lovie turned and stared, afraid to turn away for fear of what the woman might do. A few moments later, she was back, carrying a plastic jug of milk.

"Will that be all?"

Catherine put her hands on the counter and leaned forward, fixing the old woman with a cold, angry stare.

"Since I couldn't find any eye of newt or lizards' tongues, I guess it will have to do."

Lovie's face turned red. The reference to supposed witch's concoctions was not lost on her. "You don't have any call to be smart with me, young woman," she snapped.

"That remains to be seen," Catherine said. "How much for the milk?"

"Two dollars and twenty-four cents."

Catherine dug in her purse and counted out exact change, then picked up the jug by its handle. She started to leave, then stopped and turned, her eyes flashing a warning the old woman couldn't miss.

"Just so you know... I will be staying at Grannie's cabin until I'm ready to leave. You can't scare me...and you can't hurt my feelings...and I'm getting real pissed off at hearing people I don't know call my grandmother a witch."

The flush on Lovie's face deepened. "You don't know what you're talking about," she said.

"No, you're the one who's in the dark, but I'm about to enlighten you, just like I did that preacher's wife. You just tell the people of Camarune to keep talking and they're all going to wind up in court—including you."

Lovie's eyes widened. "Court? What do you mean?"

Catherine pointed her finger in Lovie's face. "Slander is a libelous offense. My grandmother was a reputable businesswoman in Texas, highly thought of in the community and president of the women's league at our church. The fact you people actually fueled rumors of her being a witch is not only ridiculous, but scandalous, as well, and I won't have it. The people of Camarune have a choice.

Either shut the hell up, or consider yourselves sued.''

Having said what she'd come in to say, Catherine took her milk and left, her head held high. She slammed the door behind her, then slammed Luke's door, as well, as she got into his car.

"Sorry," she muttered, and set the milk between her feet.

Luke sighed as he put the car in reverse. "Now can we go home?"

"Yes."

"Did you leave her bleeding?" he drawled.

Catherine snorted beneath her breath, then glanced at him, almost managing a smile. "The cut was clean. She never felt a thing."

He chuckled. God, but this woman was something. He couldn't remember when a female had so fascinated him—yet, at the same time, made him so wary. He didn't know why, but he sensed she was a woman with secrets, and in his experience, secrets could be dangerous.

As they drove away, Catherine felt vindicated. Even though she'd done little more than exchange angry words with a couple of troublemakers, she knew her grannie would have been proud.

But the figurative cut she'd made in Lovie Cleese's attitude was not, in the shopkeeper's point of view, exactly painless. It wasn't until the woman was gone that Lovie realized she'd been holding her breath. The word "sue" had taken her by surprise. Lawsuits weren't good. That meant court, and court mean emerging secrets. She didn't want any of her secrets to emerge. She exhaled nervously, then reached for the phone. She knew a lawyer down in Lexington. He could tell her where they stood. As she waited for his office to answer, she kept telling herself that she wasn't really worried. It was just good business to know all their options.

Ten minutes later, she hung up the phone, a subdued and shaken woman. Not only could the whole town be sued, but to win, they would have to provide documented proof of Annie Fane's abilities to commune with dark spirits, and a one-eyed calf recently born to a fifteen-year-old cow wouldn't cut it.

Two little towheaded boys were playing barefoot in the creek, splashing waist-high water as they ran. The tadpoles they'd been trying to catch had long since been forgotten in their frenzy to see who got wet the fastest.

A faint smile shifted the hunter's expression as he watched from the bluff above. Their laughter was infectious, their antics typical of their age and sex. He lay belly down without moving, listening to their chatter, and as he did, a sliver of memory slid into his consciousness of a time long ago, before the pain. He closed his eyes, trying to make the thoughts go away, but names came to him then, like whispers on the wind. He could see a brown-haired woman standing on a porch beside a lilac bush, heavy with blooms. Her clear, sweet voice carried across the distance as she began calling out names. Even though he knew it was part of a dream, he had an overwhelming urge to answer.

"Sup-per," she called, lingering on the syllables so that they would be easily understood. "Hank and Johnny...Charles and..."

Just before she called the last name, he flinched, and the memory was lost. He looked down. The two little boys were gone. The good feeling was gone, too. After a quick sweep of the area, he stood, his desire to withdraw stronger than usual. Without giving the children another thought, he began to move.

Fifteen minutes later, he came upon what appeared to be a thick grove of trees against the bottom of a bluff. He stood for a moment, listening to the sounds around him, then moved forward. Just when it looked as if he was going to walk into a tree, he turned to the right. The gap between brush and mountain was infinitesimal, but enough for a determined man to pass through. As he did, he stooped, and a few seconds later, entered the hidden cave beyond. A massive wooden door, shaped to fit, had been hung on one side of the opening. As soon as he walked inside, he pushed it shut, then dropped the bar to lock it. Immediately, the cave was plunged into darkness. Only a faint light from a natural opening high in the ceiling shone through, but it was enough by which to see. He stood until his eyesight adjusted to the shadows, then exhaled slowly. As if he were an animal drawn back to its lair, he found the familiarity of the place comfortable, even relaxing.

He didn't think of this place as home, although he had learned to be satisfied here. Home was where the heart yearned to be, and he yearned for nothing. He dropped his bag on a table as he moved toward his bed against the opposite wall. Normally his outings took place at night, and only occasionally, as he'd done today, did he venture out in daylight. As he dropped onto the mattress, his belly growled. He thought of the two cans of meat he'd taken from the witch's cabin, then discarded the notion. Routine was what kept him functioning, and it was time to sleep.

He pillowed his hands beneath his head, elevating it just enough to see the faint outline of the pictures on a shelf opposite his bed. One was of his mother standing beside a lilac bush, and the other was of a young, blond-haired woman, laughing and waving at the camera. Sometimes he forgot who they were, and then there would be the days when memories flooded back with such pain that it would bring him to his knees. Today, the memories were blessedly distant.

He closed his eyes, and as he did, he focused on the stranger who'd taken up residence on the mountain. A slight frown creased his forehead, but as he drifted off to sleep, it smoothed away. She wouldn't be here forever. Nothing was forever. One day soon she would be gone and he would have the mountain to himself again.

Luke was driving in second gear, taking the road as carefully as possible, and the Blazer still dragged high center.

Catherine winced. "I'm sorry. This isn't good for your car."

He shrugged. "It's seen worse." Then he braked suddenly, pointing off to their right. "Look! A deer! Did you see her?"

Catherine turned quickly, just in time to see a young doe bound into the trees. Without thinking, she grabbed Luke's arm.

"Oh! Oh, my! She's beautiful."

Luke turned, but his gaze wasn't on the doe.

"Yes, she sure is."

Catherine turned to face him, her eyes alight with joy, and caught him staring. Immediately she realized he'd been referring to her and not the deer. She yanked her hand away and looked down at her lap, then busied herself by making sure the jug of milk between her feet was riding steady.

A long moment of silence followed; then Luke put the patrol car in gear. Catherine felt giddy, and at the same time anxious. Something had happened just then, something she hadn't expected—something she wasn't ready to face. This man, however helpful and nice he was, was still a stranger. And, she reminded herself, she wouldn't be here long. No sense giving herself another reason to regret.

"Look," she began. "I—"

Luke's radio suddenly crackled with static, and then a disembodied voice interrupted what she'd been going to say.

"Hey, Luke, this is Frank in dispatch. Come in…over."

Luke picked up the receiver. "I'm here. What's up?"

"Got a report of a domestic dispute up on Benson Ridge. It's Amory Benson again. Over."

"I'll be there within the hour. Over and out."

Luke grinned to himself as he continued to drive. He had yet to get a dispatcher who could remember all the call signals and had finally given up on protocol in favor of speed, thus the rather informal manner of contact.

But Catherine didn't see his smile. She was focused on the fact that he had been called to another location.

"You can let me out here," she said. "I can walk the rest of the way to the cabin."

Luke glanced at her briefly, then back at the road. "You don't walk alone on this mountain. Remember?"

"I doubt anyone from Camarune is going to bother me. Most of them think I'll turn them into toads."

"What about thieves? Can you turn them into toads?"

She shrank back against the seat. "I forgot."

"Well, don't. Besides, we're already here."

She looked up in surprise. The cabin was right in front of them. She picked up her milk.

"I appreciate the backup and the ride," she said, and when he came to a stop, quickly opened the door and got out.

Luke frowned. This wasn't the way he'd intended to part, but duty called.

"Look, Catherine. Most likely I'll be back this way before dark. If you don't mind, I'll check in on you...just in case."

"Suit yourself," she said, and then stepped aside, giving him space to turn around.

Even though she watched him driving away, there was no denying she felt a sense of relief, knowing he would be back.

7

The moment Catherine walked into the cabin, she knew someone had been there in her absence. Nothing obvious was missing, but there was an air of intrusion she couldn't ignore. She thought of the pack rat and then dismissed the notion. An animal wouldn't leave this kind of energy behind.

Nervously, she set the jug of milk into the old refrigerator as the fading sounds of the patrol car reminded her she was all alone. Then it hit.

What if he's still here?

A quick check of the bathroom revealed nothing but a dripping faucet, and there were no other places downstairs for a grown man to hide. She looked up at the loft, then hesitantly moved toward the stairs. When her head cleared the landing, she paused, quickly looking into all the corners. There was no one under the bed, and the wardrobe in the corner was too compartmentalized for any adult to get into.

Breathing a sigh of relief, she all but ran back down the stairs and over to the door, then flipped the lock. As soon as it clicked, rationality set in. Surely she'd been imagining things. The confrontation she'd just had in Camarune had been upsetting. Maybe she'd brought too much of her emotions back here. She looked around one last time, convincing herself she was still alone, then made herself relax. The urge was great to crawl into bed and pull the covers up over her head, but Grannie had taught her to face her fears, not hide from them. Still, it didn't make her feel any better.

Her shoulders slumped. The emptiness of the cabin was a reflection of how she felt inside. With little provocation, she would load up whatever she could of her grandmother's belongings and head back to Wichita Falls as fast as the Jeep would take her. But if she did, it would be letting these people win again. They'd forced Annie into a solitary lifestyle she hadn't sought. She would be damned before she let them force her out until she was ready to go.

Having settled that, she felt better, even stronger, as she began to really study the simplistic life-style in which her grandmother had lived. She thought back to yesterday, to the first time she'd seen the cabin. Her first reaction had been the isolation, then the beauty and charm of it all. Was this what her grannie had wanted her to see?

Her chin trembled. "What is it, Grannie? What is it you want me to learn?"

Unfortunately for Catherine, Annie was in a place too far away to answer. Whatever it was, she would have to discover it for herself.

With a frustrated sigh, the daunting task of packing her grandmother's things became reality, and she began looking around, mentally sorting through the things she might want to take with her. An old metal pan with a long wooden handle and hinged lid hung on a peg near the fireplace. It was an antique corn popper. She recognized it from pictures she'd seen in magazines. She could vaguely remember Grannie once talking of popping corn over open flames—telling her how the crisp, white kernels exploded beneath the lid, then about savoring their warm and salty taste with a cup of sweet hot chocolate. If only she had paid more attention to the stories.

Her focus moved from the pan to the bookshelves, and, as it did, her eyes widened in surprise. She'd grown up reading these same authors! Gene Stratton Porter. Emily Loring. Grace Livingston Hill—even Edgar Rice Burroughs and Zane Grey. It touched Catherine to realize that her grannie had gently led her to the same authors she'd cherished. Impulsively, she reached out to them. Tracing the titles on the old, faded spines was almost like touching her grannie again. And there were dozens upon dozens of books about herbs—cultivating, identifying, harvesting, even markets in which to sell.

As she took a step back, she noticed a lone wooden box at the back of the top shelf. It was a bit larger than a shoe box and, from where she was standing, looked quite dusty. Obviously the Hollis women hadn't cleaned the cabin *that* thoroughly, believing she would only be here a short while. Curious as to what Annie might have kept so far out of reach, she pushed a chair up to the shelves, then climbed up and lifted it down. As she did, something clunked against the inside. She winced, hoping it wasn't breakable.

A thick layer of dust covered the surface, and she got a damp cloth to wipe it off. As she did, a dark, cherry wood with a trio of ornate initials on the lid was revealed. AHF. Annie Hollis Fane? She lifted the lid and turned the box toward the light.

A military medal was caught between the contents and the side of the box. That explained the clunk. It was only after she picked it up that she realized it was a Purple Heart. It was cool in her hand, but as she held it, it began to warm, giving her the impression that it was, somehow, alive. Shaking off the fantasy, she looked back in the box and found herself staring at the picture of a young man in uniform. His expression was stern, but there was a twinkle in his eye, as if he was laughing inwardly at all the pomp and circumstance with which he was posing. His hair was dark, his features rather craggy, but engaging. She turned it over, recognizing her grandmother's handwriting.

Billy—February, 1942.

So this was Billy, her grannie's great love. As she laid it aside, she kept thinking of the terror and haste with which Annie had exited this place, to have left such treasured belongings behind. She looked back in the box to the next item. It was a telegram from the United States Government—Department of Defense, fragile and yellowed with age. Sadness came as she picked it up, knowing what this must be. She unfolded the page.

Dear Mrs. Fane, We regret to inform you...

Catherine sat down in the chair, imagining a young Annie receiving the news. "Grannie." Her vision blurred. "Oh, Grannie."

She stared at the picture, trying to envision the man that he'd been and the hole his passing must have left in Annie Fane's world. Finally she laid the items aside and reached into the box again. The only things there were a handful of books. She frowned, wondering why these particular books had wound up in here, rather than on the shelves with the others. It wasn't until she opened the first that she realized these weren't books, they were her grandmother's journals—five of them, to be exact.

She picked up the earliest, all but holding her breath. What a treasure, to be able to read daily entries of her grandmother's life. As she opened the first, she couldn't help thinking that if she hadn't come, these would have been lost.

The handwriting was small and often slanted up the page, as if the woman writing the words had been in a hurry. Part of the entries were in pen, but most were in pencil. The faded words drew her, and, impulsively, she laid her palm against the surface, drawing comfort from the fact that, once upon a time, Grannie had touched the very same page. Then eagerly, she began to read.

January 4, 1940
Billy and I have been married two months to-day. He cut wood all day. I started smoking some jerky from the venison haunch Abram gave us. Emory Cleese came for some dried lungwort. I showed him how to make the tea for Lovie. She is ailing in her chest again. It's almost dark and starting to snow.

Catherine gasped. Lovie Cleese—the cranky old woman from the grocery store—had once used the herbs Grannie gathered and sold? How strange. If this was so, then what could have happened between Annie and the people down in the valley that turned them so drastically against her?

She continued to read the entries, day by day, month by month, until her stomach suddenly growled. She glanced at her wrist, then frowned. Darn that rat and his kleptomaniac ways! She had no idea what time it was. Then she remembered where she was and relaxed. Up here, clocks were secondary to more earthly things. She was hungry, therefore it must be time to eat.

Laying the journal aside, she went to the cabinet to get a tin of tuna. It wasn't her favorite food, but she was in no mood to cook. She opened the door, expecting it to be at eye level where she'd put it last night, but it wasn't there. Frowning, she shoved aside the other cans, searching label by label.

It just wasn't there.

The more she looked, the more anxious she became. She stopped, then closed her eyes and made herself think back, retracing her steps of the day before. But no matter how many times she did so, it came back to the fact that the can had been there earlier and now it was gone. She began searching further, soon realizing that a can of Spam and a can of peaches were also missing.

Her belly knotted, her hunger gone. She turned once again, surveying the room with a nervous glance. As she did, she realized she was looking at a small wooden horse on the windowsill above the sink. Her heart skipped a beat. That hadn't been there earlier. She would have seen it. What was it Luke had said about the thief always leaving something behind in trade?

As she started toward it, she kept trying to convince herself that this was something the pack rat had left. But the moment she picked it up, she knew she'd been wrong. The piece was little more than six inches high, but so perfect in detail it almost looked alive. She set it down in quick panic, then stepped to the side of the window to peer out. Someone *had* come into the cabin. It wasn't the food that he'd taken that mattered, it was the fact that he'd invaded her space. This was getting scary. It was one thing to assert her independence. It was another to be careless with her life.

In a fit of panic, she grabbed a chair and shoved it beneath the doorknob as she'd done last night, then took the journal she'd been reading and bolted for the loft. It wasn't until she had crawled into bed that she began to relax. It was hours until nightfall, but she would worry about packing stuff tomorrow. Right now, all she wanted was a connection with Grannie, and the only way she was going to get it was through the pages of her journals.

Sometime later, it started to rain. The sound of the raindrops on the roof slowly lulled her to sleep. When she woke, it was almost dark. Again hunger drew her downstairs. She rummaged through the cabinets, finally choosing to eat a bowl of cold cereal and a can of fruit cocktail instead of a real meal.

She glanced at the journals, then the bookshelves,

trying to talk herself into more reading, but it didn't work. She was angry with herself for the panic she'd felt, and frustrated by circumstances in general. Grannie would be ashamed of her for hiding. She was ashamed of herself for hiding like this, too. She glanced out the windows into the burgeoning darkness, trying to picture what her grandmother's life had been like after Billy's death. She'd lived alone with far worse things to consider than a couple of stolen cans of food. And, Catherine reminded herself, it wasn't as if the thief had offered to harm her. He'd left something he obviously valued in trade. In a skewed sort of way, it represented a strange sort of honor.

Outside, a breeze had come up. She could hear the branches nearest the house scraping against the roof. The sad sound of a whippoorwill calling to its mate made goose bumps come up on her arms. She shivered, but more from an inner longing than fear. She would soon be twenty-seven years old, and she was as alone in the world as a person could be. Would she ever have someone who loved her like Billy had loved Annie?

The moment she thought it, she thought of Luke. Of the way that he had held her, and the tenderness of his touch. Of the way his eyes crinkled at the corners when he was trying not to laugh.

Grannie, do you believe in love at first sight?

Suddenly, she needed to move, to get out of the

confines of these two rooms and get some fresh air. But that would mean going outside—in the dark—alone. Hesitantly, she moved toward the door, standing with her hand on the doorknob, contemplating the wisdom of such an act.

"Damn it," she muttered. "I will not hide."

She moved the chair aside, then opened the door. Unwilling to stand silhouetted against the light behind her, she quickly stepped outside and pulled the door shut behind her.

At first she was blinded by the darkness, but she waited, letting her eyes adjust. As they did, she realized that there were degrees of darkness beyond the house. The squares of light spilling onto the ground from the windows left soft, gray shadows at their perimeters. Lingering raindrops shimmered on the metallic surface of her Jeep, while an owl hooted from a nearby tree.

She took a few steps forward, raking the dark, muddy clearing with a nervous gaze. Nothing moved. She took a couple more steps, listening to the sounds of the forest as the cool, rain-washed breeze blew soft against her skin. Finally, convinced she was alone, she sat down on the top step, resting her chin in her hands.

Time passed, bringing with it a peace she hadn't felt in weeks. She sighed and leaned back on her hands, tilting her face to the sky. Only a few stars were visible through the cloud-streaked sky, but she didn't need to navigate the heavens to find her way. For now, she was right where she needed to be. And so she sat, finding solace in the solitude.

Sometime later the wind changed, bringing with it a strong scent of wood smoke. Immediately her posture went from relaxed to tense. Smoke meant fire and fire, meant people, and she'd been given to understand she was a long way from any other cabins. A twig snapped in the nearby trees, and then another followed. She gasped, trying to see through the inky shadows, but it was impossible.

Suddenly the darkness that had been sheltering once again became something to fear. She stood abruptly and bolted for the door, imagining footsteps at her heels. Only after she'd slammed the door and locked it behind her did she breathe a little easier. Wishing for a dead bolt and a gun, she had to settle for the chair under the doorknob. For added measure, she pushed the table and another chair forward, as well.

Shaking in every muscle, she crawled into bed, then sat cross-legged in the middle of the mattress, her gaze fixed upon the door below.

The hunter had been standing at the edge of the forest for hours—even before the rain had started. His curiosity toward the woman was stronger than his fear of being discovered. Who could she possibly be, and, more importantly, why would she stay in a place that everyone knew was haunted? When she'd come out to the porch, his first instinct had been to run, and then he realized there was no way she would ever see him. So he stayed beneath the trees—watching—barely aware of the leaves that were shedding their raindrops upon his face and clothes.

A black snake, in search of food, slithered over the toes of his boots and then into underbrush. He acknowledged its passing with nothing more than a blink. When she finally moved from beneath the porch to the steps, he stiffened, then relaxed when she stopped and sat down. Occasionally, a cloud would move past the faint glow of moonlight, and as it did, his view of her features would move from shadowed obscurity to brief moments of clarity. There was something about the shape of her face that tugged at his heart. Something familiar and sweet—but as soon as he tried to focus on the memory, it would fade. Her stillness fascinated him, and he became so accustomed to her presence that once he sensed a separation of air and, in that moment, knew that she had sighed.

He didn't know when he became aware of her sadness, but as he did, the emotions that moved through him were overwhelming. She looked so small and so lonely, sitting on that porch in the dark. He thought of the fresh grave that had been dug behind the cabin and decided that was the cause of her grief. He knew about grieving—and he knew about loneliness. But at this point in his life, reaching out to another human was impossible. His ability to communicate was dormant. Now, he simply existed.

Suddenly a twig snapped to his right. The sound so startled him that he spun to look. As he moved, a doe bolted into the underbrush and then was gone. He looked back at the cabin. To his dismay, the woman was on her feet and moving in haste toward the door. The urge to call out was strong, to tell her that she was in no danger, that it was only a deer, but to do that would be to give himself away. The sound of the slamming door echoed within the night like a gunshot.

Within seconds, he was gone.

It was almost dark when Luke started for home. The road to the right led down the mountain to Camarune. The road to the left, up past Pulpit Rock to Catherine. He glanced at his watch, thinking of the stacks of paperwork that had probably piled up on his desk, but what the hell, paperwork was endless. It would be there tomorrow, Catherine Fane might not. Debating with himself about duty versus desire, he suddenly swung to the left, his decision made. It wouldn't be the first time he'd driven these roads in the dark, but never with such anticipation.

As he drove, the grade grew steeper. He slowed

to downshift, and, as he did, a large buck suddenly bounded from the trees and into the road. He slammed on his brakes, stunned by the magnificence of the animal frozen in the glare of his headlights. For a moment, they stared—him at the deer, the deer at the lights. It was a sixteen-pointer, maybe more. Then he dimmed his lights, and as he did, the buck came to life and bolted. Luke shuddered with relief, thankful it hadn't jumped into his grill instead. It wouldn't be the first time that a deer and a truck had collided in these woods.

He drove carefully, anxious that nothing else delay him from seeing Catherine again. It occurred to him then that the first time he'd seen her, she'd looked a bit like that deer—caught in a situation not of her making. Maybe it was that vulnerability that had first attracted him to her, but that was no longer the case. After the way she'd lit into those women this morning, he couldn't think of her as vulnerable again. Catherine would be a formidable enemy. Then his gut clenched, wondering if she made love with as much passion as she fought.

A short while later, he rounded a curve and saw lights in the distance. The cabin. His heart skipped a beat. Within minutes he would see her face—hear her voice—maybe even coax a smile from her lips. Then he cursed his own foolishness. He wasn't in the habit of being a dreamer, and there was no reason to assume she saw him as anything other than a helpful stranger.

By the time he parked, he had convinced himself he was fighting a hopeless battle. He honked to announce his arrival and then got out of his truck. When he knocked on the door, he called out to her, making sure she knew the identity of her nighttime caller.

"Catherine, it's me, Luke. Let me in."

He waited. Faint sounds of someone running down the stairs, of moving furniture, then a loud thump sounded. He frowned as a second thump followed, then heard footsteps hurrying toward him. When something scooted just beyond the door, he thought, *What the hell?* This time, when he called out, his voice was loud and anxious.

"Catherine! Are you all right?"

The door swung inward. He started to speak and then looked past her to the room inside. Furniture was askew. It looked to him as if she'd barricaded herself inside. He looked back at her face, and his breath caught in his throat. Her expression was somewhere between embarrassment and panic. Without thinking, he took her by the shoulders.

"What's wrong?"

She'd never been so glad to see a man—especially one she knew she could trust. It was his concern, as much as his presence, that was her undoing. To her shame and surprise, she burst into tears.

"Son of a bitch," Luke muttered, then took her in his arms and kicked the door shut behind him.

She clung helplessly, her shoulders shaking as she wept. He held her, stroking her back with one hand, as he cupped her head with the other, holding her close against his chest.

"It's okay, Catherine, it's okay. I'm here.... I'm here."

A minute passed, and then another, until Luke's own fears were getting out of hand. He'd imagined every possible scenario that might cause this reaction until he was close to panic. Slowly, he took her by the shoulders, making her look up.

"Talk to me, darlin'."

His voice was low, as seductive as what he'd just called her. She shivered, then drew a deep breath, pointing toward the carved figure of a horse sitting on the cabinet behind him.

Luke turned, frowning. "What?"

"The horse."

He picked it up, running his thumb along the rough, unfinished surface. "What about it?"

"I think your thief was here, and for all I know, he's still out there. Earlier, I thought I heard someone in the trees."

His gut clenched as he held up the toy. "You mean this isn't your grandmother's?"

"No. It was on the windowsill when I got home, and some cans of food were missing."

He dropped the horse and grabbed her by the shoulders. "That does it! I'm taking you off this mountain. I knew it wasn't safe for you to be here by yourself."

Catherine shivered. The urge to do as he said was great, but she couldn't. Not until she did what she had come to do.

"I can't," she said, and shrugged out of his grasp.

"Why the hell not?"

Her lips firmed, and her eyes flashed angrily, reminding Luke of the fury with which she'd dealt with the preacher's wife.

"Because I haven't finished what I came to do," she said. "And because if I leave now, I will be letting the people of Camarune win again."

He cupped her cheek. "Catherine...darlin', I don't think the people of Camarune have anything to do with the thievery. There's something going on up here that is getting out of control."

His hand was warm against her skin, and the urge to turn her mouth against his palm surprised her. There was a part of her that wished they had a chance at a relationship, but the word *darlin'* had rolled off his lips too easily for her to believe he meant it. And, she reminded herself, it was just as well. She wasn't in the mood to take chances with her heart.

She took a step back, breaking the physical contact. "Whether I leave this mountain because I fear for my safety or because I'm afraid of someone's reprisal, the end result is still the same. I would still be gone, and those crazy people down in the valley would still be living in a time warp of fantasy and prejudice." Her chin jutted. "I'm not going to say I'm not scared, but I'm not leaving, and you can't make me. I may be a lot of things, but a coward isn't one of them."

He sighed, then shook his head. "God knows the last thing I would call you is a coward. I've seen you in action, remember?"

She flushed.

"So," Luke continued. "If you aren't leaving, then I'm staying."

Her mouth dropped. "But you can't...."

"Oh, but I can. I've been considering a stakeout up here anyway. I've got my sleeping bag and pup tent in the Blazer."

A moment of panic came and went. Then Catherine began to realize that, while Luke DePriest *was* technically a stranger, she'd come to depend upon his presence. If he wanted to stay, who was she to detract an officer of the law from doing his duty?

"Do what you have to do," she said shortly. "But don't use me for an excuse."

Luke started for the door.

"However, if you're bound and determined to stay around here, then please stay inside the cabin.

I don't want to keep waking up in the middle of the night, wondering if it's you walking around outside, or someone else.''

Luke saw past her bravado, but wisely chose not to comment.

"I see your point. I'll notify the dispatcher of my location and then get my bag.''

Catherine frowned, remembering his warning that communication devices were difficult to use in the mountains.

"Luke.''

He paused. "Yes?''

"How come your radio works up here and my phone won't?''

He shrugged. "Maybe because our radio tower is local—maybe because the roamer services for cell phones are too few and far between up here. Who knows?''

The answer was vague, but it bothered her, just the same. Just for a moment, an errant fear crept into her head. Even though the man was an officer of the law, he was still a local. If he had to choose, would he side with the people of Camarune—or her?

A few minutes later, she heard his footsteps on the porch and made a dash toward the bathroom. She didn't want him to know she held doubts about the wisdom of what they were about to do.

8

Luke came inside just as Catherine disappeared into the bathroom. He thought nothing of it until several minutes had passed. When she didn't come out, he began to worry. What if she'd taken sick? What if she'd passed out on the floor? He started toward the door and then hesitated. And what if she was just...busy? Finally worry overcame embarrassment.

"Catherine, are you all right in there?"

He heard a faint yes, then frowned and added, "Fine, but if you're just trying to evade the fact that I'm spending the night in here, remember you're the one who invited me inside."

Almost immediately, the door swung inward. There was a high flush on her face, but her gaze didn't waver.

"I don't hide."

"Yeah, right," he said, making no attempt to hide a grin. "Next you'll be trying to tell me that you always go to roost when it rains."

She glared. His reference to her hiding in the loft

was aggravating, but it was impossible to argue with the truth.

"I'm not trying to tell you anything," she said, and then smoothed her hands down the front of her shirt, as if she'd just remembered her manners. "I'm sure you're hungry. If you'll give me a few minutes, I'll fix you some food."

She'd changed the subject, and he was wise enough to stop the teasing.

"Food would be great, but don't go to any trouble on my account," he said.

"No trouble," she said. "No trouble at all," and wondered as she scooted past him why she'd never noticed how tall he was.

Her hands were shaking as she dug through the refrigerator. *What the hell possessed me to offer to feed him? I haven't even been feeding myself.* She turned, a polite smile on her face. "How about an omelette?"

"Have you already eaten?" he asked.

"Oh, yes, hours ago."

"What did you have?" he asked.

She flushed. "Um...a bowl of cereal and a half can of fruit cocktail."

"Sounds good."

"Oh, but you don't have to—"

"Catherine."

"What?"

"I said...the cereal sounds good."

She almost smiled. "Yes...well...all right. Cereal."

He reached over her shoulder, took the milk and the leftover fruit from the refrigerator.

"Got a bowl?"

She scrambled out from under his reach and headed for the cabinet to retrieve the cereal and bowl, muttering to herself as she went.

"Did you say something?" Luke asked.

She spun. "Who? Me? No, I didn't say a thing."

"I didn't think so," Luke said, then grinned when she turned her back.

She was nervous. But was that a good sign or a bad sign? Was it anxiety because a stranger was going to be under her roof, or was she interested in spite of herself? Luke sighed. He hoped it was the latter, because he was damn sure interested in her.

She set the bowl on the table and the cereal box next to it. "I'll let you serve yourself. That way you'll get all you want."

"No one ever gets all they want," he said softly.

She gave him a nervous look. "I was talking about cereal."

He grinned, ignoring her remarks. "Join me?"

"No, I think I've had about all I can stomach for one day," she muttered.

He grabbed the chair she'd had under the doorknob and turned it toward the table, then sat himself down. Catherine watched him the way a mouse watches a cat, expecting him to pounce at any moment. When he reached for the box of cereal, she jumped.

He paused, then looked up. "Catherine?"

"What?"

"Would you do me a favor?"

"If I can," she said, resisting the urge to bolt.

"It's rare that I get to eat a meal with anyone. Would you sit with me while I eat?"

The request was oddly touching, and Catherine began to relax as she willingly sat. Luke poured the bowl full of cornflakes, then added only a dash of milk. Catherine frowned.

"Please...feel free to use all the milk you need. I can always go back for more."

"This is fine, thanks. I don't want them to float."

The seriousness of his expression made her laugh.

Luke took a spoonful and looked up, stunned by the sound of her laughter.

"You should do that more often."

"Do what?" Catherine said, the smile still on her lips.

He pointed the bowl of his spoon at her face. "Laugh. It makes a real pretty sound."

Heat spread up her neck and cheeks. "Well... thank you."

"You're welcome," Luke said, and then took another bite.

There was a droplet of milk clinging to the corner of his mouth, and she caught herself staring, wondering if it would fall. Suddenly the tip of his tongue swept it into his mouth. She realized she'd been holding her breath.

This is crazy, Catherine. Focus on something else.

"Did you always want to be in law enforcement?" she asked.

Luke shook his head and swallowed before adding another dash of milk to the bowl.

"No, football was my career of choice," he said, and then took another healthy bite.

Eyeing the width of his shoulders from across the table, she could see where that might happen.

"But…?" she urged, knowing there was more to the story.

Luke downed the last of the cornflakes, then took the spoon to what was left of the fruit.

"I had one season with the NFL as a backup quarterback. At the beginning of my second year, I threw out my arm in a preseason game and found myself benched. It didn't heal right. I came home."

"I'm sorry," she said.

"Don't be," Luke said. "Some people never get that far. At least I was there for a while. Besides, I like what I do."

"It helps to be happy, doesn't it?"

Her question was curious, but he didn't pursue

the issue. "How about you?" he asked, once again using his spoon like a pointer. "What do you do for a living?"

"I teach high school math at a correctional center for boys."

He whistled beneath his breath, then started to smile. "No wonder you weren't buffaloed by what's been happening. Nellie Cauthorn never stood a chance, did she?"

Catherine looked a little embarrassed, then shrugged. "I've been afraid a few times in my life, I'll admit, but not of cowards, and that's what I think of the residents of Camarune."

She crossed her arms across her chest and leaned back in her chair, unaware of how defensive she looked.

"Do you have relatives there?" she asked.

"In Camarune? No. Well...not exactly."

Her instinct for self-preservation kicked in. Harboring an enemy wasn't wise.

"Either you do or you don't," she said.

"I don't see how it matters, but my mother is a distant cousin to Lucy, who owns Lucy's Eats."

"Blood is supposed to be thicker than water, remember?" she said. "If your allegiance was tested, would you follow your family or your duty?"

Luke's smile stilled. "Is that what this is all about?"

It was all she could do not to look away. "I just asked a simple question."

"No, you didn't ask a *simple* question," he countered. "What you were asking, in a damned roundabout way, was, if it came down to it, would I defend you, or side with those fools in the valley?"

She flushed, but wouldn't back down. "Okay, you're right, but you can't blame me. I'm pretty much on my own in a mess I don't understand. You've lived in the area all your life. I'm the stranger—the witch's kin—remember?"

He scooted the food out of the way, then leaned forward.

"There's something you need to understand about me. My brother gave me a job at his service station after I came home from the NFL. Granted, pumping gas was a far cry from the merry-go-round I'd been on, but I was grateful. It made me feel worthwhile to be paying my way again. One day he took my shift so I could get off early. I had a date. Forty-five minutes later, he was shot and killed in a robbery at the station. He had a wife and three kids." Then he took a deep breath. "It should have been me."

"I'm sorry," Catherine said. "But that wasn't your fault."

"I know, but it didn't make it any easier to accept. Within a month, I'd signed up at a police academy. It might have been a knee-jerk reaction to his death, and I was certainly not going to be able to help catch the man who killed him, but I needed to give something back.''

"Look, I didn't—"

"When I became a lawman, I took an oath to uphold the law, and if that meant arresting every second cousin I had between here and Lexington, then so be it.''

Catherine sat, absorbing the seriousness of what he'd just said. Finally she relaxed.

Luke stood abruptly and carried his dirty dish to the sink. When he turned around, the smile he'd worn earlier was gone.

"Do we understand each other?''

She nodded, then stood up, too, unable to meet the accusation of his look sitting down.

"There are a couple of dry towels on the bathroom shelf if you'd care to shower before going to bed.''

He sighed. Obviously this hadn't been any easier for her than it had been for him.

"Thanks, I would.''

"Well, then, is there anything else you might need before I adjourn to my roost?''

"A smile?''

She blinked, absorbing the quiet plea in his voice; then she took a deep breath and gave him what he wanted.

"Good night, Luke."

"Good night, Catherine."

She moved toward the stairs, imagining she could feel the heat of his gaze between her shoulder blades, but when she turned around, he was already moving toward the bathroom.

Moments later, he emerged minus his shirt. He glanced up at the loft, then froze. She was staring down at him as if she'd never seen him before. His heart skipped a beat. This time he could almost feel her fear, and it made him angry.

"I'm not going to jump your bones. Go to bed." Then he dug in his pack for a razor and went back to the bathroom, quietly closing the door behind him.

"Damn."

She pulled back the covers and got in bed.

"Damn, damn, damn," she repeated, unable to get rid of the notion that, once again, she'd let him down.

A short while later, she heard him come out, then followed the sounds of his footsteps around the room as he checked the window and door locks. Finally he turned out the light. As he moved toward his sleeping bag, something thumped. She heard a soft, muffled curse.

"Are you all right?"

A brief silence was followed by a low, weary sigh. "Yes, just stubbed my toe on something."

"Okay then," Catherine said. "Good night."

"Good night, darlin'," he said softly, more to himself than to her.

Catherine lay back on the bed and stared up at the ceiling until her eyes finally adjusted to the light. Everything looked the same as it had the night before, yet there was a different feeling to it all, as if the two-room cabin had suddenly become smaller. She closed her eyes, trying to think of anything except the fact that there was a very good-looking man sleeping on her living-room floor. She could hear movement, unaware that he'd just shed the rest of his clothes and crawled into the sleeping bag.

Finally there was a long silence. She took a deep breath and felt herself totally relax. For the first time since she'd arrived in this god-awful place, she wasn't afraid—and it was all because Luke had put himself between her and danger.

She rose up on one elbow, peering down into the room below.

"Luke…are you asleep?"

She heard him sigh, then thought she heard him chuckle.

"No."

"I'm glad you're here," she said softly.

There was a long moment of silence, and then he answered.

"I'm glad I'm here, too."

*   *   *

The thunderstorm moved through Camarune just before dark, leaving the streets rainwashed and glistening. The occasional light shone through curtained windows up and down the block on which Lovie Cleese lived, but there were no lights on in her house. She'd taken to her bed long ago, praying for sleep, but sleep wouldn't come. She hadn't had a moment's rest since that hearse had pulled into town. She was a superstitious woman, and the fact that a dog had died within seconds of its arrival made her cringe. Knowing the body in the casket had been Annie Fane's made it worse. Her gut feeling was that after all these years, everything was finally coming undone.

A limb from the hydrangea bush outside her window kept rubbing against the glass, like someone scratching to get in. She shuddered and pulled the covers up over her head, trying to block out sounds, as well as memories. It was hopeless.

Finally she rolled out of bed and dropped to her knees. The single braid she'd made earlier of her thin, graying hair dropped over her shoulder as she bent her head and closed her eyes. But prayer wouldn't come. She'd been trying for years to find the words to assuage herself of old sins. Tonight was no exception. She moaned and she cried, but redemption was denied. Finally she got to her feet and walked to the window. Now and then a faint flash of lightning was still visible over the mountains that surrounded the town, but the storm was long past.

She leaned her head against the window and closed her eyes. She was seventy-five—almost seventy-six—and too old to cope with what was happening again. When Annie left, she'd thought it was over. Then her shoulders slumped as a chill of foreboding swept over her. Annie Fane might be dead, but Lovie's hell wasn't over. It was just beginning.

The barn was dark, but the hunter could smell the hay stacked in an alcove to his right. He moved past it without notice. It wasn't hay he was after. It was meat. A man had to eat, and Faron Davis had pigs to spare. Sometimes, in the back of his mind, the hunter knew he was going against the way he'd been raised, but at other times, there was nothing in his mind but survival. Tonight was a night for survival. But he didn't steal—he traded—and this time was no exception.

As soon as he reached the pigpen at the end of the barn, he set down the small, handmade end table he'd been carrying and took out his knife. The blade was long and razor sharp. With hardly a sound, he leaned over the pen, and before a squeal could be heard, slit the nearest pig's throat. A few minutes later, he was gone.

It wasn't until morning that Faron Davis discovered the theft, and the fine, handmade table that had been left in the pig's place was not enough to dampen his anger. He stormed into the house, set the table down with a thump, and got the keys to his truck. His wife, Junie, looked up from the breakfast she was cooking.

"Faron, honey, where did that table come from?"

"We been robbed."

"Lord have mercy," Junie cried, eyeing the table in dismay. "The thief was here?"

Faron nodded.

"What did he get?"

"One of the shoats. I'm going down to Camarune to call the sheriff. Lock the door till I get back."

Wild-eyed, she did as she was told, then turned, curiously eyeing the table's sturdy legs and square top.

To Junie's way of thinking, the trade wasn't a total bust. The way she looked at it, the pig was gone, and the table was here. After a while, she took a reluctant shine to it. By the time Faron returned from Camarune, she had a picture of Jesus and a crocheted doily in the center of the table, figuring that the spirit of the Lord would take away whatever evil might linger in the thief's handiwork.

Faron wasn't happy, but the least he could do was let his wife get use out of the damned thing. It was obvious from the blood trail leading into the trees that the only way he would get back his pig was in barbecue form.

The report of the theft had been made to the proper authorities, but the sheriff had yet to check in with dispatch. Until he did, a missing pig would be low on the priority list of things to be done in Taney County.

Luke woke before daybreak with a backache and an empty belly. Even though it had seemed like a good idea at the time, that bowl of cereal he'd eaten last night had been sadly lacking in substance for a man of his size. With a careful glance toward the loft to make sure Catherine was still asleep, he slipped out of his sleeping bag and quickly dressed. The need for coffee was strong, but he didn't want to wake her. Instead, he took a cold Pepsi from the refrigerator. It wasn't hot, but it had caffeine. With one last look toward the loft, he eased the lock off the door and went out on the porch.

A slight breeze was already stirring the air, and the grass was still wet from last night's rain. He popped the top on the Pepsi and took a long drink, wincing slightly as the cold liquid hit his empty belly. A raccoon waddled out from the corner of the cabin and proceeded across the yard as if Luke wasn't even there. He emptied the can and then set it aside, taking joy in the quiet around him.

Minutes passed, and after a while he could see light coming over the eastern ridge. The sky was changing from dark to gray to a pale, washed-out blue. And then suddenly color swept across the sky like watercolors spilling upon paper. He stood abruptly, paying silent homage to the beauty. Only after a blue jay flew across his line of vision did he look away.

His belly growled again, and he started to go back inside and chance waking her up when he remembered a half-eaten bag of chips in the back seat of his vehicle. A few quick strides and he was unlocking the door. As he leaned inside, a gust of wind blew through, taking a small bit of paper with it.

"Damn it," he muttered, then grabbed the chips and slammed the door before anything else could blow out.

He stuffed a couple of chips in his mouth and then went to retrieve the blowing paper. The ground beneath his feet was slippery as he chased after the note. Once he almost fell. Each time he got within reach of the note, another breeze would come and carry it that much farther out of reach. It was only after it blew into the trees that he finally caught up.

It was on the ground, caught between the lower limbs of some buck brush, when he bent to pick it up. His fingers were closing around it when he suddenly froze, staring at the ground beneath it.

There was a set of footprints in the damp earth at the edge of the bush. Prints that were all too familiar. Prints with a notch on one heel. He stuffed the paper in his pocket and stood, then began walking through the trees, searching for more. Almost instantly, he found more circling the house, then a more distinct set leading away.

Catherine had been right. Someone had been here last night after the rain, and that someone was the thief.

"Luke? Luke? Are you there?"

He pivoted sharply. Damn. She was awake.

"Here," he called, and walked out of the trees.

Catherine turned toward the sound of his voice with a smile on her face. She was holding the empty Pepsi can.

"Breakfast?"

"Caffeine," he said, and tried to smile, but all he could think of was what might have happened to her if he hadn't stayed.

"Coffee is brewing," she said. "And I'm frying some bacon. How do you want your eggs?"

He hesitated, then made a quick decision. He would tell her later, after she'd gotten some food in her belly.

"Whatever's easiest," he said.

"Fried, then," she said, and added, "one less dish to wash."

"I'll help," he offered.

"Nothing left to do but the eggs. Give me five minutes, okay?"

"Five minutes," he repeated, knowing what he had to tell her would kill that pretty smile in her eyes. "I'll just check in with dispatch while you're finishing up."

He waited until she'd gone inside and then headed for the Blazer again. This time, when he opened the door, he got inside and shut it behind him, then took the paper out of his pocket, curious as to what it was that he'd chased. It was a receipt for an oil change. He frowned, then tossed it back on the seat, thinking had it not been for that slip of paper, he might have chalked her fears up to the isolation, rather than a real threat.

He picked up the receiver.

"Headquarters…this is DePriest. Do you copy?"

A burst of static preceded the response. "This is Frank. We copy. Been trying to contact you for about thirty minutes. Over."

He frowned. "What's up? Over."

"It's your pack-rat thief. He hit Faron Davis's place last night. Carried off a pig. Davis is pretty upset. Over."

"They sure it's him? Over."

"Traded old Faron a table for a shoat. Over."

Luke sighed. "I'll check in with him later this morning. Right now I'm investigating a similar report that may be connected. I'm in the mountains above Camarune, in the Pulpit Rock area. Probably be here most of the day. If you have any emergencies, tell the deputy on duty to handle it. Over and out.''

Then he got out of the car and started toward the cabin. By the time he got to the door, he had his game face on. When he realized she hadn't heard him come in, he paused, watching her from across the room. Her head was bent, her attention so focused on what she was doing that it made him smile. He wondered about the kind of man who would let her come all this way alone to bury her grandmother in such an out-of-the-way place. It never occurred to him that she would be unattached. Not a woman this pretty.

"Smells good," he said.

She turned. "Oh! I didn't hear you come in. Breakfast is ready."

"Give me a second to wash up," he said, and hurried into the bathroom.

When he came back, she was sitting at the table, waiting for him to return. He slid into his seat without hesitation and had started to pick up his fork when Catherine took him by the hand and then bowed her head.

In the back of his mind, he knew she was blessing their food, but he couldn't get past the feel of her fingers curled around his hand. Somewhere between one breath and the next, he heard her whisper, "Amen." He shuddered, then looked up. She was staring at him and trying to smile.

"What?" he said.

"My fingers. I'm going to need them to eat."

Embarrassed, he turned her loose, then took a big bite of bacon, figuring that if he had food in his mouth, he couldn't say or do anything else wrong.

"Tastes good," he said. "I really appreciate it."

"No, I'm the one who should be saying thanks," she said. "Last night was the first good night's sleep I've had in months."

He held comment for later. No use ruining their meal.

A few minutes later, he got up and set his dirty dishes in the sink, then poured himself a second cup of coffee.

"Want a refill?" he asked.

She shook her head. "Not much of a coffee drinker. One is enough for me, but thanks."

He sat the pot down and then strolled to the window, letting the hot brew cool. Again his gaze fell on the tree line. He wondered how long the man had stood there, watching her.

Was he there when I came? Did he see her run into my arms? Does it please him to know he brings fear to women's hearts?

He turned. Catherine was clearing the table. The quiet way in which she was working intrigued him. He hadn't known many women who knew how to be satisfied with their own company. Most of them had to be talking, either to him or about someone else. It pleased him to see the peace within this woman's soul.

"Catherine."

She looked up.

"Sit down for a minute, will you? We need to talk."

A little surprised by the tension in his voice, Catherine sat.

"Have any of the Hollis men been back to visit you since the day we buried your grandmother?"

She shook her head. "No, although I expect Abram will be back before I leave. He knows that I would contact him if I needed any kind of help. Why? Do you need to talk to him?"

"Oh, no, just curious."

Then he took a slow sip of coffee, trying to figure out how to tell her what he'd found without scaring her to death. But he waited too long. Catherine sensed something was wrong. She stood abruptly.

"Something's wrong, isn't it? When you checked in with headquarters, did they tell you something bad that concerns me?"

He shook his head. "No, but you were right in believing someone was outside last night. I found a set of footprints that circled the cabin. And someone stole a young pig from Faron Davis's farm last night. His place is in a direct line with this cabin, about two miles down.''

She blanched, then covered her face with her hands. Within seconds, Luke had her by the shoulders.

''Look at me.''

She lifted her head.

''I won't let you be hurt.''

''Don't make an impossible promise.''

A tinge of anger sounded in his voice. ''If I promise someone protection, then I will deliver protection,'' he snapped. ''I am good at what I do.''

''I'm sorry. I didn't mean you couldn't do it because you were incapable. I just meant...'' She sighed. ''Dear God, Luke, this is a nightmare. I don't know what to do. It's bad enough that I'll go home to Texas without Grannie. I don't want to leave all of her things behind, too. But I can't help thinking that if I stay, I'll be risking my life.'' Then she grabbed him, curling her fingers into his forearms. ''What should I do?''

''I can't tell you what to do. Honestly, I don't think the thief poses an actual physical threat, simply because of the fact that he's never offered to hurt anyone before. However, there's no guarantee.''

''Damn,'' she muttered, then turned away.

He reached for her, pulling her against his chest and holding her close.

"Like I said, I won't tell you what to do, but if you decide to stay, so will I."

She slumped against him. "Isn't that a little above and beyond your personal call of duty?"

"Yes."

The husky drawl in his voice made her pulse skip a beat. She turned, needing to see him when he answered.

"What are you saying?" she asked.

He touched the side of her face with a fingertip, then withdrew it as quickly. "Right now, not much, darlin'. But I'll have to admit, I've got a lot on my mind and most of it concerns you."

She made no attempt to hide her shock. Finally she shook her head, almost smiling.

"Isn't this where I'm supposed to say, this is all so sudden?"

He grinned. "I'd a whole lot rather you didn't."

"You're something else, aren't you, Luke De-Priest?"

"So I've been told. So, what's the verdict?"

She sighed. "Hope that sleeping bag's padding is good. You just bought yourself a few more nights on my floor."

Luke felt a little like he had the day he'd signed his NFL contract. It was somewhere between elated that he'd reached an unattainable plateau and afraid to look at what was there. He turned and headed for the sleeping bag, then dug something out of the covers. When he turned again, he was wearing a gun.

"What are you going to do?" she asked.

"Follow those footprints, then see a man about a missing pig. If you're afraid, I can put a deputy on guard until I get back."

She shook her head. "No. I have plenty to do to keep me busy. In fact, I may go into Camarune. We'll be needing some more food, and I need to get some boxes to pack up some of Grannie's things."

He frowned. "Do you think that's wise…going into town again?"

"Probably not," she said. "But the sooner I get this over with, the sooner I can get back home."

That wasn't what Luke wanted to hear. Again he thought of who might be waiting for her when she got back.

"Yeah, I can see where you'd feel that way," he said. "You've probably got a boyfriend who is worrying about you."

Catherine turned, giving Luke a slow, considering look, then shook her head.

"There's no one like that in my life."

"Well, then," he drawled, trying not to gloat, "that just proves what I always thought about Texans."

"What's that?" Catherine asked.

"That their hats are bigger than their brains."

9

Catherine was nervous all the way into town. Confrontations made her sick to her stomach, and there was no guarantee that her warning of a lawsuit would be enough to make the citizens of Camarune keep their distance. Besides that, this time she was without Luke's backup.

She sighed. Just thinking of him brought goose bumps. He was big. He was good-looking, and Lord knew he was sexy. Kissing that mouth of his might be dangerous, but she would be willing to give it a try. And, if they spent much more time together, she had every expectation that it would happen. She knew he was interested. He'd asked if she had someone special back home. She'd had friends, and a couple of serious relationships in her lifetime, but nothing that she hadn't been able to walk away from. In the past, that had bothered her from time to time, but right now, she was glad to be unattached. Luke DePriest was what Grannie would have called a looker. And, it would seem, he was looking at her in an interested way.

When she realized she was coming to the outskirts of town, thoughts of Luke moved aside as
she bolstered herself for what might lie ahead. Her
grocery list was in her pocket, and the Jeep was
low on gas. First things first, she thought, and
wheeled into Maynard's station and parked at the
pump.

Without waiting to see if someone would come
help, she began filling her tank. As usual, several
pickup trucks were parked around the building,
probably the same crew of men she'd seen there
before. She could only imagine what they must be
saying, but she refused to turn and look. Their behavior was not going to become her problem.

A small bee flew past her face as she held the
nozzle in the tank. She swiped at a loose strand of
hair, wishing she'd taken time to put it up. The
weight of it hung on the back of her neck just
enough to be uncomfortable. Suddenly the squeak-
ing hinges of a door behind her warned that someone was emerging from the station. She held her
breath, refusing to look, afraid her anxiety would
show.

"Need some help with that, ma'am?"

It was Maynard, the owner. "I've got it...but
thanks," she said, hiding her surprise.

"I'll just be washing off your windows, then,"
he said, and reached for a squeegee and a rag.

Catherine was stunned. His attitude was certainly

different from the first time she'd seen him. She wondered if it had anything to do with her confrontation with the two women, or if Luke had had a hand in it. Either way, she was relieved to be facing one less problem.

The pump stopped. She topped off the tank and then reached in the Jeep to get her purse, quietly counting out her money to Maynard.

"I appreciate the business, ma'am," he said.

She looked at him, then slowly smiled. "And I appreciate the courtesy."

To her surprise, Maynard blushed. "Yes, ma'am. Well, then, if there's anything else you'd be needin' while you're here, don't hesitate to ask." Then he added. "About the other day…"

"I don't hold grudges," she said, and then smiled.

His face turned red, and he ducked his head, more than embarrassed. "My wife tore into me good about not helping you with your grannie. She comes from Lexington and don't believe in witches and hexes."

"Smart woman you married," Catherine said.

"Yes, ma'am," Maynard said. "Like I said. If there's anything you need…"

"Well…actually there is."

"Yes, ma'am?"

She pointed toward the left rear tire. "It looks a little low. Do you have time to take a look? I may have picked up a nail, and I'd hate to have a flat on the mountain.''

''Sure thing. You can take a seat inside if you want,'' he said, then nervously glanced toward the store, remembering his other customers inside.

Catherine realized his dilemma and opted for a less confrontational climate. ''Thanks, but I believe I'll just walk around a bit. How long will you be?''

''Give me half an hour and it'll be ready and waitin'.''

She handed him the keys and slung her purse over her shoulder, relieved that things were beginning to seem more normal. Without giving him time to change his mind, she started walking, seeking shelter in the shade of the tree-lined streets as she began her first real look at the town of Camarune.

The structures were old, as were most of the vehicles she saw parked in the drives. In the middle of the first block, a man was standing on a ladder painting the eaves of a house. He stared as she walked past, then returned to his task. Across the street, on the corner, an elderly woman was on her knees in her yard, digging up weeds. A large yellow tabby cat lay in the sun beside her wheelbarrow, while a pair of robins hopped about on the ground nearby. The scene made Catherine smile. The cat was either too old or too well-fed to care about pouncing on birds. The woman paused in the act of tossing a handful of weeds into the barrow to watch

Catherine's passing. Catherine hesitated, then waved. To her surprise, the old woman waved back.

"Well, this isn't so bad," Catherine muttered. "Maybe there are some decent people living here after all." Then she frowned. "And maybe they just don't know who I am."

A few minutes later, she turned a corner and stopped beneath the shade of a large oak to catch her breath. As she did, she noticed an old man in a wheelchair on the porch across the street. His shoulders were slumped forward, as if he was about to get up. His thin, bony hands lay in his lap, curled in upon themselves as if he'd forgotten what function they were supposed to fill. In spite of the heat of the day, someone had covered his lap and legs with a faded brown throw, hiding all of his lower body save the toes of his slippers. His hair was matted, just brushing the edge of his collar, and his unkempt beard had a yellowish cast in the center, as if stained by too many bites of food that had missed his mouth.

How sad, she thought, to be trapped in a body that wouldn't obey.

She started to walk on when a woman abruptly exited the house and poked something in his mouth. Catherine watched as she pushed his head back, then tilted a glass to his lips. She frowned, watching as the old man struggled to drink. A few moments later, his caretaker carelessly dabbed at the dribbles that had fallen from his mouth, then yanked at the blanket across his legs, as if irked at having to straighten something she'd already settled. Her voice was strident, her behavior less gentle than it should have been.

Catherine thought of her grandmother's last days and how her entire survival had depended upon someone else's mercy. She wondered if the woman was family and was sorry for what the man was enduring. Moments later, she saw him look up. Embarrassed to be caught staring, she turned away, wondering if Maynard was through with her tire.

Just as she started to leave, a young boy of about ten or eleven came wheeling down the street on a bicycle, tossing newspapers into yards. She waited for him to pass, then started to cross the street when he yelled out to the old man on the porch.

"Jubal, Jubal, Jubal Blair, someone ought to wash your hair."

"Get on out of here or I'll tell your daddy," the woman yelled, waving her fist at the paperboy. After he was gone, she got her paper and went back into the house, leaving the old man unattended.

Catherine had gone pale. Jubal Blair? Horror washed over her in a continuous wave. She couldn't have heard him right. Jubal Blair was dead. Grannie Annie had told her so. But the old man on the porch was real enough. Maybe she'd misunderstood the boy.

Then she thought of the woman who'd been her mother, running for her life through the dark of night from a man called Jubal Blair. She thought of Turner, her father, killed by that same man—the man he'd called father. There was no way she could leave until she knew for sure.

Her heart began pounding as she stepped off the sidewalk into the street. Her stomach was beginning to roll as she started toward the porch, needing to look into the eyes of a man who could so casually end people's lives. She had no way of knowing that the sway of her walk was so like her father's that they could have been twins, or that the sunlight on her hair gave it a blue-black sheen—the single distinguishing feature by which the Blairs had once been known.

When the woman was halfway across the street, Jubal's sight began to focus, and as it did, his mind suddenly jerked, catching on bits of faded memory like the worn and rusty cogs in a gear. Something skittered along the byways of his thoughts like a bad dream, but it had been so long since he'd tried to think that the act didn't come easy. She was still coming this way, staring at him like something foul she'd just found on the bottom of her shoe.

Damn her—damn them all. They think I don't feel. They think I don't care. Let them live for one day inside a weak and rotting carcass.

Then she was standing at the foot of the steps, staring up at him. He wanted to shout at her, but the only thing to come out of his mouth was a dribble of drool. And then she took a step forward, and he looked into her eyes. The hate blazing there startled him. In sudden panic, he began to fidget, his hands jerking spasmodically in his lap as he struggled to move. He wanted to know why she was here, but all he got from her was a blinding look of hate. And then she spoke, and the sound of her voice almost stopped his heart.

"Jubal Blair?"

He grunted. That voice and face were so familiar. If he closed his eyes, he could believe it was his wife standing before him. But that was impossible. She'd been dead for more years than he could remember. A gurgle came up his throat, causing him to choke momentarily. By the time he caught his breath, his face was blue from lack of oxygen. Was this it? Was he finally dying? Was this the ghost of his wife, coming to take him away? She spoke again.

"Are you Jubal Blair?"

He blinked, then nodded once.

She inhaled sharply, as if someone had just punched her in the stomach.

"You're not dead," she muttered, more to herself than to him.

He watched horror spread across her face, puzzled by its origin. What the hell could it matter to her one way or the other? Besides that, couldn't she tell he was as good as dead?

He struggled to raise his arm, angrily grunting and pointing with what was left of his fist for her to get away.

Catherine felt as if she'd been blindsided, but before she could move, the woman who was his caretaker stormed out of the house.

"Who are you?"

Catherine glanced at her but didn't bother to answer. Her entire focus was on the man in the chair.

Jubal's grunts increased as he began thumping his fists against his lap.

"What have you done to him?" the caretaker yelled.

"It's more a case of what he's done to me," Catherine muttered, and then took a step back, unwilling to look at him any longer for fear she would see something of herself in his eyes.

"You get on out," the woman spluttered. "We don't need no strangers." At the word stranger, a look of recognition suddenly spread over her face. "I know who you are," she gasped, and grabbed the handles of Jubal's wheelchair. "You're the one claiming to be Annie Fane's granddaughter. You're the one who brought the witch back to Camarune. You're the one who's causin' all the bad luck."

"The only evil that ever lived in this place came from people like you."

The woman sneered. "That witch never had no child, and I oughta know. I midwifed the babies born around here for the last fifty years."

Catherine glanced at Jubal and was shocked by the intensity of his gaze. It hit her then that his body might be useless, but his mind was still there. She could almost see the wheels turning in his mind.

"I never claimed we were blood kin." Then she stared straight into Jubal Blair's eyes. "She just took in a lost mountain baby that nobody else wanted."

Jubal jerked up as if someone had just punched him beneath the chin, his dark eyes glittering wildly as he stared upon her face. That hair...that walk...that voice. He closed his eyes, remembering Turner screaming for a baby—his and Fancy's baby. He looked again and saw his son in her face. Disbelief gave way to panic, and then panic to rage.

Catherine gasped. In that moment, she realized he knew. She thought of her little mother, dying in the dark at Pulpit Rock, then leaned forward until she could see her own reflection in his eyes and whispered, "You thought it was over, didn't you, old man?"

All the muscles in his right cheek began to twitch. Catherine stared, willing him to speak. Nothing came out but a grunt.

She turned away, disgusted by even being in his presence.

Behind her, Jubal started to shriek. The sound was something between a gut-wrenching wail and pure hate.

"What did you say to him?" the woman screamed.

Catherine kept on walking.

Jubal's face turned dark, the veins in his neck distending like blue markers on a relief map. The caretaker gasped, certain that he was going to expire before her eyes. Then she started to moan.

"She put a curse on him...Lord have mercy... maybe she put a curse on us all."

She threw up her hands and ran for his medicine. All the while she was forcing it down his throat, she kept saying a prayer, trying to overcome the power of a witch's hex.

Luke lost the trail of footprints at the edge of a creek about a half mile below the house, then stepped into the water, continuing through the swift-flowing stream while searching both sides of the creek for signs of an exit. He walked until his boots were soaked and his feet were numb, and still no luck.

Finally he gave up the hunt and got back on dry ground. There was nothing for him to do but get back to the cabin to his patrol car.

Frustrated with his lack of success, he kept going over the identities of all the people he knew who lived up here, trying to put a face with a man who had the skills of his thief. As always, he came up with nothing. To his knowledge, no one on the mountain was any good at woodworking—at least not in the way this man was. And the things that he stole were never worth all that much money. Just simple things that a person might need to get through life. Which always brought Luke back to his one continuing question. If the man's needs were so simple, then why didn't he just buy what he needed? Granted the incomes of some of these people were spare, but even the poorest of families managed to raise a cash crop of tobacco now and then, or worked bringing out coal from some of the neighboring mines. Who among them was so poverty-stricken that he was reduced to stealing cans of tuna and fruit?

And the mountains were full of game. It wouldn't be the first time a deer had been poached out of season, and most everyone in Taney County knew that Luke would be the last person who would send a man to jail for trying to feed his family. He doubted that there was a man on the mountain who didn't own at least one gun, so why not hunt for his food?

Even though the logic of his supposition was sound, it didn't give him the answer he needed. By the time he got back to his vehicle and headed toward Faron Davis's farm to investigate the theft of the pig, it was almost ten. The fact that Catherine's Jeep was missing made him nervous. She'd gone into Camarune after all. The urge to follow her was strong. This constant need he kept feeling to protect her was rooted deeper than the oath he'd taken as an officer of the law. It bothered him—more than he cared to admit—that within days she could be gone. When he reached the turn leading toward the Davis farm, he gunned the engine. The sooner he finished taking Faron Davis's report, the sooner he could get back to her. Minutes later, he topped a rise. Below, he could see a part in the heavy growth of trees, revealing the gray, weathered shingles of a house. He braked at the top of the hill and reached for the handset on his radio.

"DePriest to base, do you copy?"

"This is Frank, go ahead."

"I'm at Davis's farm if you need me."

"Roger, that. Over and out."

"DePriest out," Luke said, and then put his vehicle in gear. He still had to see a man about a pig.

It was just past one when Luke started back to the cabin. After he'd taken Davis's report, he'd gone into headquarters and picked up some files, leaving word where he could be reached. Officially, he was on stakeout. In reality, he was hoping he caught more than the thief. After clearing up details at the department and making sure his duties would be covered, he swung by his apartment, picking up some clothes and a sackful of groceries. If he was going to camp out on Catherine's doorstep, the least he could do was furnish some of the food. Soon he was back on the road, heading to Catherine.

By the time he passed Pulpit Rock, he was beginning to get nervous. Last night there'd been a prowler at the cabin, and he'd gone off this morning as if nothing had happened. Now he'd been gone for more than half a day. Granted, she hadn't been there all that time alone, but she was bound to be home by now. What if the thief had come back? What if she'd walked in on him? His belly lurched. Hellfire—he should have taken her with him.

By the time he got to the cabin, his gut was in knots. He barely glanced at the Jeep parked outside, expecting Catherine to come out of the house at any moment.

But she didn't.

He started toward the door. It wasn't until he got even with her car that he realized she was still behind the wheel. Relief hit. Like him, she'd only just arrived. He bent down and tapped on the window.

"Hey, there, looks like I got here just in time to help carry stuff in."

The fact that she didn't respond wasn't apparent until he opened the door. He took her by the elbow, expecting to help her exit. She didn't move. He touched the side of her face.

"Catherine...are you all right?"

Other than a slight moan, she didn't answer.

The knot in his belly tightened. "Catherine...darlin'?"

She inhaled slowly, then turned, staring at him with blank confusion.

He looked past her into the seat. Condensation had all but dissolved one of the paper sacks beside her. My God, he thought. How long had she been sitting here?

"Are you sick, honey?"

"He's alive," she muttered, then started to shake.

Luke frowned. "Who, Catherine? Who's alive?"

"Jubal Blair," she said, then fell into his arms in a faint.

The sun was hovering at the crest of the ridge when Catherine sat up with a jerk. Confused, she tried to reconcile her surroundings with what she remembered last and couldn't figure out why she was sitting on the floor. Seconds later, Luke was kneeling before her.

"Catherine...do you know where you are?"

"In Grannie's cabin?"

Luke exhaled softly. At least that was a positive response.

"But why am I on the floor?" she asked.

He brushed a lock of dark hair away from her face and smiled.

"Didn't think I could get you up those damned narrow stairs without dropping you."

Her confusion spread. "But why would you need to—"

"You fainted."

Her lips parted in disbelief. "I didn't!"

"Yes, you did. In my arms, as a matter of fact. Scared the hell out of me, too."

She swept her hands across her face, feeling for fever. Her skin was cool, almost clammy.

"Was I sick?"

"I don't know, darlin'. When I drove up, you were sitting in your car. You muttered something about Jubal Blair being alive and then went out like the proverbial light."

She paled. Memory hit with the force of a fist to the gut, then she started to shake.

"He's not dead," she muttered, then grabbed Luke by the arm. "Did you know he's not dead?"

Luke frowned. "Yes, darlin', I knew."

"My God...oh, my God. Grannie said he was dead."

"Well, the way I heard it, he came darn close."

"He shot him. Why didn't he die?"

Luke's heart skipped a beat. He knew the story. Someone had ambushed Jubal and his sons one night while they were running their dogs. They'd killed all the dogs, as well as Jubal's sons—except the youngest, who'd taken himself off to greener pastures earlier that very day. Jubal was still alive when they found them, but had suffered a massive stroke. To this day, the incident was still a mystery. He took her by the shoulders, but to his dismay, her head rolled on her neck like a limp rag doll.

"Who shot him, Catherine?"

Her eyes wouldn't focus, and then suddenly she stilled, as if suddenly realizing what she'd said.

"How would I know? I wasn't here."

"Then why did you say *he* shot him? What do you know that we don't know?"

She looked at him then, wondering how much of her past she could reveal without putting herself in danger. If only she knew what the situation was between those two families. Were there any still living who carried on the hate, or had society and sanity finally intervened? She wanted to tell, but the secret was so old, and she was so new to the revelations.

"Nothing," she said, and shrugged out of his grasp. "I don't know anything. Grannie just told me he was dead."

His mind began to whirl with possibilities the law had never considered. Pulpit Rock was only a short distance from the cabin. Years ago he'd heard the tale about the witch putting a curse on the Blairs that had caused their deaths. As a kid, he'd laughed it off, but there was another possibility that now made more sense. Had Annie Fane seen something that night that sent her into hiding? And if she had, what horrible thing would have made her run?

"Why would Jubal Blair's death even be a point of discussion between you two?"

Catherine struggled to her feet and began smoothing out the wrinkles in her shirt.

"It wasn't a *point* of anything, just something she said." She looked at Luke then, gauging his expression. Even though he didn't press her further, she could tell he wasn't satisfied with the answer she'd given. "What time is it?" she asked.

"Almost six."

"I'd planned to cook chicken for supper tonight."

"I can wait," Luke said.

She managed a smile. "Well, then, I suppose I'd better get busy."

"Can I help?" Luke asked.

"Not right now, maybe later."

She headed toward the kitchen area, well aware that Luke was watching her every move. After she opened the old refrigerator, it dawned on her that Luke had put up all the groceries she'd bought earlier.

"Luke?"

"What?"

"Thanks for taking care of me...and the food."

"You're welcome."

In some way, Catherine felt the need to put the moment at ease. Making herself smile, she turned to face him.

"I wish I could offer you a drink and tell you to put your feet up and watch TV until dinner is ready, but I can't. You'll have to settle for a chair and a book."

"I like the view too much to put my nose in a book."

The fact that he was staring intently at her was too pointed to mistake. Guilt hit. How could she follow through on her feelings for him when she'd just lied to his face?

"Luke...I don't—"

"Don't say it," he said shortly. "I don't want to hear anyone else tell me no, especially you. Especially not today. And, since you don't need any help right now, I think I'll take a shower."

Tears blurred Catherine's vision as Luke disappeared. This wasn't what she wanted. Her shoulders slumped. But what *did* she want? Starting a relationship with this man would be crazy. Even if something did develop between them, she couldn't and wouldn't live in a place where her face and name were reviled on a daily basis.

She swiped at the tears on her face and grabbed a knife. Grannie had always claimed that peeling potatoes was therapeutic. She was about to test that theory.

By the time Luke came out of the bathroom, the food was almost done.

They ate without making eye contact and washed the dishes afterward in total silence. When she went to take her shower, she heard Luke go outside. He didn't come back in until she was upstairs in bed.

She was almost asleep when Luke's voice drifted upward toward the loft.

"Hey, Catherine."

"Yes?"

"If Jubal Blair means nothing to you, and your grannie didn't tell you anything important about the death of his sons, then why did learning he was alive upset you so much that you fainted?"

There was a long moment of silence.

"Catherine?"

"I'm tired, Luke. Go to sleep."

It wasn't the answer he wanted to hear.

10

Nellie Cauthorn bolted across the street toward the grocery, her purse clutched against her breasts like a shield. Even though Preacher had told her to stay out of the fray, she considered it her duty as Lovie's best friend to make sure Lovie knew all that was going on in Camarune. The door jingled as she entered the store.

"Lovie, where are you?"

"Here!"

Nellie found her in the cereal aisle, stamping prices on boxes of cornflakes.

"There you are," she gasped, then looked over her shoulder to make sure they weren't overheard. "Are we alone?"

Lovie straightened and then brushed some dust off the front of her dress, absently noting a loose button she needed to fix.

"Yes, what's up?"

Nellie leaned forward. "Did you hear?"

"Hear what?"

Nellie lowered her voice. "About that woman and Jubal Blair?"

Lovie's heart skipped a beat. She knew exactly which woman Nellie was referring to, but after the talk she'd had with that lawyer, she was aiming for a more neutral position. Still, her curiosity was piqued.

"What about them?" she asked.

Nellie was so excited, it was all she could do to stand in one place.

"Well...you know Myrtle Ross, who takes care of Jubal Blair?"

Lovie resisted the urge to roll her eyes. "Yes, Nellie, I know Myrtle. She lives five houses down from me, and I see Jubal on her porch nearly every day."

"Oh! Yes...well...anyway... Myrtle came to the house this morning to see Preacher. She wanted him to perform an exorcism at her house."

"Good Lord. Has she started drinking again?"

"No, no, nothing like that," Nellie cried. "Just listen. I'm trying to tell you something."

Knowing Nellie, this would take some time. "I'm listening," she said, and resumed marking the cereal boxes and placing them on the shelves.

"Myrtle said that Fane woman did something to Jubal yesterday that got him all stirred up. She said he was carrying on something fierce after she left, and it took her forever to get him to sleep last night.

Then she said he moaned and groaned in his sleep like a man possessed. That's when she decided that the woman, being that witch Annie Fane's grand-daughter and such, had probably put a spell on him. Anyway, Preacher has gone over there to pray with her and Jubal.''

Lovie slammed a box of cereal on the shelf and then turned to Nellie.

''My lawyer says we'll be in a whole lot of trou-ble if we don't stop calling her a witch. We don't really know anything about her except that she brought Annie Fane back to bury. He says she could presses charges against us for libel.''

Nellie's lips pursed. ''I know that. It's not like I'm telling it on the streets. I just came to tell you.'' Then her eyes narrowed thoughtfully, as if some-thing had just occurred to her. ''Just because *she's* not a witch, that doesn't mean her grandmother wasn't. You know the stories about her.''

Lovie turned away. She knew the stories. She knew them all too well.

''Anyway,'' Nellie added, ''didn't that same law-yer tell you that if we had proof of witchery, we would be protected against any lawsuit?''

''Yes.''

''So what about this? She obviously did some-thing to poor Jubal.''

''Exactly what did she do to Jubal?''

Nellie began to fidget. ''Well, Myrtle didn't

know for sure, but she said the woman said something to him, and then he started to have a fit.''

"She didn't hear what she said?"

Nellie shook her head.

"Then what makes Myrtle think it was something bad? That Fane woman doesn't know Jubal Blair. Maybe she was just asking directions and he got all upset because he couldn't answer. Lord have mercy, Nellie, it's a wonder he's still alive. Maybe that woman didn't have anything to do with his upset. Maybe his time is just coming to an end.''

Nellie was stunned by Lovie's lack of interest. "But yesterday you said—"

"That was yesterday," Lovie snapped. "And if I was you, I wouldn't say any more about what your husband was doing. After all, isn't there some code of privacy that preachers are supposed to observe?''

Nellie flushed. "Well, I never. See if I ever come tell you anything again," she muttered, and headed for the door.

Lovie watched her go, well aware that she'd hurt Nellie's feelings. But it couldn't be helped. Nellie didn't know everything. When the door slammed behind her, Lovie sighed, then turned and picked up another box of cereal and put it on the shelf. It wasn't so much that Lovie had developed a kinder heart or had a religious epiphany about her fellow man. It was guilt that was eating her alive. All the stories that were going on about a one-eyed calf and food turning to blood might be happening, but she would bet her life that Catherine Fane's coming had nothing to do with hexes or spells any more than Annie Fane had been a real witch.

She picked up the carton she'd just emptied and carried it to the back of the store, passing the refrigerated case where she kept the milk that she sold. As she did, she caught a glimpse of her reflection. She paused, staring at the old woman looking back, imagining the guilt she felt was plastered all over her face.

"You did it," she muttered.

I didn't mean for everyone to hate her.

"You could have stopped it years ago."

It just got out of hand.

"You could still make amends."

I'm too old, and it's too late. Besides that, the woman is dead. Now leave me alone.

Lovie did as she'd been told, thinking nothing of the fact that she'd just had an argument with herself—and lost.

Sunlight was coming through a crack in the shutters as Catherine rolled over in bed and sat up. Just as she did, a small, dark shadow moved out from under her bed and across the floor. She leaned over for a closer look, then let out a scream.

Luke came out of the sleeping bag with his gun in his hand, thankful that he'd gone to sleep in his underwear instead of stripping as usual. After all these years of hunting that damned thief, he would hate to have to arrest him in the nude.

He turned in a circle, expecting to see an intruder, and saw Catherine coming down the stairs instead, still screaming.

"What?" he yelled. "What's wrong?"

She pointed. "It's the rat! The rat! He was under my bed!"

Luke swung in the direction that she'd pointed. Sure enough, there was a rat on the floor, running for all it was worth. He took quick aim.

"Don't shoot!" Catherine screamed. "If you kill him, I won't find my watch."

"Christ almighty," Luke muttered, and reached for his pants as the rat aimed for the hole in the wall beneath the bookcase.

Seconds later, Luke was running for the door, following on Catherine's heels.

Catherine bounded outside and jumped off the porch, heading toward the back of the house. If the rat got outside before she got around the corner, she would lose him for sure. She cleared the south porch just as the rat darted into the grass.

"There it goes," she shouted, and took off after it, unmindful of the fact that there might be anything from snakes to sharp rocks beneath her feet.

"Be careful!" Luke yelled, then winced as his heel came down on a stone.

By the time he looked up, Catherine was disappearing into the trees. He groaned. Damn it to hell, he'd been in the NFL. He was supposed to be the fast one, and she was leaving him in the dust. Forgetting about pain, he kicked into stride. Within seconds, she was back in sight.

Suddenly she stopped. "There!" she screamed, pointing somewhere toward the ground. "He went there!"

Luke was right beside her. "Where, honey? Where did he go?"

"That tree," Catherine said, pointing to a hole between the roots of an old dead tree.

"I'll be damned," Luke said, and squatted down to peer inside. When he stood, he was grinning. "You found him out after all, didn't you, girl?"

Catherine's chest was heaving, the hem of her nightgown was damp from lingering dew on some of the underbrush, and the bottoms of her feet were beginning to burn. She looked up at Luke, at the smile on his face, and then down a few inches to the expanse of his bare chest. It was then that it hit her. Except for a bit of flimsy fabric, there was precious little hiding her body. Resisting the urge to cross her arms over her breasts, she turned away, hoping he couldn't see through her gown, then peered into the hole.

"How can we get to his stash?"

"First we're going back to the house to get

dressed," Luke said. "I'm not cutting down a tree barefoot. And then we're—"

"But he might get away," Catherine wailed.

Luke started to laugh. "Hell, Catherine, even if he does, he's hardly going to take everything with him. I thought you were after your watch, not a hunting trophy. Besides, I don't think a pack rat would mount very well."

Heat spread up her face as she turned and punched him on the arm with a playful swat.

"Just shut up and help me get my watch."

Luke grabbed her wrist. "Say please."

Catherine froze. She knew he was teasing, but there was a look in his eyes that made her weak in the knees.

"Please?"

He moved closer. "Now, darlin', I think I heard a question in that word. You want to clarify your sweet needs for me?"

She could feel the heat of his body as he took a step closer. Her mind was spinning. Sweet needs? Lord have mercy. She'd thought *Texans* were talkers. She took a deep breath, then got lost in his gaze.

"Catherine...I'm waiting."

She exhaled slowly. "Me, too."

The game had gone too far. He stuck his gun in the back waistband of his jeans and then took her by the arms.

Her head tilted, as if waiting for his kiss. The last thing she saw was his face, coming closer—closer. She closed her eyes. The waiting was over.

His mouth came down hard upon her lips, then instantly softened. His arms encircled her waist, pulling her close against his body. When she moaned, he lifted his head, a questioning look on his face.

Catherine locked her hands behind his neck.

Grannie, do you believe in love at first sight?

"Yes…please," she said.

He picked her up in his arms and started toward the house.

The woods had grown silent; the air barely stirred. The faint smell of damp earth and new grass blended with the scent of warm bodies and the thunder of fast-beating hearts. Catherine was afraid, yet, at the same time, certain that this was right. Luke was a strong man a good man. She laid her head against his shoulder and flattened the palm of her hand against his chest. His heartbeat was steady, unlike hers.

Moments later, he kicked the front door shut and then stopped, looking first at his sleeping bag, then up the stairs to the loft.

"The bed," she said softly. "And I'll walk."

He put her down, then cupped her face, unwilling to turn loose of her. This time his kisses were sweet, gentle nips—tasting first of her lower lip, then her upper, then the edge of her chin. Catherine swayed. Luke took her by the hand and led her toward the sleeping bag instead.

"Too damned far," he said softly, pointing toward the loft with his chin.

Her legs were trembling so much now that she was forced to agree. When her feet touched the down-filled comforter, she jerked as if she'd been burned. Luke stopped, searching her face for signs of regret.

"Are you okay with this?"

Her eyes felt heavy, her skin hot to the touch. She touched the side of his face, then his mouth, tracing the shape with her fingers.

"I may never be okay again."

A slight frown appeared between his eyebrows. "Are you afraid?" When she hesitated, a soft moan slid up and out of his throat. "Darlin'...the last thing I want is for you to be afraid of me. Just say the word now and this is over."

Instead of an answer, she knelt on the sleeping bag and then held out her hand. He took it—and her—without waiting, moving them both until they were centered upon the satin-slick surface.

Catherine sighed. The weight of his body felt right—almost familiar—as if she'd waited all her life for this man.

Luke was shaking. He had been in need plenty of times in his life, but he'd never before been in love. It was a sobering revelation to an independent man. He looked down at the woman in his arms, wanting to lay permanent claim but knowing that, for now, all she'd offered was her body. It remained to be seen if she would give him her heart.

"Catherine…I promise I—" Then he froze, his head tilted to one side as he listened.

"What?" she asked. "What is it?"

He rolled. Within seconds, he was up and grabbing for a shirt.

"Someone's coming."

Catherine bolted to her feet and headed for the bathroom and the change of clothes she'd left in there last night.

By the time the car pulled into the yard, Luke was fully dressed and standing on the porch, silently cursing fate and the arrival of one of his deputies, Donny Mott.

"Hey, Donny, you're out early this morning."

Donny was short and stocky, with a slight roll to his gait, compliments of a motorcycle wreck he'd had when he was a kid.

"Not early, boss. Late. I've yet to get to bed."

Luke frowned. Something was wrong.

"Talk to me."

Donny glanced toward the house, then lowered his voice.

"Uh…it's about Miss Fane."

"What about Miss Fane?"

Donny hooked his thumb behind him, toward the valley below.

"Hell, Luke, they're goin' crazy down there. Some woman's got half the town up in arms about Miss Fane and Jubal Blair. They've had to call the doctor in twice for him, and there's a death watch in front of his house. They're sayin' she put some kind of spell on him and that she's got to come take it off or he'll die."

"Jesus Blessed Christ," Luke whispered, and it was a true prayer.

He swiped a hand across his face. This was getting serious. A crowd of frightened people would do things that a man alone would not.

"What do you want me to do?" Donny asked.

Before Luke could answer, Catherine came outside, carrying two cups of coffee in her hand. Her smile was sweet, but the nervous glance she gave Luke was somewhere between an apology for interrupting their conversation and regret that they'd been interrupted, as well.

"Thought you gentleman might like some coffee," she said.

Donny Mott had grown up in Camarune, and it had taken every ounce of grit he'd had to drive up to this place to find his boss. But when Catherine came out the door, every assumption he'd made regarding Annie Fane's kin turned to dust. This stunning, black-haired beauty with that sweet, childlike smile was about as witchlike as his aunt Margaret. He took off his hat and then reached for the cup she was offering.

"Don't mind if I do," he said.

Luke stifled a grin. He'd never seen Donny blush. It would seem that, once again, Catherine had conquered, this time with nothing more than a smile. He, too, took the coffee she offered. When she turned to go inside, he spoke.

"Wait, Catherine."

She stopped and turned.

"This is Donny Mott, one of my deputies. Donny—Catherine Fane."

They both smiled and nodded, then Catherine turned to Luke.

"Is everything okay?" she asked.

The hesitance in her voice was to be expected. Ever since her arrival, most of his problems had been because of her.

"Not exactly," he said. "I'll tell you about it later."

She frowned, but went back inside, trusting that he would do as he said.

Luke waited until the door was closed; then he stepped off the porch and walked out into the yard. Donny followed.

"Are they making threats?" he asked.

"Not yet," Donny said. "Just talkin' crazy."

Luke sighed. "One always leads to the other."

Donny nodded, waiting for instructions.

"You did good in coming to tell me," Luke said. "But I want you to go home and get some rest. I'm thinking I need to pay a call on old Jubal—just to see if there's anything he wants to tell me."

Donny gaped. "But, Luke, the old man can't talk—hasn't talked for nigh onto thirty years."

"There's always a way...if the spirit's willing." Then he added, "And as my momma used to say, 'and the creek don't rise.'"

Donny laughed. "Yeah, I heard that one before."

A few minutes later he was gone, leaving Luke with an empty coffee cup and a sinking feeling in his belly. In a way, he wasn't surprised. This old wound had been festering for years and had re-opened the day that hearse had pulled into town. It stood to reason there would be trouble, but he couldn't help wondering about her reticence to speak of Jubal Blair. It would help to know what had really happened yesterday between her and that old man, but he had a feeling she wasn't going to tell him.

Catherine looked up as Luke came in the door. "Another cup?" she asked, lifting the coffeepot in his direction.

"Not just yet."

A little embarrassed, she set the coffeepot down on the stove and opened the refrigerator to get out some eggs.

"Breakfast will be ready soon. I thought since they came looking for you that you would have to go. I didn't want to delay you any more than—"

"Catherine."

His voice scared her. When she turned, the look on her face only made her fear worse.

"What?"

"Do you trust me?"

"Yes, of course I trust you," she said, and then looked away, pretending to busy herself with the food.

Luke grabbed her wrist. "Look at me and say that again."

Her stomach lurched. Something was really, really wrong. *Oh, Grannie, what have you gotten me into?*

"I trust you," she muttered, but once again her gaze slid sideways as she spoke.

"Like hell," he said softly, and thrust his hands in his hair and strode out to the porch.

Catherine followed. "Look, Luke, we haven't known each other long, but—"

He spun, his voice thick with anger. "Long enough to let me make love to you, but not enough to tell me what the hell's going on? Is that what you're about, Catherine Fane? Is it all about you, and the rest is nobody else's business?"

"No, no," she begged, reaching for his arm. "You don't understand."

"Then make me," he growled, and pulled her into his arms. "Tell me what happened between you and Jubal Blair."

"Why? Why do you need to know?"

"Because there's a crowd in town that's verging on the edge of insanity. These people were raised with prejudice, steeped in religion, and practice superstitions on a daily basis. In their minds, your grandmother was a witch. I don't know why they think that, but they do. And, by reason of birth and blood, that makes you one, too. They think you put a curse on Jubal Blair, and they want you to take it off."

She blanched, then swayed. Luke caught her before she could fall, then pulled her into his arms.

"For God's sake, Catherine, tell me something I don't already know."

"Annie Fane was no blood kin to me at all. All she did was take in a baby that nobody else wanted."

The poignancy in her voice was hard to hear. At once he felt shame, as if he'd trespassed in a place he shouldn't have been, and, at the same time, sadness for her.

"What happened to your parents?" he asked.

She hesitated, then told herself that one more truth couldn't hurt.

"They died. I don't know about details, just that I was only hours old when she took me. She was my world." Her voice broke. "And now she's gone."

Luke held her where they stood, trying to decide what to do next, when she pulled away from him and walked into the house. He followed her in, noticing almost immediately that she'd rolled up his sleeping bag and put it by the fireplace.

So much for that.

"I'm going into town. Will you be all right here by yourself for a while?"

She turned. The look in her eyes said one thing, while she said another.

"I'll be fine."

"I'd take you, but until I get some of this mess sorted out, it might make things worse."

She nodded. "I understand. Besides, I've still got some sorting to do, and I want to read some more in Grannie's journals."

He wanted to kiss that frightened look off her face, but when he reached for her, she moved away. Hope sank. Back to square one.

"I won't be long. Lock the door after I'm gone."

"I don't like this feeling," she said.

"What feeling?"

"Like I'm the prisoner and everyone else is a victim."

There was nothing he could say to make it better.

"Like I said, I won't be long."

She followed him outside, then watched as he

drove away. After he was gone, she walked off the porch and into the yard, then turned in a circle, silently staring into the trees.

"If you're out there," she shouted, "look your fill. I'm here, and I'm not going away until I'm good and ready."

Having said it, she stomped back into the house, punctuating her vow by slamming the door.

Luke was pulling into town before it dawned on him that she still hadn't told him what she'd said to Jubal Blair. He sighed. The omission alone was telling. Obviously she'd said something—something that must have mattered to Jubal Blair, if not to anyone else.

Maynard waved at him as he passed the station. A little of the tension he'd been feeling began to recede. At least everyone in town wasn't involved.

He drove the two-block length of the main street, then turned left. Almost immediately, his hopes fell. He could hear them singing.

11

It was "Onward Christian Soldiers," and Preacher Cauthorn was leading the fray, which did not make Luke feel any better. Soldiers fought wars, and the last thing he needed was for a crowd of zealots to decide they needed to purge Camarune of Catherine Fane. As he parked, a few on the outskirts of the crowd saw him arrive. Word began to spread that he was there, and by the time he reached the edge of the crowd, the song had dwindled to a murmur. Everyone seemed to be waiting.

"Excuse me. I need to get through."

The crowd parted to let him pass, then closed behind him as he moved toward the house. Shouts followed him. Some of the voices he recognized, others he did not.

"Hey, Luke, what are you going to—"

"Sheriff, you've got to do something about—"

"You've got to arrest—"

"It ain't right that—"

The demands didn't stop, but neither did he. By the time he got to the front door, he was sweating.

The anger of the crowd was so strong he could almost feel it. Unless he did something soon, Catherine could be in real danger.

Preacher mopped at his brow with a snow-white handkerchief, then offered Luke his hand.

"Real glad to see you here, Sheriff. I fear we've got a crisis on our hands."

Luke shook the preacher's hand. "Yes, I'd say that you do," he said. "What are you going to do about it?"

Preacher looked stunned. "I don't understand. Haven't you come to help us rid Camarune of Catherine Fane?"

"For what?"

Nellie Cauthorn stepped out of the crowd, waving her Bible over her head.

"For putting a curse on Jubal Blair!" she shrieked.

Luke turned, fixing her with a cool, steady glare.

"What did you say?"

"For putting a curse on Jubal Blair," she muttered.

"That's what I thought you said." Then Luke shook his head. "It seems to me that you didn't pay very good attention to the warning Miss Fane gave you the other day."

Preacher stared at his wife in disbelief. "Warning? What warning? You didn't tell me you'd conversed with this woman."

Nellie started to sputter. "It didn't amount to all that—"

"She was threatened with a lawsuit if she didn't stop libeling the Fane name by calling them all witches," Luke said.

"Have mercy," Preacher gasped, then gave his wife a stern look. "We'll discuss this further at home."

Nellie's color heightened, and her lips sucked into a tight, angry pout. She couldn't believe that Preacher had just reprimanded her in front of God and everybody. They would discuss it, all right, but not in the way he had planned.

"Damn it, Luke, you owe us an explanation!" someone shouted.

He spun, his own anger visible as he faced the crowd.

"On the contrary," he snapped. "You people are the ones owing an explanation. You're disturbing the peace! You've stomped all over Frances Parker's prize begonias, and you're blocking the street! And I can only imagine how Pete and Sammi Frost feel about this noise you've been making. They live on the next block and just brought their little boy home from the hospital last week. How the hell is she supposed to get that baby to sleep with all this noise?"

There was an audible gasp and then sudden silence. The last thing they'd expected was to be the ones in the wrong. They'd come to crucify, not be crucified. Then someone in the back of the crowd got brave enough to challenge his authority.

"What about Jubal? He's dyin' because of the witch's kin!"

"Bullshit," Luke said, for once disregarding his manners in the presence of the female sex. "If Jubal Blair is dying, then it's because of his age and health, not some so-called spell. As for calling Annie Fane a witch, you've all been warned that you could be sued for slander if you don't cease and desist."

"But everyone knows that—"

"Knows what?" Luke interrupted. "I want someone to step up and tell me what they know. I want an eyewitness to an actual event, not some fourth-generation gossip hardly worthy of being told over a Halloween campfire."

The crowd shifted nervously, eyeing Preacher and waiting to see what he did. But Preacher's vehemence had dampened considerably when he'd heard the word *sue*. If word got back to the church superintendent, he could lose his job, and he was too old to move and start over again. So he stood to one side, clutching his Bible in one hand and his songbook in the other, with what he hoped was a benevolent expression on his face.

The rest of the crowd was starting to divide. To some, Luke was beginning to make sense, while others were still doubtful. They had been ingrained with too many years of superstition to be easily swayed.

Then Luke added, "As for saying Catherine Fane is kin to a witch, not only are you maligning Annie Fane, you'd best get your facts straight before you start calling names. Miss Fane is no blood relation to Annie Fane."

"No, sir! That ain't right!" someone shouted. "I heard her call that woman Grannie."

Luke had to raise his voice to be heard over the murmur that followed.

"I never said Annie Fane didn't raise her." Then he pointed to a tall, thin woman with frosty-red hair standing a head taller than most in the middle of the crowd. "I've been calling Sadie Hutch there Aunt Sadie for as long as I've lived, and to my knowledge, we're not related. Every one of you knows that it's the mountain way of showing respect for our elders."

Sadie giggled nervously and waved, then realized what she'd done and looked away. But the damage had been done. He'd broken the hostility of the crowd by becoming one of them.

"My information is that Miss Fane was orphaned soon after her birth. All Annie Fane did was take in a baby nobody else wanted. I don't know what Bible you people have been reading, but in mine, that's the Christian thing to do. There's also a passage in mine that says something about those without sin casting the first stones, so the only people I want to talk to in this crowd are the sinless ones.''

He paused, looking out across their faces. By now, a few were already walking away, while others had their heads together in quiet conversation.

''That's what I thought,'' he said shortly. ''I'm going in the house now and talk to Jubal myself.''

''That old man can't talk.''

Luke didn't bother to acknowledge the shout. All he did was point to a group of about twenty or so who were standing to his right.

''If you people don't get out of Hazel's roses, I'm going to arrest you for vandalism.''

They moved en masse, scurrying toward the street.

''And don't be blocking traffic, either!'' he yelled, then turned and knocked on the door.

Myrtle appeared almost instantly, her face flushed, her eyes snapping in anger. Luke supposed she'd been listening and hadn't liked what she'd heard.

He took off his hat and nodded. ''Morning, Myrtle. I need to talk to Jubal.''

She started fussing with the front of her apron and then smoothing down her hair as she stood in the doorway, blocking his entrance.

''Now, Sheriff, I don't know as how I can allow that. The Commonwealth of Kentucky pays me to take care of Mr. Blair, and his doctor said to keep him quiet. Besides, you know he don't talk none.''

Luke stared her straight in the eyes. "I doubt I'll be making as much noise as that crowd you had on your lawn, and I'm well aware he can't talk, but he can listen, now, can't he?''

Her voice began to waver as Luke started past her. "Yes, but—''

"If you'd be so kind as to take me to him, I'd be obliged.''

Myrtle's options had just run out, and she knew it. She stepped back to let him pass, then shut the door behind him.

"This way,'' she grumbled. "But I'll have to stay with you when you talk.'' Then she added quickly, lest Luke read her comment as a threat, "Just in case he needs me, you understand.''

"Fine with me,'' Luke said, and wished she'd left the front door open as they walked toward the back of the house. The smell of age and urine was strong within the old walls.

Jubal Blair was, quite literally, fit to be tied. He'd worked himself into such a state that what was left of his body had given out. He couldn't swallow without choking, and he hadn't been able to sit up for over a day. Lying in this stinking bed, with nothing to look at but Myrtle's fat, ugly face and the water stains on the ceiling above him, was true hell.

He wanted to die. He'd been trying to die for so many years that he'd lost count. But that was before he'd seen *her*. Now he was afraid his secrets would come out before they buried him in the ground. Would she tell? He groaned. Would it matter? There was little the law could do to him that the years hadn't already done.

If he could, he would have laughed at the quixotic justice of fate, but even that ability had been taken away from him years ago on the mountain beneath Pulpit Rock.

He moaned, then moaned a little louder. Where the hell was Myrtle? She knew he couldn't lie in one place for too long. Didn't she know his bones were coming through his flesh from the weight of his body? He needed to be turned, God damn it!

Finally he hushed. Even if she was standing by his bed, she still wouldn't hear him over that noise going on outside. Earlier he'd heard bits and pieces of Myrtle's mania and had a pretty good idea of what had started it all. But what the hell did they expect? Any man would have reacted the same when faced with a ghost—even if this one was walking and talking.

He closed his eyes, trying to get her face out of his mind, but it was no use. He could still see the accusation in her eyes. She knew! Somehow she knew what had happened, just like he'd known her the moment he'd seen her. When he thought about it, it wasn't too far-fetched to believe. After all, a man should be able to recognize his own kin—even if she'd been tainted with a Joslin's blood.

He shuddered, then sighed, trying to figure out how she'd survived. For all these years he'd assumed she'd been lost in the hills and considered it justice for the sons that he'd lost. Granted, he damn sure hadn't known Turner had fathered the child when the whole thing started, and he still didn't know if it would have made any difference. His hate had been strong then, like his body. Now the only thing he hated more than himself was God, for taking it all away.

It took him a while to realize that the singing had stopped. He didn't know why and didn't much care. He was just grateful for the blessed peace. Then the front door slammed, and he heard the sound of footsteps. Myrtle's he recognized. They were a shuffling scoot. But the distinct stride of boots on a hardwood floor was impossible to miss. He opened his eyes, expecting to see Myrtle parading a different doctor into the room.

The last thing he expected was the man wearing a badge. In that moment, every fear he'd lived with for the past twenty-odd years came crashing down on him at once. *So,* he thought, *the girl told and they've come to take me away.*

* * *

"He might be asleep," Myrtle hissed.

Luke found himself staring into a face full of hate. "He's not," he said shortly, and then nodded at Jubal. "Mr. Blair, I doubt you remember me, although I've spoken to you off and on over the years. My name is Luke DePriest. Matthew De-Priest from over in Crying River was my dad. I'm sheriff of Taney County now. Have been for almost eight years."

Jubal tried to put as much anger into his stare as he could. The son of a bitch could take his behavior any way he chose.

Luke was surprised by the life in the old man's eyes and knew instantly that he wasn't as close to death as everyone believed. He pulled up a chair without being asked and sat down beside Jubal's bed.

"I understand you haven't been feeling too good."

Jubal refused to respond, thinking that the man would give up and leave, but he hadn't counted on Luke's tenacity.

"I thought you and I needed to have a little talk," Luke said. "Did a young woman come to see you yesterday?"

Jubal's heart jumped, then settled. He looked away, still refusing to respond.

Luke turned to Myrtle. "If he doesn't even remember her visit, then I fail to see why you think she's caused him to take to his bed.''

Myrtle's mouth dropped, and she began talking in fits and starts, pointing toward Jubal as she spoke.

"You didn't see him. After she left, he started howling like a dog at the moon. Why, it scared me to death, it did. I had to call in the doctor to calm him down.''

The whole time Myrtle was talking, Luke never took his eyes from Jubal's face. To the old man's credit, if something had disturbed him then, he wasn't revealing it now.

"He looks fine to me," Luke said, then laid his hand on the man's arm. "Jubal? Jubal?''

Jubal silently cursed him, hating him for his youth and for his health. Then he turned, fixing the sheriff with a steely gaze.

"Are you fine, Mr. Blair? Because if you're not, then I might need to call in Miss Fane to give her version of what happened between you two.''

Jubal's heart jerked again, only this time it took longer for the rate to settle as he shook his head vehemently from side to side.

Luke frowned. "You're not fine?''

Jubal grunted angrily and thumped the bed with a fist.

"You look fine to me.''

Jubal nodded.

"Oh," Luke said. "You were telling me that you didn't need me to call in Miss Fane."

Again Jubal indicated a yes.

"Then I won't," Luke said.

When Jubal visibly relaxed, Luke's frown deepened. This was odd. The old man seemed as adamant about keeping secrets as Catherine had.

"There are a couple of other matters I think we need to clear up," Luke said. "I don't know if you're aware of it or not, but there are a good hundred or so people outside this house who think you're in here dying because of something Catherine Fane said to you." At this point Luke chuckled and patted Jubal on the arm, well aware that the man was in no mood to laugh. "Isn't that crazy?"

Jubal took a deep breath, glaring first at Myrtle for causing all this fuss, and then at Luke for not letting it go. Finally, he nodded.

"Well, I never," Myrtle muttered.

"They're saying she's a witch. Do you believe in witches, Mr. Blair?"

Jubal snorted and rolled his eyes. Luke grinned. "Neither do I." Then he turned to Myrtle. "You know, I believe you misinterpreted Mr. Blair's behavior yesterday." Then he looked back at Jubal. "Yesterday, when you upset Myrtle, were you just angry about something, or were you feeling sick?"

Jubal nodded and thumped the bed with both fists.

"Both?" Luke asked.

Jubal nodded again.

Luke slapped his knee and then stood, still watching Jubal's face.

"Well, I think that about covers all the questions I had for you. Now, if you don't mind, I'll just go outside and send the vultures packing. I don't think you're anywhere ready to die, and damn sure not from some fictional curse."

Jubal blinked once. If the man only knew. The curse was real, but it hadn't come from that girl. She was just a by-product of a hate that had ruined them all years before she was ever born.

Luke watched Jubal's face, wishing with all he had that the old man could speak, but that wasn't going to happen. If he got answers, they would have to come from Catherine herself.

He nodded at Jubal. "Mr. Blair, it's been a pleasure to see you again. I'll look forward to seeing you back on the porch real soon now, you hear?"

Jubal glared. He got the message. For things to return to normal, he was going to have to act normal, too, which meant sitting out on that damned porch in his own pee and shit until Myrtle decided to clean him up.

Luke nodded at Myrtle. "I'll see myself out," he said, leaving Myrtle to do as she chose.

She chose to follow him to the door.

When Luke stepped outside, the crowd's attention refocused on him, rather than the gossip they'd been trading. Preacher Cauthorn was standing off to one side, in deep conversation with his wife. Luke stifled a grin. If nothing else was accomplished today, at least Nellie Cauthorn was getting what for.

"What's the verdict?" a man shouted. "Is old man Blair going to die?"

"Not today," Luke said. "And if I'm any judge of character, not for a good long time. That old man is tougher than most of you standing. And Myrtle can vouch for me when I tell you that he wasn't upset by anything Catherine Fane did. Let's just say that Myrtle misunderstood his demands." Then he winked at Myrtle, trying to soften the fact that she'd raised a fuss for no reason. "But it's easily understood. After all, he can't speak, and she was only doing her job."

"Is that so, Myrtle? Is Jubal all right?"

Luke saw her waver. He could tell that it was killing her to have to admit to being wrong.

"I never heard him act up like that," Myrtle said. "How was I to know what he wanted?"

"Well, good Lord," someone muttered. "Here I've gone and wasted a day, and my green beans are past needin' to be picked."

Preacher took this as his cue to disassemble that which he'd wrought.

"Well, now," he said, "it seems we've been

misled.'' He gave Myrtle a hard look, willing for her to take the blame, rather than himself and Nellie for their impulsive behavior. ''I say we go on about our business and let the sheriff do his.''

For the first time since he'd arrived, Luke began to relax. ''I second Preacher's suggestion,'' he said. ''You people go on home. And next time you hear gossip, I remind you to think what the consequences could be. I came damned near arresting the lot of you.''

They began to disperse by twos and threes. The silence in which they left was as noticeable as the noise they'd been making earlier. Luke turned, pulled his hat a little lower on his forehead and then touched his finger to the brim.

''Preacher...Nellie...you all take care now, you hear?''

They nodded and smiled.

He heard them arguing all the way to his car. It wasn't until he slid behind the wheel that he turned loose his fear.

''Thank you, Jesus,'' he whispered, and then reached for the radio. ''Sheriff to base. Over.''

''This is Joe. Frank's off. Go ahead. Over.''

Luke shook his head. If the Lexington police force ever heard these transmissions, they would laugh their heads off.

''Crowd dispersed on Bleeker Street. I'm coming in. Over and out.''

He started the engine, then glanced at his watch. It would take half an hour to check in at headquarters, then another hour to get back to Catherine, and it wasn't even noon. Even though he hated to leave her alone, he felt she would be safe. In his opinion, her greater danger had been the crowd he'd just sent home, not a petty thief who, if one didn't count livestock, had yet to harm a soul.

Catherine rocked back on her heels in frustration, staring at the pack rat's den. The poker she'd filched from the fireplace had gone only so far into the hole before striking something solid—probably the other side of the tree. Obviously the den was farther up inside. What she needed was a saw. She stood, then gave the tree a sharp whack with the poker in frustration.

"In the words of the inimitable Arnold...I'll be back."

Then, grinning at her own bit of wit, she started toward the house.

The day was sunny and getting warmer by the hour, although if the gathering clouds overhead were any indication, there could be more rain before night. A pair of squirrels scolded from the branches of a tree as she moved beneath its shade. An accumulation of last year's acorns crunched beneath her feet, sending a faint, musty scent into the air. A bit of spider's web caught in her hair, and she gasped, sidestepping the path and swiping at her face as she went. She hated spiders. Next to snakes, they were tops on her list of things to avoid.

In the distance, she could see the lip of Pulpit Rock hanging out over the mountain and the valley below. Such a difference between that place and this. Here, everything grew in abundance. Down there, even the ground was barren.

She shivered, remembering Grannie's story, imagining the blood spreading upon the earth, then, later, the rain washing it deep into the soil. Gripping the poker a little bit tighter, she hastened her steps, breathing easier as soon as the back of the house came in view.

She paused, letting the peace of it all ease her fears. It gave her a good feeling to know that she was walking in places where her grannie had walked and sleeping in the same house that Grannie and her Billy had built. Suddenly her stomach growled, and she remembered the breakfast she'd been going to cook for herself and Luke.

Guilt slowed her steps. Luke. What was she going to do about him? Better yet, what was he going to do about her? He was going to want answers about Jubal Blair, she just knew it. And there was a part of her that wanted to tell. But how much? She could admit to being Fancy Joslin's daughter, but what would happen if she said her father's name? She shook her head and started walking again. She would worry about it later. Right now, she was hungry. Until Luke came back, she would have to find something else to do. She thought of Annie's journals. Maybe the answers she was searching for would be between the covers of those books.

A short while later, she settled down on the porch with another journal, a bacon sandwich and a glass of milk.

12

May 12, 1941

They're saying in town that we might go to war. I can't bear the thought. Billy's quiet, but the look in his eyes says it all. If we do, he won't wait for the draft. That's not his way.

Catherine turned the page, almost dreading to read the next entry. As she did, from the corner of her eye she saw something move among the trees. She turned. A doe and fawn were grazing at the edge of the clearing. She held her breath, the journal momentarily forgotten in the beauty of the scene. She wondered how many times over the years Annie Fane had sat in this very place, admiring such a peaceful scene. Then it hit her how much Annie had given up for a stranger's child.

"Oh, Grannie," she whispered. "I'm so sorry you had to leave this place because of me."

A few moments later, the doe moved on, taking her baby with her. Catherine exhaled slowly, then looked down at the place she'd been holding and began reading the penciled-in notes.

May 30, 1941
Emory Cleese is back again, this time for him-self. He suffers from ulcers, I think. I gave him some marigold water. He says it helps the pain. I told him to see a doctor, but I don't think he will. Emory is grudging and penuri-ous. Billy laughs at my words. He says the man is just hateful and tight.

Catherine chuckled. Some of Emory's ways had obviously rubbed off on his wife. She continued to read, going through the journal month by month until she reached December. There was only one entry, and it nearly broke her heart.

December 7, 1941
It's almost midnight, and I've been crying for hours. The worst has happened. Japan bombed Pearl Harbor. We are at war. Billy is packed. He's leaving tomorrow to sign up. Dear Lord, I won't try to stop him, but I pray that you please bring him home.

Catherine flipped through the pages. There were no more entries for the year. She stood, saddened by Annie's devastation. Somehow, it was worse reading those words because she already knew the outcome of Billy Fane's selfless act.

The melancholy she was feeling sent her back in the house. There was a restlessness to her spirit that she couldn't identify. So much to do, and yet she couldn't bring herself to do it. Billy was gone—had been gone for all these many years. But if she emptied this house of Annie's things, then the fact of her death would be official, too. She picked up another journal and then stood for a moment, absorbing the comfort of being among her grandmother's things. Suddenly she shook her head and moved toward the door. She wasn't ready to give Grannie up. Her belongings were here. What could it hurt to leave them a little while longer?

She settled in her chair once again, anxiously turning the pages, wondering how the first entries would read. The United States of America was at war.

March 1, 1942
It snowed last night. I'm almost out of wood. I never noticed what a lonesome sound the wind made until I listened to it by myself. I write to Billy almost every day but have received only a handful of letters from him, and they are all old. Sometimes I wish I knew where he was, other times I think it's better I don't.

Catherine's vision blurred. She wiped her eyes, then read on, noting that Annie wrote less frequently and about different things. Now, everything she was writing came from her inner thoughts, rather than her daily chores.

August 10, 1942
Camarune feels like a ghost town. There aren't enough men left to put out a good fire. Talked to Lovie today. I traded some of my gas coupons to her for some of her sugar coupons. She needed the extra to go to Lexington to see a doctor, she said. I don't need them. I rarely get off the mountain. She seems embarrassed by the fact that Emory is 4F. I told her she should be thankful every day of her life that her husband was born with flat feet. I don't think things are going well for them.

October 12, 1942
Billy is dead. I am, too.

Catherine caught herself sobbing and closed the book, unable to read any more. She stood and walked off the porch toward the trees without thinking, needing to get away. She moved without aim, following the road and the patches of shade. Halfway down the drive, she realized she was still carrying the journal. She debated with herself about taking it back, then decided to keep going. It never occurred to her that she was moving away from safety. Her mind and heart were in the past, with Annie.

It wasn't until she saw the silhouette of Pulpit Rock to her left that she realized how far she'd come. Her heart skipped a beat and then calmed almost as quickly. Everything seemed normal. Birds and squirrels were abundant, and every now and then she would see a rabbit bounding through the bushes.

The warmth of the day enveloped her, lulling her into a sense of security. As she glanced toward Pulpit Rock, she thought of her meeting with Jubal Blair. After what her grannie had told her about that horrible night, she couldn't believe that he'd survived. Why him? Why not her mother or, at the least, her father. Then she sighed. She could almost hear her grannie saying that life isn't always fair, but it's the only life you've been given. Live it to the fullest. Impulsively, she stepped off the road and into the trees, her destination Pulpit Rock.

It took only a few minutes before she reached the clearing, and again she was struck by the emptiness of the place. It wasn't just the lack of grass and brush that seemed strange, it was the silence, as well. There were no birds flying from tree to tree, no squirrels chattering rudely at her presence. Just the looming presence of the rock itself, jutting out over a dark swath of bare earth. At that moment she almost turned and went back, and then she reminded herself that evil came from people, not from the places they inhabited.

Clutching the journal, she started toward the rock and couldn't help thinking of how afraid Fancy must have been, knowing that she was going to die all alone—knowing that within seconds Jubal's dogs would be upon her.

Halfway there, her toe caught on a partially embedded rock, and she stumbled and fell. The journal flew out of her hands as she braced herself for the jolt. It was brief, but painful, skinning her knees and the palms of her hands. She groaned as she rolled over, and sat up, leaning forward to inspect the damage. It was nothing that soap and water and some antiseptic wouldn't cure.

"That hurt," she muttered, then lay back on the ground, giving herself time to relax.

Shading her eyes with her hands, she looked up. The clouds that earlier had been pretty white puffballs were piling one on top of the other, gathering in strength. Something crawled on her leg, and she sat up, finding an ant halfway up her shin. She brushed it off and then gingerly stood, wincing as she moved first one leg, then the other, testing them for soreness.

Suddenly a snapping sound came out of the woods, breaking the unnatural silence. She spun around, expecting maybe a deer. Nothing emerged. She told herself that if it had been a deer, she'd probably scared it away, then looked around for the journal, seeing it a short distance away. As she started toward it, another snap came, this time louder—closer. She stopped again, anxiety heightening.

At first there was nothing, and then he was there, standing deep in the shadows—watching. From a distance, his features were nothing more than vague images in a face framed with hair—dark, wild hair flowing out from under a shapeless felt hat, and a long, bushy beard interspersed with gray, hanging halfway down the front of his chest. She had a moment's impression of old, ill-fitting clothes and great height, then she went blank.

Fear came at her from all sides, binding her in place until she forgot to breathe, forgot to move. Was he the thief, or was he someone from the valley, coming to get rid of the witch's kin?

He moved forward. She took a step backward. He moved again, coming closer to the edge of the clearing. His silence was more frightening than any shout could have been.

Wordlessly, Catherine spun. Her first step was a leap, and then she started to run.

Out of the clearing.

Into the trees.

As fast as she could go.

Limbs from the underbrush slapped at her face, stinging imprints to remind her that she'd over-stepped her bounds.

She kept on running.

Too frightened to look back.

Too winded to scream.

All she could hear was her own gasping for breath and the thunder of her own footsteps crashing through the dead leaves. She didn't know if he'd given chase. There was no time to look and see.

Suddenly there was a tug on the back of her shirt. A scream ripped up her throat as she spun, swinging her arms wildly. A sob bubbled out of her throat as she realized her shirt had caught on a tree. With a yank, she ripped herself free. Seconds later, she burst out of the trees into the road, only to fall head-first into the path of an oncoming car. She screamed again, then covered her head with her hands, ready to die.

Luke was a man who believed in acting upon instinct, which was why he'd cut his business at headquarters short. He was driving these roads faster than he'd ever taken them before, and yet there was a feeling inside him that he would still be too late. But too late for what? He'd left feeling certain that Catherine would be safe. And after dispersing the crowd at Myrtle's house, he'd been even more certain that any immediate danger was over. But the more time passed, the more nervous he'd become. It was a feeling and nothing more that had sent him back up the mountain.

The Blazer was in high gear as he rounded the curve at Pulpit Rock. The last thing he expected to see was Catherine, coming out of the trees on the run. He was already braking when she fell into the road, and he was out and running before she started to scream.

He grabbed her by the hands, yanking them away from her head and pulling her to her feet and into his arms. The blood on her knees and hands could have come from the fall he'd just witnessed, but not the scratches on her face. When she saw who he was, she began sobbing hysterically, clutching at him with both hands.

"It's you, it's you.... Oh, my God, it's you."

Frantic, he tried to pull her free so he could assess her injuries, but she wouldn't let go.

"Catherine, sweetheart, let me look at you. Please."

But she kept clinging, burying her face against his chest and sobbing.

"In the trees—in the trees—he was watching me from the trees!"

Luke flinched and then pushed her away as he spun around. He saw nothing, but in woods this dense, that didn't mean a damn thing. He yanked his gun from the holster, then pointed toward his car.

"Get to the house and lock yourself in!"

Catherine reached for him, unwilling to be left alone. "No! Don't leave me," she begged.

"Do as I say!" he yelled. He was already running.

She moaned, then bolted toward the car. Her hands were trembling as she slid behind the wheel and slammed the door. With one frantic look back at the place where Luke had disappeared, she shifted into gear and gunned the engine. Moments later, there was nothing to mark their presence but a lingering cloud of dust.

Luke ran with his gun drawn, knowing that he could be running directly into trouble. Every tree was a possible hiding place, every bush a place to be ambushed. But hesitation would mean losing the opportunity to finally catch this man. The fear on Catherine's face had been real. Whatever was happening out here needed to stop.

Ahead, he could just make out the clearing beneath Pulpit Rock, but when he came to the edge of the trees, he paused, unwilling to put himself in full view of a rifle sight. Instead, he began circling the clearing. About halfway around he found the footsteps. He crouched, eyeing the imprints, then frowned. It was the thief, all right. Same size shoe, same notch in the left heel.

"Christ," he muttered, and quickly stood, eyeing the surrounding area.

The footprints led into the clearing. He followed them reluctantly, imagining someone taking aim at his back. But no shots rang out. The footprints stopped, then turned. He could tell the man was running now. His stride had lengthened. About a hundred yards inside the tree line, he lost the trail. Frustrated, he began to circle, but it was no use. It was as if the man had taken to the sky.

He checked the time. It was almost an hour since he'd given chase. Catherine was at the cabin alone—and no telling in what condition. With a rueful sigh, he holstered his gun and started toward the cabin at a jog.

The hunter was less than a hundred yards away when the sheriff finally stopped pursuit. He'd been watching the man for the better part of an hour, admiring the skill with which he tracked, yet well aware that he would never be caught. This mountain and the forest that covered it were as familiar to him as the breaths that he took. He knew the nooks, the caves and the hollow trees large enough to hide a full-grown man. The rock-strewn slopes he traversed left no prints to mark his passage, and the trees that sheltered the wildlife formed dense green barriers between him and his fellow man. He'd spent too many years eluding such men as this one to be caught so easily now.

When the sheriff gave up the chase, the hunter knew a moment of regret. Now he would be alone again. The book he was holding felt damp. He brushed it off on his jacket, then opened it up. It had been so long since he'd held such a thing that the words were a jumble on the page.

He thought of the girl who'd dropped it. It wasn't the first time he'd seen her, and he would have stayed away. But he'd seen her lying on the ground, and he'd thought she was dead. People died at Pulpit Rock. It wasn't a good place to be.

But then she'd sat up, and he'd been so relieved that he'd moved without first looking where he stepped. Making noise wasn't like him. He frowned, disgusted with himself. This wasn't the first time he'd given himself away around her. Curiosity was dangerous for him, and, even worse, he'd frightened her. That made him sad. He let the book fall shut, then slipped it in his bag and started through the trees. It would rain soon. He didn't like the rain. It reminded him of things he would rather forget.

Luke hit the porch running. There was a stitch in his side, and his legs were shaking, but his thoughts were on Catherine.

He grabbed the doorknob and turned. It was locked. He began pounding the door with his fists.

"Catherine, it's me, Luke! Let me in!"

Seconds later, the door swung open and she fell into his arms.

"Thank God, thank God. I thought something had happened to you. I've never been so scared in my life."

He pulled her inside, shutting and locking the door behind them. Then he took her by the shoulders and turned her toward the light. His touch was gentle but sure as his fingers swept her face and the faint pink scratches.

"Did he touch you? Did he do this to you?"

"No, no, he was too far away. When I saw him, I ran."

Luke breathed a quick sigh of relief and pulled her back into his arms.

"Sweet Jesus, I have never been so scared in my life. Do you know how close I came to running over you?"

She nodded, clinging to his warmth and his strength.

His voice lowered to a growl. "This just proves what I've said all along. You aren't safe up here, and you're damn sure not staying by yourself again. If I have to go down, you're going with me. Is that understood?"

"Yes," Catherine said, and then sighed. "I still

don't know why my grannie wanted me to come here, but I should probably just pack up and go home. This is so crazy. I'm causing a mess down in the valley and putting myself in danger up here. If I was honest with myself, I'd say that the only reason I'm still here is you.''

Luke went still. It was the last thing he'd expected her to say, and yet the most wonderful.

He pushed her back, needing to look at her face.

"What did you say?"

"That I'm a shameless hussy?"

He shook his head and then cupped her face, pressing soft, gentle kisses on every scratch.

"No, darlin', I'm pretty sure I heard you say that you're the answer to my prayers."

She swayed toward him. "Make love to me, Luke. I don't want to go to my Maker without knowing what it feels like to come apart in your arms."

"I'm already in pieces, darlin'. Let me show you the way."

He took her by the hand and led her upstairs, undressing her with his eyes, then with his hands, until there was nothing between them but desire.

In all her life, Catherine had never seen such a beautiful man. His body was hard, his muscles taut and long, but it was the look in his eyes that she would never forget. She held up her arms, welcoming him to her bed.

"I don't expect you to promise me something you can't give," she said. "Just know that for now...for me...this is enough."

He stood above her, imprinting her image in his mind. Her flat belly and slender waist that flared into the woman shape of her hips. Black hair fanning out on the pillow beneath her head. Nipples hard and pink, like half-ripe berries waiting to be tasted. She watched him from under heavy lashes, her lips slack with desire. When he leaned over her, her nostrils flared, and she took a deep breath.

"No, Catherine, this will never ever be enough."

He stretched out beside her, then leaned over until his lips were against her cheek. In slow, colorful detail, he began telling her what he was going to do and how she was going to feel. By the time they got to the first kiss, she was shaking. And when he rolled her nipple between his fingers, then slipped a hand between her legs, she came so hard and so fast that she screamed.

And that was only the beginning.

They made love all through the night, sleeping only when their bodies were worn out from the passion. Then one of them would rouse just enough to remember where they were, and it would start all over again.

Sometime after midnight it started to rain. Catherine woke to the sound of raindrops pelting the roof above her head and wondered if this was normal weather or if this was a sign. Maybe these were angels' tears, being shed over all the wasted lives and twisted lies.

Luke's breath was warm against her back, his arm heavy across her waist. She was pinned so that any movement she made would alert him. Her body was achy, but in such a sweet way. And the hunger he'd awakened in her had yet to be filled. She closed her eyes, savoring the memories of his face above her, etched in ecstasy. Remembering the shudder of his body as he climaxed with a mighty groan, and then the tenderness with which he'd held her afterward. She'd told him she didn't need promises, but she'd lied. God help her, she wanted this man forever, not just for a while. She turned over, and as he was coming awake, reached down and took him into her hands. She heard his breath catch, then heard a soft groan.

"Catherine...Catherine..."

"Ssh," she whispered, then slid down his body, replacing her hands with her mouth.

He groaned again, his back arching as his blood began to pulse. Time ceased. There was nothing on which to focus but the pull of flesh against flesh. He gave himself up to the feelings and went quietly out of his mind.

When Catherine woke again, the rain was still coming down, with intermittent flashes of lightning and thunder to punctuate the act. Beads of sweat ran out from under the tangled hair lying heavily against her neck. She rolled out from under Luke's arm and then grabbed for her gown, slipping it over her head as she moved toward the stairs. Afraid to turn on a light for fear of waking him, she felt, rather than saw, her way down.

She headed for the bathroom, the wooden floor cool against her feet. As soon as she'd closed the door, she flipped on the lights. After attending to bodily functions, she turned on the faucet to wash. Even the tepid water coming out of the taps was welcome as she splashed it on her face. She kept thinking of the rainfall and how good it would feel against her skin, but this wasn't the place or time for a midnight walk in the rain. The rain-washed air, however, was bound to be cooler than the inside of this cabin.

She came out of the bathroom, glanced up at the loft, then toward the door, agonizing as to the wisdom of such a move. Earlier, all she'd done was go for a walk, and look where that had wound up. But, she reminded herself, she'd been alone then. Luke was here now. And she wouldn't go any farther than the edge of the porch. Just far enough to get cool.

Giving the loft one backward glance, she unlocked the door and gave the doorknob a turn. Immediately the wind came through the opening, plastering her nightgown to her body. She lifted her chin and inhaled deeply, savoring the rush of cool air.

Thunder rumbled, momentarily rattling the windows. As she peered out into the darkness, she suddenly shivered, but from anxiety, not cold. She took a step forward, and as she did, stepped on something soft and flat. She gasped and jumped back. Whatever it was, it wasn't supposed to be there. Lighting flashed, momentarily illuminating the area, as well as the object. She saw a scrap of old fabric, and as she reached down to pick it up, the fabric blew back, revealing what lay beneath.

It was Grannie's journal—the one she'd dropped at Pulpit Rock. In her fright, she'd forgotten that she'd left it behind—and it would have been ruined.

She took a step back, clutching the journal like a shield, and stared intently into the curtain of rain. Almost immediately, the sky spat another bolt of lightning, brighter and closer than the last. And in that instant between light and dark, she saw him standing not fifty feet away. Like before, he was immobile, but staring intently at her face.

Frozen to the spot, it occurred to her that he could be dashing toward her in the night and she would never know it, but in the same instant, she discarded the notion. This man meant her no harm. In returning the book, he'd made the only apology he knew how to for her fright and her pain.

She held her breath, waiting for the next flash of light, and when it came, she jerked, as if someone had punched her in the stomach. It was just as she'd guessed. He was gone.

"Catherine...what the hell are you doing out here in the rain, never mind the danger you could be in?"

Without waiting for an answer, Luke pulled her back into the house, and shut and locked the door.

"We were wrong," Catherine said.

"About what?"

"He won't hurt me."

Luke frowned. "And how do you know that? Have you become psychic, too?"

She handed him the journal. "I dropped this when I fell at Pulpit Rock. When I saw him, I forgot it and ran."

"Then how did you—"

He froze, his gaze focusing on her face and then moving to the window.

"He was here?"

She nodded. "I stepped on it when I opened the door. Then I saw him in a flash of lightning. One moment he was there, the next he was gone." She looked at Luke. "It would have been ruined."

"Son of a bitch," Luke muttered, thrust the journal into her hands and started for the door.

She grabbed him. "No. Let him go. He doesn't mean any harm."

"He scared you. He stole from you."

"I scared myself, and he didn't actually steal, he traded. As for the journal, I left it behind. All he did was return it."

Luke combed his hands through his hair and then turned in a frustrated circle.

"This is crazy. Don't start romanticizing what he's done. You're still not safe up here."

"Maybe so. But the danger won't come from him. I'd bet my life on it."

Luke's eyes glittered darkly as he laid his palms against the sides of her face.

"But that's my point, my darlin' Catherine. If you insist on staying here alone, that's exactly what you'll be doing."

13

The hunter slid the bar across the door to the cave, locking himself inside. Only after he heard the solid thump of wood against wood did he begin to relax. With the assurance born of years of repetition, he moved through the darkness until he reached the table. Feeling his way along the surface, he found his lantern, then the matches in the box beside it. One strike of match against box and a small flash of light pierced the black. He put flame to wick and then adjusted the fire before replacing the globe. Once he could see, he stripped where he stood, ridding himself of the sodden garments he'd been wearing, then hung them on pegs in the walls. Satisfied with that, he moved to the middle of the floor and struck another match, lighting the kindling to the fire he'd built earlier. Again light flared, this time illuminating the walls and the interior of the cave.

He laid dry moss onto the spitting flames, then straightened, staring in satisfaction as it caught and flared. The flickering flames cast ominous shadows

on the man's naked body, highlighting a round
puckered scar on his back and one in his leg. Before
long, his body was warm and his hair nearly dry.
His belly rumbled, which meant it was time for
food. He ate not for taste, but for sustenance, caring
little for what it was or how it was prepared. Only
now and then did he remember something like the
taste of fresh yellow corn, dripping with sweet butter and sprinkled with pepper, or the flaky crust of
biscuits, hot from the oven. But those times were
rare, and unwelcome. Always, with the memories,
came the faces of the people who'd been there with
him—and with that came pain.

He grabbed a knife and the lantern, and moved
toward the back of the cave, stooping as he entered
a smaller, narrower opening that led into a separate
chamber. As he lifted the lantern, the light refracted
off the hovering haze, giving the room a foggy
look. But it wasn't fog, it was hickory smoke, cur-
ing what was left of Faron Davis's pig. He reached
for the meat hanging from cross poles over a smol-
dering log and hacked off a slab, then carried it
back to the table and dropped it in a black, cast-
iron skillet and set it on the fire. Soon the scent of
frying pork filled the air. With nothing to do but
wait, he picked up a knife and a small piece of
walnut wood, then sat down on his cot and began
peeling away the excess from the bluebird he'd
seen in the wood.

As he worked, he thought of the woman he'd seen at Pulpit Rock. Curiosity had made him watch her, but he regretted that he'd revealed himself to her. She'd been afraid then. But she hadn't been afraid when she'd come out on the porch. He paused in his whittling, remembering the way she'd stood on the porch, bravely staring into the rain, as if she'd known he was there. It had been impulse that had made him give back her book, but he only traded for things he needed, and he'd had no need for it. It seemed fair to return it.

Grease sizzled and popped into the fire, causing a brief flare. He set down his work and got up. There was never a thought of putting on other clothes. His choice of garments was limited at best, and he saw no need to cover himself when there was no one to see.

With a rag for a pot holder, he pulled the pan from the fire and then the meat from the pan. Spearing it with the knife that he'd used earlier, he ate it like a Popsicle on a stick, biting off only small bits and pieces until it had cooled enough to eat. When his belly was full, he blew out the lantern and made his way to bed by the light of the dwindling fire.

Within minutes, he'd fallen asleep, and as he slept, he dreamed of dogs and dying and babies crying in the rain.

Nellie buttoned her floor-length nightgown all the way to the top, then primly straightened the long sleeves and high collar before exiting the bathroom.

Preacher was sitting on the edge of the mattress in his undershorts, with his Bible in hand, waiting for her to come to bed. Nellie hated it when he did that. It seemed sacrilegious to be reading the Bible without wearing clothes. His soft, pudgy belly hung over the waistband of his shorts—an odd accompaniment to his thin, knobby knees and legs. His hair, once abundant and red, was little more than a circlet of fluff around the back of his head. It looked to Nellie a little like a fuzzy headband that had slipped backward upon his neck. She pursed her lips and clasped her hands over her belly, trying not to judge the man she'd promised to honor.

"It's time," Preacher said.

Nellie flushed. They'd been married almost thirty-seven years, and she was still uncomfortable with the intimacy of husband and wife. But it *was* Friday. Preacher always wanted it on Friday.

"I know what day it is," she snapped, and laid herself out on her side of the bed like a body in a coffin, ready to do her duty, while the rain peppered hard against the window beside their bed.

Preacher opened the Bible, then cleared his throat just as a crack of thunder split the sky.

Nellie bit her lip. She loved sleeping when it rained, but it would be a while before she was allowed the privilege. This was the part she liked least—staying awake through all eight chapters of the Song of Solomon before he was ready to proceed. She figured she was the only woman on the face of the earth whose husband had to read the same Bible verses every Friday before he could get it up.

Save me, Jesus, she thought, and then set her jaw for the evening to come.

Four blocks over and three houses down, Lovie Cleese slept alone. Widowed now for more years than she cared to remember, she'd almost forgotten what it was like to give in to a man. But there'd been a time in her life when that wasn't so. A time when she was young and vital and yearning for more than a glimpse of the world beyond the deep, green valley in which they'd lived.

But Emory's wanderlust had not matched his wife's, and little by little, year after year, Lovie forgot what it was that she'd wanted to see. Only now and then did she wonder what her life would have been like if she'd taken that first step alone.

Tonight, her dreams were dark and ugly, taking her to places in her past that she'd tried to forget. But the lies had been told, and the years of deception had spun a web that was strong—too strong to let Lovie go.

A flash of lightning outside the window revealed a grimace as she slept. Her long gray braid had somehow become wound about her neck. Her hands fluttered restlessly, and she seemed to be gasping for air. In the midst of a breath, a particularly loud crack of thunder ripped through the sky. She came awake within seconds, screaming out a name and grabbing at what she thought was a rope around her neck. It took several seconds for her to realize that she'd been dreaming, and that she wasn't really about to be hanged. She rolled over and turned on the lamp. At once a small yellow glow bounced off the wall behind the shade, shedding a small patch of light into the dark, lonely room. But instead of lying back down, she crawled out of bed, afraid to close her eyes for fear the dream would come back. Her heart was hammering erratically as she staggered into the bathroom. Just for a moment, she caught a glimpse of herself in the mirror and thought she was looking at a stranger. She shuddered. In a way, she was.

She flipped the switch, then began splashing her face with water, trying to wash away the memories of where her dreams had taken her. But the thoughts were still there, as was the name of the woman she'd screamed out in her sleep.

Annie. She'd screamed Annie's name.

She leaned forward, bracing both hands on the side of the counter and staring into her own face.

"Liar," she said.

For once, the woman didn't argue.

"You're going to hell."

The woman looked away.

Lovie turned out the light, then stood in the doorway, staring into the shadows of the small, lonely room. So this was what her life had come to.

An empty bed.

An empty life.

An empty heart.

She shuffled back toward the bed, then suddenly bypassed it for a straight-back rocker near the window. Gathering a cover from the foot of the bed, she turned off the lamp, then wrapped the quilt around her shoulders and sat down with a plop.

As the minutes passed, her eyes began to burn from lack of sleep, but the fear of going back to that place she'd been was enough to keep her upright. Finally, age overcame determination and her head began to bob. Her eyes closed, and she slumped forward, her chin resting upon her chest.

For Lovie, morning could come none too soon.

Day broke with a clear sky and a promise of heat. Already, the air felt damp and heavy from last night's rain. Catherine woke to the feel of Luke's mouth upon her breasts and arched into his touch with a soft, satisfied moan.

He lifted his head, his eyes dark and full of need.

"Good morning, darlin'."

"It sure is," she said.

He smiled. "Is that a compliment?"

"That would be an affirmative, sir."

Cupping his hands beneath her hips, he raised her up and then slid her beneath him.

"It's dangerous to play fast and loose with an officer of the law."

"How fast can you play?" she asked, then opened her legs and guided him in, taking pleasure in the groan that slipped out of his mouth.

"If you don't slow down...it'll be too damned fast," he said.

She laughed and wrapped her legs around his waist, pulling him deeper.

This wasn't an argument that he needed to win. He let her lead the way until she forgot where she was going. After that, it didn't matter. It was downhill all the way, and they were both out of control.

Catherine was tying the last lace on her tennis shoe when Luke opened the door and looked in.

"You ready?" he asked.

"Just about," she said, then looked down at her legs. "Should I be wearing jeans instead of these shorts?"

He grinned. "Not from where I'm standing."

"Be serious," she said. "We're going to cut down a tree. I don't want to get all itchy or get into spiders or stuff."

"Your knees still look pretty raw. The shorts are more comfortable for you, aren't they?"

She nodded.

"Then the shorts it is. If we see spiders, I'll slay them for you."

"My hero," she said, then threw her arms around Luke's neck and planted a hard kiss in the middle of his mouth.

"Be careful with those," he said. "They could get you in trouble."

She arched an eyebrow, giving him a wicked smile. "I think they already have," she said.

He laughed aloud, then picked her up and swung her in a circle while her feet dangled aimlessly against his shins.

His laughter filled her, completing the healing that his love had begun. With a satisfied sigh, she closed her eyes and held on while the world spun around her.

It wasn't until they heard footsteps on the porch that Luke stopped. He turned, still holding Catherine aloft, to find Abram Hollis and his sons.

Abram's expression was slightly shocked, but his sons were grinning broadly. Belatedly, Luke put Catherine down. She pulled down the hem of her T-shirt and sauntered to the door as if this was her normal method of greeting her guests.

"Abram, how nice of you to call. Come in! Come in!"

The men took off their hats and stepped over the threshold, carefully eyeing Luke as they did.

Technically, these people were all the family Catherine had left. Luke didn't know whether to smile or start apologizing. He started with a handshake, figuring if they refused it, the apology would be wise. To his relief, they all shook hands and refrained from comment.

"Would you care for some coffee?" Catherine asked. "And there are biscuits left over from breakfast. I could fix something."

"We ate," Abram said. "But thanks."

"I'm sorry there isn't a sofa, but I have some chairs. Would you sit?"

Abram shook his head as he continued to look around the room. "We were working up this way. Thought we'd stop in and see how you're doing." He gave Catherine a curious look. "You haven't done much packing."

She turned, letting her gaze sweep the rooms from ceiling to floor. Finally, she sighed. "I know...and I don't think I will."

"Why?" Abram asked.

Catherine smiled, her eyes misting a little as she looked in the old man's face.

"Oh, I don't know. Somehow it doesn't seem right. The stuff just belongs here, that's all. You and your family have been using the cabin off and on for all these years, and now that I know it's here, I'd like to think that by leaving it as is, a part of Annie and Billy lives on."

A rare smile broke the somberness of Abram's face. "That's a real thoughty thing to do, girl. I think Annie would be proud."

Catherine struggled for words, trying hard not to cry.

At that point, Luke decided it was time to change the subject.

"You men in any kind of hurry?" he asked.

They all shook their heads.

"Got any interest in helping me chop down a tree?"

Abram frowned. "If it's a bee tree, count me out. I'm allergic to the stings."

"No, we're after a pack rat that ran off with Catherine's watch. She found the nest. We're hoping the watch is in there."

"Grannie gave it to me. Even if it's ruined, I want it back," Catherine added.

"We're in," the boys said.

"I reckon that might be a thing to see," Abram added. "Count me in, too."

"Catherine, you show them where we're going. I picked up my chain saw yesterday, when I went back to the department, but it's still in the Blazer."

They parted at the porch, Luke going one way, while Catherine and the Hollis men went the other.

"Nice day," Abram said.

Catherine nodded. "It rained hard last night."

He nodded back. "Good for the herbs."

She smiled. "That's what Grannie always said."

"You miss her, don't you, girl?"

Catherine sighed. "So much that I can hardly bear to consider what home is going to be like without her."

"Then why go?" Abram asked.

Catherine paused, staring at him in disbelief. "Don't you know what's been going on around here?"

"Some," he said. "But it didn't stop Annie from staying."

"I'm a teacher," Catherine said. "How can I teach people who think I'm a witch? Besides that, they wouldn't hire me, even if I was willing to try."

"Have you asked?" Abram said.

She looked startled. "Well...no, but—"

He gave her a slow, steady look. "Never know till you ask, girl."

"How much farther?" Jefferson asked.

"Just a little way into the trees," she said, pointing uphill, toward the north.

They began walking again, the conversation seemingly over. A few moments later, Luke caught up, and, other than the animals, the only sounds to be heard were footsteps crunching through the underbrush.

"There it is," Catherine said, pointing toward a tall dead tree with skeletal limbs that pointed toward the sky in accusation. The trunk was bare, the bark long ago shed. The small hole at the base of the trunk was like a single black eye, staring out into the woods.

"He ran in there," she said, pointing toward the hole. "I dug in there a bit yesterday with the poker, but had no luck. I think the den must be somewhere up inside."

Cleveland Hollis started to grin. "The trick is going to be finding how high to saw. Dang, Dancy, remember when we sawed down that old tree on Granddad's place and a whole nest of hornets came out?"

Catherine's eyes widened. "Yikes."

Luke grinned. "I sort of doubt that a pack rat and a nest of hornets would be sharing a tree. However, if you're afraid, then stand back a ways."

She hesitated. The urge to do as he suggested was strong, but the men were all looking at her in a condescending way, and because they expected her to hide, she decided to stay.

"No, I'm fine."

Abram nodded approvingly. "Just like Annie, she is. Annie always faced everything with the same gentle strength. Good or bad, she was with you all the way."

Luke looked at Catherine then, and the love in his heart was there on his face.

"If a man had a woman like that, I suppose he could do about anything."

Catherine blushed. The Hollis brothers grinned.

"About that rat," Abram said.

Luke winked at her, then pulled the rope on the chain saw, taking comfort in the noise of the loud, angry purr.

The saw blade bit into the wood about four feet up from the ground, sending sawdust flying. Catherine moved a little farther back, resisting the urge to cover her ears. The men were staring at the tree Luke was cutting as if gold dust might come pouring out. They looked so like little boys at play that she had to smile.

The muscles in Luke's arms were knotted from exertion, and as he continued to saw, a line of sweat began darkening the center of his blue shirt. She found herself staring at the breadth of his shoulders and remembering that he'd played professional sports. She thought of last night and the way he made love. If he'd been as good at football as he was at making love, he would have been the highest paid player in the NFL. She knew his strengths—and his weaknesses—all too well. Leaving him wasn't something she could even think about, yet how in the world could she stay?

Abram's words kept coming back to her, but it was nothing short of folly to consider it. In less than two weeks, she'd gotten into more trouble in Camarune than she had in her entire life.

Suddenly Cleveland danced sideways, and she jumped back in fright.

"There he goes! There he goes!" Cleveland shouted.

Sure enough, the pack rat was abandoning the proverbial ship in favor of less noisy surroundings. They laughed, watching as the sleek brown rodent made a beeline for parts unknown. A few minutes later, Luke pulled the chain saw out of the tree, then killed the engine and stood back.

"Tim-ber," he said, and with a playful Paul Bunyan stance, gave it a push.

It creaked—and then a series of loud, snapping sounds followed as it began to fall, its branches ripping through nearby trees and taking other limbs with it.

"Would you look at that!" Jefferson cried, pointing into the stump that was left. "That old rat must have been holed up in here for some time."

They moved forward, each peering into the hollow core that had been revealed. But it was Catherine who had the most to gain. Immediately she began digging through the nest, tossing out everything from glass and bottle caps to wire.

"Oh, I don't see it," she cried.

"Let me look," Luke said, and dug deeper into the nest, picking it apart as he went farther and farther down the hollow trunk. When it got to the point where Luke was reaching as far into the trunk as his arm would go, Abram offered up a suggestion.

"Maybe you should cut off another foot or so on the trunk."

Luke nodded. "Yeah, maybe you're—" He stopped. "Wait! I think I've found something."

Catherine watched as he pulled out a handful of dried moss and then laid it on the ground.

"There's something in here. I can feel it," he said.

She squatted down beside him, watching intently as he sorted through the tangle of leaves and moss. Then he rocked back on his heels, holding a small lady's watch with a thin leather band.

"My watch!"

He dropped it into her hands.

Immediately, she held it up to her ear and then laughed. "It's still running. Oh, Luke, can you believe it? It's still running!"

She stood abruptly, showing it to Abram and his sons. They looked suitably impressed, both with the fact that Luke had felled the tree like a seasoned woodsman and that her watch was still working.

Luke brushed the sawdust from his clothes and was looking for the guard to put back on his saw when Catherine threw her arms around his neck in wild abandon.

"You don't know how much this means to me. How can I ever thank you?"

He gave her a hug and then whispered softly, so that only she could hear, "I'll think of a way."

She blushed and then laughed, too overjoyed to care what Abram might think.

"Well now," Abram said, "this is something Polly will get a kick out of hearing. She's not too partial to rats. It'll do her good to know you got the best of the deal."

"You'll have to bring her next time you come," Catherine said. "I'd love to meet her."

"Didn't think you planned on stayin' all that long," Abram drawled.

Luke went very still. Did Abram Hollis know something about Catherine that he didn't know? He looked at her then, dreading to hear her answer.

"That's the good thing about plans," she said. "They're always changing."

Luke turned away before anyone saw how afraid he'd been and picked up his saw.

"Ready to go?"

"I'm ready," Catherine said, and then winced when she moved too close to some bushes. "Ouch," she muttered, and looked down at the scrapes on her knees.

Luke heard her cry and turned, reaching to steady her in case she was about to fall.

"Catherine, are you all right?"

"Yes. I just walked too close to that bush and scratched my sore knee."

"What happened to you, anyway?" Jefferson asked.

She hesitated, and then shrugged. "Nothing much, just a fall."

"Did you fall face first?" Cleveland asked, lightly teasing her about the faint red scratches still evident on her face.

"Not exactly."

"She got those running from that damned thief," Luke said.

The men looked startled. "What thief?" they echoed.

"He doesn't steal, exactly," Catherine said. "It's more of a trade."

Luke frowned. "No, Catherine, that only applies when both parties are aware that there's a trade going on. When you take something without asking, it doesn't matter what the hell you leave behind. It's still theft."

"You talkin' about that old hermit?" Abram asked.

Luke stared. "You mean you *know* him?"

Abram looked at Luke and then looked away. "Not exactly."

"How exactly?" Luke asked.

Abram turned. "We see him from time to time. He don't bother us. We don't bother him."

Luke couldn't believe what he was hearing. "Do you know where he lives?"

Abram shook his head. "No, nothing like that. But me and the boys are in the woods a lot. Sometimes we see things, you know. But we mind our own business."

"That man has stolen livestock, he's trespassed in people's homes, he's taken clothing from clotheslines, and basically terrorized a community of people for more years than I can count."

"What's there to be scared about?" Jefferson asked. "I didn't think anyone'd ever seen him up close."

"I have," Catherine said. "Twice."

The Hollis men stared in disbelief.

"He ain't one to show himself to people," Abram said.

"Well, he showed himself to me," Catherine said. "And he returned a book to me that I'd lost."

"I'll be danged," Abram said. "That's odd. I ain't never heard him speak."

"We didn't speak. He just left the book on my porch where I could find it."

"He saved Jefferson's life," Cleveland said. "Tell them, Daddy."

"Are you serious?" Luke said.

Abram nodded. "It was the spring that Jefferson turned four. Polly wanted to go mushroomin', so we loaded up in the truck and drove all the way around the mountain to come up here and hunt. There's a place on the far side of Annie's cabin where morels grow. Polly is real partial to morels. Anyway, we'd been at it for about an hour when we looked up and realized Jefferson was gone. Polly panicked and started callin' out his name, but he wasn't nowhere in sight. Just when we was about to go into Camarune and organize a search party, this tall, skinny man come out of the woods, carrying Jefferson in his arms. Jefferson was wet and cold and scared half to death, but he was alive. The man never said a word to us. He just stared at Polly, then put my boy down and walked away."

"He saved my life," Jefferson said. "I remember falling into the river and then someone yanking me out by the hair. I know I howled for about half a mile, but the man never said a harsh word. He just held me close and kept walking, as if he knew where to go. I still remember how soft his beard felt against my face."

"Well, I'll be damned," Luke muttered. This didn't fit the profile of the man he thought he'd been hunting.

"Come on," Catherine said. "I don't know about you, but I want something cold to drink."

"I'm with you, cousin," Dancy said. "And, about those biscuits you said you had left over...?"

Everyone laughed, except Dancy.

"When a man's hungry, he's hungry," he said.

"You ain't never been full," Abram said, eyeing his youngest son's lanky form.

"'Cause I've had to feed behind too many long-armed garbage disposals," he said.

They were still laughing when Annie's cabin came into view.

14

The radio in Luke's vehicle was squawking as they came around the side of the cabin. He dropped the chain saw and ran, quickly covering the distance in long strides. Catherine smiled to herself, picturing him running down a football field, and wished she'd known him back then.

"Anything wrong?" Abram asked, as Luke hurried toward his car.

"Not necessarily," Catherine said, then smiled at Dancy. "Let's go see about those biscuits."

"Get 'em to go," Abram told his son. "We need to be gettin' on back."

"Yes, sir," Dancy said and followed Catherine inside, while Abram picked up the chain saw and carried it to the porch, then settled down to wait for Luke.

A few moments later, he was back.

"Sorry about that," Luke said, and then pointed at the saw. "Thanks for carrying it to the porch...and for helping find Catherine's watch."

"It was a good show," Abram said.

"That it was," Jefferson said.

Cleveland laughed. "That rat's probably still running."

"Which reminds me," Luke said. "I'd better fix that hole in the outside wall of the cabin. We don't want to go through this again."

"You stayin' up here long?" Abram asked.

Immediately his sons made themselves scarce, unwilling to be a part of the inquisition.

In a way, Luke had been expecting this ever since they'd walked in and caught him kissing Catherine.

"As long as she needs me," he said.

Abram hesitated. He hadn't expected Luke to be so forthright. Maybe he was reading the man wrong. But then he reminded himself that, in Annie's stead, it was up to him to make sure that no one did Catherine wrong.

"I wouldn't like to see her hurt."

"Neither would I," Luke said.

Again there was a long, stilted silence. Luke knew it was up to him to put the man at ease. But how? How much could he say to Abram when so little had been said between himself and Catherine? Yes, they'd made love with a passion that had stunned him, and losing her seemed impossible to consider. But he had no claim on her—regardless of where his heart might lie. Finally, he was the one who spoke up.

"Can I ask you something personal?"

Abram hesitated, then finally nodded. "You can ask. Don't mean I'll answer."

Luke grinned. "Fair enough."

"Then ask away," Abram said.

"Do you believe in love at first sight?"

Abram shoved his hat to the back of his head, then thoughtfully scratched at a spot on his chin.

"I don't know as I do. I'm not one to swear by somethin' I ain't never experienced."

"Then let me tell you something, Abram, it's a thing to behold. You feel hot and then cold—all over—all at once. All the spit in your mouth goes dry. You couldn't make a complete sentence if your life depended on it, and the worst of it is, you forget to breathe."

Abram stared at him then—at the steady look in his eyes and the truth on his face.

"You had yourself a feelin' like that, have you?"

"Yes, sir, that I have," Luke said.

"She know anything about it?"

"Oh, she knows that I'm smitten, she just doesn't know how bad."

Abram frowned, giving his next words serious consideration; then he gave Luke's shoulder one solid but friendly thump.

"My advice is to keep the worst of it to yourself until you know where you stand."

Luke tried not to stagger from the weight of the blow. "Yes, sir. I appreciate your wisdom."

"I ain't all that smart about women," Abram said. "I just lived a long time with one."

"In my eyes, that makes you the expert," Luke said.

"Hey, Daddy, I'm ready to go," Dancy shouted.

They turned. Abram's youngest was waving at them from the porch with a biscuit in one hand and the last bite of another in his mouth.

Abram hesitated, then once again offered Luke his hand.

"I reckon we'll be goin' now. I'm trustin' you to take care of Annie's girl."

"Like I said…for as long as she needs me."

Then Abram grinned. "Just make sure you're so darn good at what you do that she doesn't think she can live without you."

Luke was still laughing when the Hollis men walked away.

"What's so funny?" Catherine asked.

He gave her a hug. "Nothing much. It was one of those 'you had to be there' moments."

She didn't think she believed him, but she let it go. Then she pointed toward his car.

"The call—was anything wrong at headquarters?"

"Not wrong, but something I've got to take care

of," he said. "Grab your purse. We're going for a ride."

She started to pull back. "I think I'll be fine here by—"

He shook his head. "This isn't up for discussion."

"But you heard what Abram said about—"

"I don't ever want to be as scared as I was yesterday when I saw you coming out of the woods. My God, Catherine, I nearly ran over you. I'm not leaving you up here alone again. Willingly or not, you're coming. Which will it be?"

She sighed. "I need to brush my hair and get my purse."

"I'll wait."

She started back to the cabin, then hesitated and turned.

"What if I just—"

"Damn it, Catherine, for once, do as you're told."

Her chin jutted mutinously, and just for a moment, Luke thought she would balk. Then she stomped into the house, returning minutes later with her purse and a handful of books.

"What are those?" he asked.

"Grannie's journals. I'm not good at twiddling my thumbs."

Luke caught her up in his arms, trying to tease her into a good mood.

"No, darlin', I'm inclined to disagree. You're real good at twiddling."

She grinned and then socked him playfully on the arm. "You're real close to being an obnoxious chauvinist, you know."

"Oh, darlin', I'm afraid Kentucky is full of 'em."

She laughed. "Just my luck, huh?"

He nuzzled his nose against the side of her neck, then gave her a sweet kiss. When they parted, they were both more than breathless.

"You call that luck?" he whispered.

"No," Catherine drawled. "I call it foreplay, and if you keep it up, you're the one who'll get lucky."

Luke threw back his head and laughed. The sound rang out within the clearing, then echoed against the backside of the mountain like the disappearing chimes of a bell.

Catherine laughed with him, knowing she would never forget this moment, or the man to whom she'd given her heart.

Catherine had never been to Crying River, but she was getting a first-class tour of the town. Not only was it the town closest to where Luke had grown up, it was the county seat of Taney County. It was an old-fashioned town, built in 1874 around a town square. Huge trees with drooping branches ringed the square, shading the sidewalk around the perimeter. A weathered gazebo sat off to one side, while a series of sidewalks criss-crossed the greens. Swatches of pink and purple petunias graced the flower beds along the walks like patches in a green crazy quilt. She was instantly charmed and wondered why this town had thrived while Camarune had all but shriveled and died.

"What do you think?" Luke asked, as he finally pulled up in front of an old redbrick building.

"It's amazing," she said. "Is this where you work?"

He nodded. "Come in with me. This might take a while."

She hesitated, then pointed toward the square. "If you don't mind, I'd rather go sit out there and read."

He leaned over and kissed her square on the lips, unmindful of who might see.

"I don't care what you do, as long as you stay within shouting distance of me."

She frowned. "I don't need a jailer."

"No, just a keeper," he said. "And before you argue with me anymore, you've got to give me a break. Abram all but threatened to have my hide if I let anything happen to you."

She blushed. "I'm so sorry. He doesn't have any right to—"

Luke put a finger on her lips, stopping her complaint.

"But that's where you're wrong," he said softly. "He's now the closest thing to a relative you have, and in Kentucky, that makes him responsible."

Catherine's heart skipped a beat. Luke was wrong, but she wasn't going to argue. She thought of Jubal and then gave herself a mental shake. If it was left up to her, no one would ever know.

"Okay, you win. I'll be sitting on the bench nearest your building, and if I get tired of reading, I won't go farther than inside the square."

"Deal," he said.

They parted company on the street. He watched until she had settled on a bench and opened one of her books. When she looked up and waved, he waved back, then went inside, for the moment satisfied she was safe.

Catherine sat for a while, savoring the peacefulness of small-town living, and tried to picture herself in such a place. But after living her whole life in Wichita Falls, it was difficult to do. She was used to busy streets and traffic.

It occurred to her as she sat that Luke hadn't shown her the school. She wondered what it was like, and if they ever had openings. The moment she thought it, she frowned. These mind games were dangerous. She had no claim on Luke De-Priest. She'd made sure of that by making that stupid declaration before they'd made love. Now there was no telling what he thought of her.

She sighed, then opened the next of Grannie's journals. The present was such a mess that, for now, it was better to get lost in the past.

October 28, 1942
Lovie has been here for nearly a week. It was kind of her to come and help out, but I think I'm ready for her to go home. Everyone seems to think I won't be able to go on without Billy. They don't know that he's still with me every time I close my eyes.

Catherine was stunned by the entry—more concrete evidence that Lovie Cleese had once been close to Annie. She read on, noting that nothing much changed until late in March the next year.

March 25, 1943
Something is wrong between Emory and Lovie. I can tell it. I went to the store. Emory was the only one there. When I asked about Lovie, his face turned red and he snapped at me, saying something about me being nosy. I don't know what to make of it. This isn't like either of them.

May 12, 1943
It's been raining off and on for more than a week. All the main roads going in and out of

town are flooded, except the one up the moun-
tain. I walked the four miles down the moun-
tain today to get groceries rather than try to
drive my old truck. The road is too treacherous
to get behind the wheel. Thank God I'm not
completely cutoff.

May 14, 1943
Last night, Emory Cleese knocked on my door,
begging me to come with him to town. He said
Lovie was dying. I asked him if he'd called the
doctor. He said they couldn't get through. I
took some of my tinctures and went with him,
although I didn't hold out much hope that I
could effect any cures. My work is in herbs,
not miracles.

She was miscarrying. I gave her an extract
of mistletoe for internal hemorrhage and then
prayed. God was good. Somehow she survived.

So sad for her. Billy and I always planned
on a large family, too.

Someone honked, breaking Catherine's concentration. She looked up. It was a young boy in a
truck who'd honked at a girl on the street. She
watched them talking and smiled. Young love. She
thought of Luke. If they'd known each other as
children, would they have fallen in love? A few

moments later, the boy drove on and the girl continued down the street, almost skipping. Again she thought of Luke and knew just how the young girl felt.

A trio of butterflies flitted past her line of vision and landed on a nearby bed of petunias. Catherine leaned back to watch, taking refuge in the idyllic quality of the day. Yet no matter how long she watched, she couldn't turn loose the tragedies of the past.

Poor Grannie.

Poor Lovie.

Life wasn't just about finding someone to love. It was about learning how to live with the losses, as well.

She glanced at her watch, gently rubbing at the face with her fingertip and so thankful that she'd found it. Then she looked at the time, unable to believe she'd been out here for more than an hour. She glanced up at Luke's office, wondering how many times he'd looked out to make sure she was all right and thought about taking a walk around the square. The urge to read more was too strong. The more she read, the more convinced she became that the answer to Annie's trouble was in these books. If she only knew what the question was, it would be easier to find the answer. She opened the book and read on.

May 20, 1943
Emory Cleese hanged himself. The whole town is talking about it. I'm heartbroken for Lovie. First her child, now her husband. How can life be this cruel? I offered to stay with her, like she'd stayed with me. She closed the door in my face.

May 30, 1943
I went into town today to mail some ginseng roots to my buyer. With the war going on, I don't get much money for it, but every little bit helps.

Something is wrong in Camarune, but I can't quite put my finger on what. People turn away from me when I speak, and Lovie still won't talk. I don't understand.

July 4, 1943
I went down into the valley today for the Fourth of July celebration. A little boy threw a rock at me and called me a witch. I thought he was just playing, until I saw the look on his father's face. The whole town has turned against me, and Lovie refused to sell me any food. I drove all the way to Crying River to buy my groceries. I don't know what's wrong, but I don't think I will be going to Camarune again.

I cried myself to sleep.

Catherine turned to the next page. To her surprise, it was blank, as were the rest of the pages in the book. She picked up the last journal and opened it. There was only one entry, and it was dated almost thirty years later.

October 28, 1973
I buried her beneath the black walnut tree
about fifty feet north of Billy. My God, my
God, the horror of this night. I'm afraid—so
afraid of what might happen to me and her
baby.

Catherine stood with a jerk as the reality of what she'd just read sank in. That was her birthday, and if Annie had buried a woman that night, it had to have been Fancy. All this time... She'd been in Annie's backyard all this time.

She opened the book again, just to reassure herself that she hadn't imagined what she'd read, but it was there in her grannie's familiar scrawl. The haste with which Annie had written it was obvious. The words were large and slanted sharply toward the right corner of the page, as if she'd cared little for style in her need to get it out of her system.

"Dear God," she murmured. "What do I do?"

The urge to tell Luke was so strong, but if she did, what would it change? In his capacity as an officer of the law, would he be obliged to reveal what she'd told? How could she prove that what she said was the truth? Everyone but Jubal was dead. And the way people in Camarune had been behaving, the words in Annie's journal could just as easily be confirmation of the blame they'd laid on her all those years ago for the deaths at Pulpit Rock.

No one had known about Fancy's part in the drama, because Annie had carried her away before the others had been found. And no one had known about Fancy and Turner—at least, not until that night. Now the only living person who could have verified her story was Jubal, and he quite obviously hated her guts.

While she was still contemplating her options, Luke exited the office.

"Catherine!"

She looked up. He was waving at her from across the street.

She let the book fall shut. "Coming," she yelled, grabbed the rest of her things and ran to meet him.

George Henry Lee had never been all that stable. Folks said it was because his daddy's work mule had kicked him in the head when he was seven, but there were others who said the trait just ran in the family. George Henry's daddy had shot himself in the foot to keep from being drafted back in World War Two, and George Henry's brother, Dunbar, was serving a ten-year prison sentence for messing with a neighbor's daughter. The fact that the neighbor's daughter was only eight years old at the time had incited a near riot in Camarune. They were ready to hang the man when Luke DePriest had intervened. George Henry's brother had been glad to go to jail.

Now George Henry and his father lived alone up on the mountain, about a quarter of a mile as the crow flies from Faron Davis's farm.

George Henry had heard all about Faron's one-eyed calf. He'd even made the trek on foot through the woods to see it for himself. That night, he'd dreamed his house was full of mirrors and everywhere he looked, he saw himself, but with only one eye. It took a couple of days before the memory faded enough that he could look at himself when he shaved. Everything seemed to smooth out after that. His daddy, who'd been failing in health, even took a good turn and seemed more like himself than he had in years. He'd done a little hoeing out in the tobacco patch and gathered the eggs for George Henry two days in a row. George Henry was feeling real good about life in general. And then he began finding snakes.

The first one had been in the chicken house when he'd gone to gather eggs. It wasn't the first time he'd caught a black snake trying to steal eggs, but George Henry hated snakes with a passion. He took a hoe to the snake and, in the process, accidentally killed one of his setting hens, too.

Still shaken from the encounter, he headed for the barn, the milk bucket banging against his leg. The milk cow was already in the lot, bawling. George Henry opened the gate to let her into the barn, then turned to follow her in. As he did, something dropped from the rafters above his head and onto his shoulders.

He shrieked and then danced sideways, instinctively, swatting at the weight. When another black snake slid to the ground at his feet, he stood frozen in horror. That it was not poisonous was immaterial to the fact that it was the second one he'd seen this morning, and this one had been around his neck.

The milk cow was still bawling, waiting for her grain, as well as to be relieved of the milk she was carrying. It was all he could do to fasten her into the stanchion. By the time he sat down to milk her, he was sick to his stomach. George Henry was big on omens, and these were too obvious to miss. Something bad was happening, and he feared it would get worse. In a panic to get pack to the house, he grabbed the cow's teats and began pulling in earnest, anxious to finish the job.

Finally he was through. He turned her loose and gave her a quick slap on the rump to hurry her through the gate. Unused to the rough treatment, the old cow tossed her head and looked back at George Henry, as if to say, what's the deal?

It was a trick of light and a little paranoia that caused the mirage, but when she turned and bawled, he saw only one eye in her head.

At that point he started toward the house on the run, the bucket of warm milk slopping against his leg as he went. By the time he got to the back door, he was crying and yelling his daddy's name.

The old man met him at the door with the broom in one hand and something long and dark in the other.

"Look here what I killed in the kitchen," he said.

George Henry's eyes rolled back in his head, and he staggered backward off the porch.

"What's wrong with you, boy?" the old man muttered, and reached for the milk before George Henry let it spill.

But George Henry was past answers. The way he figured it, they'd been cursed. He headed for his truck, praying with every step. If the prayers didn't get rid of the curse, then it was going to be up to him to get rid of the witch that had laid it.

It was just after 1:00 P.M. when Luke reached the outskirts of Camarune. Catherine had been unusually quiet all the way back, and he feared she was still angry with him for not letting her stay at the cabin. He reached for her hand and gave it a gentle tug. When she smiled at him, he breathed a sigh of relief. If she was mad, it didn't amount to much.

"Darlin', are you hungry?"

"A little."

"Want to give Lucy's Eats another try?"

She smiled. "I'm game if you are, and I promise not to make any more scenes."

He frowned. "It won't be you who's in trouble if there are."

"Thank you for being on my side about this," she said.

"It's about being on the right side, darlin'. I've had just about all of that witch crap I'm willing to handle. The next person who even gives you a nervous look is going to have to answer to me."

"Thanks."

He gave her hand a quick squeeze, then returned his attention to the road. A couple of minutes later, he parked in front of the town's only café, then jumped out to open the door for her.

"You, sir, as my grannie would have said, are a gentleman and a scholar."

He grinned. "I don't know about scholar, but I do what I can in the other department."

"You're not too shabby as a lover, either," she added, giving him a prim little smile to punctuate the suggestive remark.

His grin widened even more. "Are you flirting with me?"

"Yes, I believe that I am."

"You know that could get you into all kinds of trouble."

"Exactly *what* kinds did you have in mind?" she asked.

He leaned over and whispered in her ear.

Her eyebrows arched. "Why, Sheriff, that sounds positively indecent."

He chuckled, then impulsively kissed her on the cheek as he started to lead her inside. They were all the way at the door before Catherine spun around.

"Oh, wait! I forgot my purse."

Before Luke could stop her, she was running back toward his car.

He started to follow her, then looked past her instead, to the man across the street. In the back of his mind, he recognized George Henry's face. But it was the rifle George Henry was carrying that he focused on first. After that, everything seemed to happen in slow motion.

George Henry lifting the rifle and taking aim.

Catherine grabbing her purse from the seat and closing the door.

Luke running toward her with his gun drawn, shouting for her to get down.

The pop of rifle fire echoing within the small valley.

The stunned expression on Catherine's face as the shot knocked her on her face.

The red stain spreading on the back of her shirt.

The knowledge that he'd just let down the only woman he'd ever loved.

And then everything that had been in slow motion became a frantic series of vignettes.

Maynard Phillips wrestling George Henry to the ground before Luke could kill him.

Luke screaming into his two-way for someone to dispatch a Medflight chopper to Camarune

George Henry being led away in handcuffs to await the arrival of Luke's deputy, Donny Mott.

Luke's frantic efforts to stop the flow of blood from Catherine's shoulder.

And the look of guilt and horror on Lovie Cleese's face.

15

It was just after midnight when Catherine woke up, expecting to see the open rafters of Annie's cabin above her head. Then she moved, and the pain that racked her body sent her gasping for breath. Almost immediately, Luke was at her side.

"Darlin', don't move."

She moaned.

Luke put a steadying hand on her shoulder as she started to shift.

"Easy, baby, you'll hurt yourself."

Her eyelids fluttered, adjusting to the dim light. Then she wrinkled her nose, sensing unfamiliar scents.

"Where am I?"

"In Lexington," he said, and then added, "you're in a hospital."

A frown creased her forehead. "Hospital? Why?"

Luke hesitated, but telling her a lie wouldn't make her pain any less. He spat out the answer as if the words had a bad taste.

"You were shot."

"I was what?"

He sighed. He could understand her confusion. It was a nightmare to him, and he'd witnessed it all.

"Someone shot you...in the back."

"Oh, my God," she moaned, and then clutched at his hand. "Am I going to die?"

Luke's chin trembled. "No, darlin', but there for a while I thought I might."

She sighed, trying to concentrate past the need to sleep.

"Who?" she whispered.

"George Henry Lee."

Her eyes drooped, and then she licked her lips.

"Do I know him?"

The fear in her voice made him sick. It was all he could do to keep talking.

"I don't think so, sweetheart."

When she started to cry, his own vision blurred.

"Catherine, I am so sorry. I promised I would protect you, and I nearly got you killed instead."

"Not you," she muttered. "Them."

Then she closed her eyes. Moments later, she'd drifted back to sleep.

Luke felt little satisfaction in the knowledge that George Henry was behind bars and that, after the crazy way he'd been talking, might never see daylight again. He felt her forehead and then rang for a nurse. The fever they'd predicted was on the rise.

* * *

Lovie was on her knees in the floor, praying for all she was worth. She'd asked God for plenty of things in her lifetime and received precious few. But after all the years of living that she'd done, she finally knew why. Her prayers had been selfish and self-serving, making promises and deals with a God who only wanted her heart. But now she was being forced to see herself as what she'd ultimately become, and the truth was, she was physically sick of the sight. Not only had her sins ruined a good woman's life, but now they were spilling over into the next generation, as well.

She laid her head on her forearms as she knelt by the bed, trying to get the images of George Henry's capture out of her mind. Spit had been rolling from his mouth as they threw him to the ground, and he'd kept screaming about snakes and curses and killing the witch.

She moaned, then slumped sideways into a heap on the floor. Her heart was fluttering with an erratic beat—sometimes too fast and then hardly at all. Her skin felt clammy, her legs heavy and weak. It occurred to her then that she could die where she lay, and no one would ever know the truth of what she'd done. Just the thought of going to meet her Maker with that sin on her conscience struck terror in her heart. If she died before she was able to confess her guilt, then she would go right where her husband had gone for the sin of killing himself—to hell.

Dear God, she didn't want to have to spend eternity with that man. It had been bad enough living with him here on earth.

It was that thought alone that made her get to her feet. With staggering steps, she dragged herself to a chair near the phone and then sat with a plop. Her fingers were shaking as she dialed the phone; then she held her breath as it began to ring.

"Central Baptist Hospital."

"I'm inquiring as to the condition of Catherine Fane."

"One moment please."

Lovie leaned forward and dropped her head between her knees, trying hard not to pass out before she learned what she needed to know.

"Nurses' station."

She stifled a sob and sat up. "I'm calling for an update on Catherine Fane's condition."

"She's out of surgery. Her condition is listed as serious but stable."

"Thank you, Jesus," Lovie muttered, and hung up the phone.

That news was what she needed to hear. Maybe there would be time after all to rectify what she'd done.

Five houses down, another soul was restless and unable to sleep. All during the dinner Myrtle had been feeding him, Jubal had been treated to a play-by-play of the day's events, right down to the telling of George Henry shooting the witch and being carted off to jail. Added to Myrtle's astonishment had been the unique experience of seeing a Medflight helicopter set down in Susie Bell Watley's backyard on the outskirts of town to take away that woman who'd been shot.

At that point, Jubal had choked on his food and Myrtle had to abandon her tale in order to keep him from dying with one of her dumplings in his mouth.

But now that everything was quiet, Jubal Blair couldn't sleep. He kept thinking of that woman, so like his wife, being gunned down in the back in the middle of the street. He grimaced with frustration and pounded the bed with a fist. There was a time in his life when he would have taken care of George Henry Lee in his own way.

Almost instantly, he heard the thump of Myrtle's feet hitting the floor and wished for the ability to speak. He would tell her to get her fat ass back in bed.

"You all right in here?" Myrtle asked, sniffing the air for signs that he'd messed the diaper he wore, anxious to get it off before he messed up the bed.

He grunted and waved his arm, indicating he wanted her out.

She ignored him, as she would have a fly, turned on the light and lifted the sheet from his body, inspecting him as she would have a baby in a crib.

His eyes glittered with hate, his lips stretching thinly over pale gums and yellowed teeth. In the harsh glow of the overhead light, he more resembled a snarling dog than a man.

To his dismay, Myrtle shook out a pill and forced it between his teeth, then put a glass of water to his lips and lifted his head, helping him drink. He had two choices—choke or swallow. He chose the latter, mentally cursing her as she exited his room.

A short while later, in spite of his fury, the sleeping pill began to work and Jubal's eyelids dropped. He slept, less restless than before, but locked into a nightmare without any end.

Up on the mountain, the hunter had taken refuge inside his cave; for the moment, the need for scavenging was past. He moved within the shadows, sleeping when he grew weary, eating when his body grew weak. His focus now was on the objects he dug out of the wood. They were many and lined up on shelves, on the floor; a few were even packed in rags and in boxes.

Eagles in flight, their feathers so distinct they looked real.

Horses pawing the sky, with nostrils flared, and manes and tails in seemingly fluid motion.

A bird on a nest, suspended for all time above her openmouthed babies with a worm dangling down from her beak.

A strutting rooster.

A setting hen with a single chick's head peeping out from under her wing.

They were nothing to him but a means to a trade. He wasn't aware of their simple beauty, or even conscious of his skill. It was just something he did.

So he sat in the cave, like a mole in the ground, moving blindly through the hours and the days of his life. Only now and then did he venture out of the cocoon, and when he did, it was more often in pursuit of the nightmare that played in an endless loop inside of his head—the never-ending cry of a newborn baby's wail.

Four days after Catherine's surgery, her condition was upgraded from serious to good. No one was more relieved than Luke. That first night he'd spent at her side, he'd come to a decision. The day she was released from the hospital, he was going to ask her to marry him. If he had to, he would pack up and go with her to Texas. He'd almost lost her before he'd had a chance to tell her that he loved her, and to hell with fear and pride. He wasn't going to lose his chance again.

Catherine's days had run together. She had little concept of how long she'd been there, or how close

she'd come to dying. All she knew was that every
time she'd opened her eyes, Luke had been standing
by her side. During that time, she'd made a decision. She was going to tell him how she felt. Life
was too short for regrets.

A couple of days later, she was on her way back
to her room from physical therapy, shaky and weak,
but well-pleased with her prognosis. She would not
lose any function or mobility in her right shoulder.
The bullet had been deflected by a rib, sending it
on a different path than the one aimed straight at
her heart. She was lucky, the doctors said, but Catherine knew better. She didn't believe in luck, only
blessings, and it had been a blessing from God that
had saved her, not chance.

As the orderly turned her wheelchair around the
corner, she saw Luke standing in the doorway,
awaiting her return. She hadn't seen him since last
night, when she'd made him go home to his bed.

"Good morning," she said, waving at him as
they came up the hall.

"Same to you, darlin'," he said, and laid the
palm of his hand on her head as they passed, needing to reconnect physically with the woman who
held his heart. "Did you sleep well?"

"Thanks to those little miracle pills, just fine,"
she said, and then started to stand. Almost immediately, the room began to spin. "I'm getting

dizzy,'' she said, and sank back into the seat as the
orderly reached to steady her descent.

"Let me," Luke said, and lifted Catherine bodily
from the wheelchair, then laid her in bed.

As soon as her head touched the pillow, she
breathed a quiet sigh of relief and closed her eyes.

"Thank you," she said, waiting until the room
stopped spinning before she opened them again.

"Are you all right, Miss Fane?" the orderly
asked.

"Yes," Catherine said. "At least, I will be as
soon as everything lands."

"You've had a pretty rigorous workout. I suggest
you get some rest," he said, then wheeled the chair
out of the room, leaving Luke and Catherine alone.

"Just lie still, baby," he said softly. "Don't talk
until you feel like it."

Then he began fiddling with her covers, pulling
them straight and tucking them beneath her arms
the way she liked.

Catherine caught his hand and pulled it to her
face, then laid her cheek against his palm.

"I'm all right."

He sighed, then kissed her, then kissed her again.
When he raised his head, there were tears in his
eyes.

"I love you, you know," she said softly.

He shook his head in disbelief. All this time he'd
been afraid he would never hear those words from

her lips, and now they come without warning—and so easily.

"Ah, God, darlin', I love you, too...more than you will ever know."

"Hold me, Luke."

"I'm afraid I'll hurt you."

She smiled. "I can take the pain. I just can't take losing you."

He eased onto the side of the bed, watching her face for a sign of distress. All he saw was love. His hands were trembling as he slid them beneath her shoulders. Her breath was soft against his face as he laid his head on the pillow next to hers. She slid one arm around his neck, holding on to him as tight as she could.

"Oh, Luke, I'm so scared. I'm not as strong as Annie. I won't stay in this place anymore. They won't let me. But I can't bear to lose you."

He hated the fear in her voice and the people who'd put it there.

"Don't worry about it right now. You need to concentrate on getting well. I don't know how, but we're going to work this out."

Tears slid from the corners of her eyes onto her pillow.

"Promise?" she asked.

"Promise."

"Seal it with a kiss," she begged.

He smiled, then lowered his head. It was the best deal he'd ever made.

Late that afternoon, Catherine was asleep when her first visitors arrived. Luke looked up to see Abram Hollis and a woman he assumed was his wife standing in the doorway. The woman was plump and fair, with a healthy sprinkling of gray in her short brown hair. Like Abram, who still favored his overalls, she was dressed simply—a plain cotton dress, with tiny pink flowers in the print that matched the pink in her cheeks. Luke got up from his chair and motioned for them to come in.

He lowered his voice, speaking just above a whisper, so as not to disturb her sleep. "Abram, it's good to see you."

"And you, boy," Abram said. "Though I'll have to say I'm not happy about the reason. This is my wife, Polly. Polly, this here is Luke DePriest, the sheriff I was tellin' you about."

"Oh, the man who's sweet on Catherine?"

Luke grinned. "The same. It's a pleasure to meet you."

She started to smile, and then looked at Catherine. The smile stopped as she looked to Luke.

"How is she doing?"

"Better…in fact, much better."

A cold look came on Abram's face. "I'm expect-in' to hear that you have the man in custody who did this to her.''

"He's there, and there he'll stay," Luke said shortly.

"That's good," Abram said.

Behind them, Catherine began to stir. They turned, watching as she slowly opened her eyes.

"Abram! You came," Catherine said, and then held out her hand.

Abram grasped it gently, as if someone had just given him a baby chick to hold.

"Course we came," he said gruffly. "You're family. And speaking of family, it's about time you met the most important part of mine. This here is Polly."

The older woman moved to the side of the bed and patted Catherine's cheek, as if she'd known her for years.

"Annie wrote of you so often, I feel as if I already know you," she said.

Tears came.

"Now, none of that," Polly said. "It was Annie's time, and you did what was right in bringing her home. You're the one who matters now. You've got to concentrate on getting well so you can come to dinner. I make the best chicken and dumplings in Kentucky, just ask my men.''

Abram smiled, and it struck Catherine then that she'd never seen him smile before. She watched as the trio began to converse about the man who'd tried to kill her. But her concentration was on another subject. She kept watching the way Abram and Polly leaned toward each other as they spoke, and the way he would often touch her arm or her shoulder if she moved too far away.

She loved Luke like that. That pressure in your chest when you hear your loved one laugh—and the fear in your gut when you know that they're in pain.

"Catherine, are you all right?" Luke asked.

She blinked. "I'm sorry, what did you say?"

He laid the back of his hand against her forehead, checking for fever.

"I asked if you were all right."

"Yes, I was just woolgathering."

"Abram and Polly just invited you to their house for Christmas dinner."

Surprised, Catherine grinned. "Christmas? That's a good six months away."

"Not for Polly," Abram said. "She's already working on her presents."

"Really?"

"I always give homemade presents," Polly said. "They're so much more personal."

"I agree," Catherine said. "Grannie used to do the same."

"Then you'll come?" Polly asked.

Catherine hesitated, then looked at Luke. He winked. That settled it for her.

"I'd be honored," she said. "I'll bring pecan pies. They're my speciality."

"Better bring a bunch," Abram said. "They're my favorite."

Polly blushed. "Abram! I do declare."

Catherine grinned. "Don't worry, Polly. I'm not insulted. Dancy's already been at my biscuits, so I think I'm getting the picture."

Polly had to laugh along with the others. It was a well-known fact in their family that feeding behind Dancy could be risky to your health.

The Closed sign was still on the door at Cleese's Grocery. It had caused quite a stir in Camarune. No one could ever remember Lovie closing in the middle of the week—not even for a holiday.

Nellie Cauthorn had already made it her duty to check on Lovie's health and was at her front door, knocking repeatedly without getting an answer. It wasn't until Lovie's next-door neighbor came out to water her roses that the mystery was solved.

"She's not home," Hester Amarind shouted.

Nellie turned. "She's not at the store, either. Do you know where she's gone?"

Hester shook her head. "She left early. Before eight, I think." Then she added, "She was driving her car."

Nellie frowned. She couldn't remember the last time she'd seen Lovie behind the wheel.

"Thank you," she said, and bolted off the porch, making a beeline for the church. Maybe Preacher knew something she didn't. Of course, there was every possibility that he wouldn't tell her once she'd asked. Ever since that day at Myrtle Ross's house when the sheriff had come to break up the crowd, he'd been giving her judgmental looks.

It wasn't her fault that everything in Camarune was in a mess. Everyone knew it was that woman, Catherine Fane, who'd picked the scabs off old wounds. Of course she was sorry that the woman had been shot, but that was George Henry's doing. Nellie's conscience was clear as she scurried toward the church. Her mission today was to find out where Lovie had gone.

She would have been shocked to know that Lovie was, at that very moment, in Lexington, pulling into the parking lot of Central Baptist Hospital.

Lovie parked, then glanced at herself in the rearview mirror. Her right eye was twitching. A sure sign of distress. Right now, there was nothing she could do about the twitch, but she was about to do something to correct the distress. The trip had been harrowing for a woman her age, especially one who hadn't been past the city limits of Camarune in years. But she'd made it. And now that she was here, she felt an obligation to look her best when she faced Catherine Fane.

She licked her finger and then stroked a wayward piece of hair, smoothing it back into the tight roll twisted to the back of her head. But there was nothing she could do about the wrinkles the years had put on her face. Resigned to her fate, she hooked her purse over her arm, then reached for the flowers that she'd cut from her own yard. The vase in which she'd arranged them was one of her favorites. The way she looked at it, giving away a vase was the least she could do.

Cradling it carefully against her breasts, she got out of the car. The scent of hydrangea and bougainvillea was sweet beneath her nose as she made her way to the door. A man on his way out stopped to hold the door for her. She nodded and smiled a quick thanks as she moved through. She missed little courtesies like that. The only men she came in contact with these days were shopping for their wives, or coming to buy beer. She couldn't think of a one, except maybe Luke DePriest or Preacher, who would bother, and right now, she was not on the top of their friendship lists.

She stopped at the information desk for directions to Catherine's room, then moved toward the elevator. As she stepped on, careful not to spill the water in the vase, a cool draft of air-conditioned air slipped down the back of her neck. She gasped and then turned, expecting the devil himself to be standing there smiling. But she was alone in the car.

She pressed the fourth-floor button, then braced herself against the wall as the door slid shut. Before she was ready, it had opened again. It was get off or go home.

She exited quickly, pausing to get her bearings. A few moments later, she started down the hall, in search of room 416.

When she arrived outside the door, she hesitated, listening to the muted sound of laughter coming from inside. The urge to leave before they saw her was strong, but then she thought of what was at stake. She set her jaw and knocked, knowing full well that when they saw her face, the laughter would cease.

"Someone's at the door," Catherine said. "It can't be hospital staff. They don't bother to knock."

"I'll see," Luke said, and got up from the side of her bed and quickly strode to the door.

To say he was surprised when he saw who was waiting to come in would have been understating the obvious. His first instinct was to tell her to get lost, and then he saw the flowers she was holding and the plea on her face.

"I need to talk to her," Lovie said. When Luke hesitated, she added, "Please. It's important."

"Who is it?" Catherine called.

Luke stepped back, holding the door ajar. Lovie moved past him and came inside.

Catherine's first instinct was to put something between her and the woman, but she knew of nothing that would counter sharp words. She looked to Luke for support. He nodded. At that point she relaxed.

Lovie set the vase on the table beside Catherine's bed.

"I brought you flowers," she said, and then resisted the urge to roll her eyes for stating the obvious. "They're from my yard."

"They're lovely," Catherine said.

Lovie shifted nervously, then glanced up at Luke, who'd stationed himself beside Catherine's bed.

"She's doing well, I hear."

"No thanks to George Henry," Luke snapped.

Catherine reached for his hand, then tugged gently until he moved to sit beside her on the bed.

"Yes, I am," Catherine said, and then added, "I have to say, I'm surprised you're here. I hope it's more than curiosity that brought you so far."

Lovie wanted to smile, but there was too much guilt in her soul for joy to come through.

"I needed to see for myself that you were going to be okay."

"Why would you care?" Catherine asked. "In fact, why would anyone in Camarune suddenly care? They didn't exactly send out a great welcome when I came."

It was all Lovie could do to look her in the eye.

"I know," she said. "And that's partly why I'm here."

Catherine glanced at Luke. He shrugged, as if to say he was as puzzled as she.

"So...you're the one they elected to assess the witch's condition?"

Lovie paled beneath her paint and powder. "Don't," she moaned, and reached for the foot rail of the bed to steady herself. "Don't say that."

"Say what?"

"Witch," Lovie whispered, then pressed her fingers against her lips to keep from crying. It took her a few moments to gather her wits, but it was enough for Luke and Catherine to see she was truly upset.

"Luke, maybe you should get her a chair," Catherine said.

"No, no," Lovie said, taking a step away from the bed. "I won't pretend I'm welcome, and justly so. Just give me leave to say what I came to say."

"I'm listening," Catherine said.

Lovie dabbed at her eyes with a handkerchief and then took a deep breath.

"When will you be released?" she asked.

"Tomorrow evening."

Lovie nodded with approval. "Tomorrow's Saturday, the next day is Sunday."

"Your point being?" Catherine asked.

"I want you both to come to Sunday services in Camarune."

Catherine was already shaking her head before Lovie had finished.

"Wait, here me out," Lovie said. "Both you and Luke, and all of Annie Fane's family, must be there. You have to tell Abram and Polly and their sons and wives. They deserve to hear what I have to say, as much as you do."

"And what's to keep someone else from finishing the job George Henry started?" Catherine snapped.

Lovie kept shaking her head. "That's what I'm trying to tell you. After this Sunday service, you'll never hear anyone call your grandmother a witch again."

Catherine leaned forward before she thought, then winced in pain.

Instantly, Luke had his arm around her, coaxing her back against her pillows.

"What is it?" Catherine begged. "What do you know that we don't?"

Lovie would only shake her head.

"Not now," she said. "On Sunday. And you'd better be there, because I'll never have the nerve to say it again."

"I knew there was something," Catherine muttered. "All the way through Grannie's journals, you were the friend who stood by her."

Lovie gasped. "She kept journals?"

Catherine frowned. "For years...as far back as her marriage to Billy, then up to the time everyone turned against her. After that, nothing."

"What kinds of things did she write?" Lovie asked.

"Just day-to-day stuff...like the people who came to her for help, and the kind of herbs and tinctures she would give them."

Lovie stilled. "Did she write about me?"

Catherine nodded. "Many times." She hesitated before adding, "Even about your misfortunes."

"Dear God," Lovie muttered, and looked away. This was worse than she'd thought. Who could have known there would be a written record that, if the right people had read it, would have ended the lie years ago?

"Why does that matter?" Catherine said. "Lots of people keep journals."

But Lovie would only shake her head. "You'll know. They'll all know soon enough."

Having said what she'd come to say, she turned to go.

"Wait!" Catherine cried.

"No," Lovie said. "No more. Not now. Just come to church on Sunday. That's all that I ask."

Moments later she was gone, leaving as abruptly as she'd arrived.

"What do you make of that?" Luke asked.

Catherine frowned. "I don't know, but I need to be there. If there's an answer to why everyone turned against my grandmother, I deserve to know."

Luke didn't like the odds, but he knew how to even them.

"Okay, darlin', I'll make sure you're there. But we're not going in alone."

16

Catherine was dressed and waiting for Luke to come and get her when a nurse walked into her room with a wheelchair.

"Looks like you're ready," she said. "I take it that good-looking man who's been hovering around your bed is coming to take you home?"

"Yes, but it will be a while before I really go home."

"You're not from here?" the nurse said.

Catherine shook her head.

"Where *do* you live?"

"Texas."

"Humph. Well, then do me a favor, okay?"

"Like what?" Catherine asked.

"Tell me when you're leaving. I'd hate to see him pining away all alone."

Catherine laughed, but the nurse's teasing hit a sore spot. Things couldn't get much worse in Camarune, and the good Lord knew she wasn't ever going back there again once she'd heard Lovie out and gotten her things from Annie's cabin. Luke seemed so sure that they would work things out, but she didn't see how.

"I'll just leave the wheelchair. You'll need it when they take you down to the lobby," the nurse said. "And good luck to you, Miss Fane."

"I'm going to need it," Catherine said.

After the nurse left, she moved to the window. But the parking lot was on the other side of the building, so watching for Luke wasn't possible. There was nothing to do but wait. She settled into a chair where she could see the door and then proceeded to fall asleep.

Typically, everything at the sheriff's department had gone to hell in the proverbial handbasket just as Luke was walking out the door. A tractor-trailer rig hauling crude oil had run into the back end of a truckload of hay, spilling both loads all over the road and into the ditches that ran along both sides of it. By the time the hazardous-material crew arrived to clean up the spill, it looked like someone had tried to tar and feather the place and failed.

After two hours of hassling with both companies and the HazMat team, Luke left Donny Mott in charge and headed toward Lexington, resisting the urge to run lights all the way. When he finally pulled into the parking lot of Central Baptist, he breathed a sigh of relief. A few more minutes and he would get Catherine; then maybe their lives would return to a semblance of normal. He exited the elevator, resisting the urge to run. But by the time he got to room 416, he was breathless. But when he pushed the door open, instead of hurrying inside, he stopped, mesmerized by what he saw.

Catherine was asleep in the chair, her head tilted slightly to one side, her hands folded primly in her lap. She was wearing the clothes he'd brought for her yesterday—a blouse that buttoned up the front and a pair of clean jeans. It was all he could find in her suitcase that was clean. He'd loaded everything up then, including her dirty clothes, and brought them back to his house. She didn't know it yet, but he was taking her home—to his home. At least there, he knew she would be safe.

She sighed and then shifted her position, wincing as the movement caused her pain.

Luke felt sick all over again, remembering the look on her face as the bullet had ripped through her back. He'd come so close to losing her. It wouldn't happen again.

He walked toward her, then squatted down beside her chair and brushed his hand across her knee.

"Catherine…sweetheart, it's me."

She was smiling before she opened her eyes.

"You're here!" she said, her voice still slurred from sleep, and laid her head on his shoulder.

He brushed the side of her cheek with a kiss. "As

they say in my business, I was unavoidably detained. I'm sorry.''

"You're here now. Whatever it was, it didn't matter.''

"Yeah, well, tell that to the trucker who just lost his load outside of Crying River this morning.''

"Oh, no, was anyone hurt?''

Luke grinned. ''Just their feelings. The HazMat crew wasn't too happy with the mess they made. Picture a load of crude oil spilled on top of a truck-load of hay. It looked like someone had poured chocolate syrup all over the Jolly Green Giant's bowl of shredded wheat.''

Catherine laughed, although the image was staggering. She could only imagine the mess that it had made.

Luke stood, then held out his hand. ''Are you ready to go?''

"As long as it's with you, always.''

"Good to hear,'' Luke said. ''Because you're coming home with me. I've already moved your stuff down from the cabin and—''

"You don't have to sell me,'' she said. ''I'm relieved.''

He grinned, then shook his head. ''Darlin', you don't know how many ways I've practiced telling you that. How dare you agree with me before I can get it all said? What's a man to do with someone like you, anyway?''

"Love me?"

He cupped her face, then kissed her, lingering longer on her bottom lip than he had any right to do.

Catherine was the first to pull back, and then only because she heard someone coming.

"That kind of stuff could get you in trouble."

Luke sighed. "I'm already in so deep I can't see over."

She sat down in the wheelchair and then took his hand. "So hold my hand and maybe neither one of us will sink."

Too moved to speak, Luke grabbed her hand. He was still holding it when the nurse came in to take them down.

"Aren't you going to take your flowers?" she asked, pointing to the vase Lovie had brought.

Catherine started to say no, then relented. "Yes, I suppose I should," she said.

"I'll get them," Luke said, and carried them downstairs, then handed them to Catherine after he'd buckled her in the front seat of his car.

"You going to be able to hold these all the way home?" he asked. "I can pour out the water and prop them in the backseat if you think it will hurt you."

"No, I'll be fine. I've never been given a peace offering before. I'd hate for something to happen to it before it's had time to work."

"Amen to that," Luke muttered, then shut her door and hurried around to the other side.

Luke's home was oddly comfortable, something she hadn't expected from a bachelor. Furnished in oversize, overstuffed chairs and sofas in shades of brown and blue, everything fit his size and his life-style to a T. The pieces were large enough for him to slouch down in, with colors muted enough not to show dirt. Lamps were scattered about the room, ready to light dark corners, and there were some interesting pictures on the wall that she suspected were of his family.

Luke's boots echoed on the hardwood floor as he helped her into the room.

"I'll show you the bedroom first, then you can lie down wherever you want. There's a television in my bedroom, as well as the one in the living room." Then he touched the side of her face and smiled. "And you won't hurt my feelings if you would rather sleep in the spare room. I want you to be comfortable, wherever that might be."

"In your arms?"

"Good answer, darlin'."

She shivered. God, but she loved that sexy growl in his voice.

"Maybe you could show me the rest of the house, and then I think I will lie down, but in here on your sofa. Except for a couple of programs I saw in the hospital, I haven't seen a newspaper or a news report since I got to Kentucky.''

"You haven't missed anything," Luke said. "The government's still messed up, and both parties are blaming each other."

She laughed. "I think you missed your calling. You should have gone into broadcasting. You summed it up so well."

"One does what one can," Luke said, and then took her by the elbow. "Now for the grand tour."

Catherine was asleep on the sofa with the remote still in her hand. Soup was heating on the stove, and Luke was on the phone, issuing orders as he stirred.

"Just make sure they get at least one lane open before nightfall," he told Donny, "and don't let them give you any bull. I'm home for the rest of the day, so if you need me, you know where to call. Yeah, I'm glad she's here, too. The trick is going to be to get her to stay."

He disconnected, then turned the fire out under the pan and set it on a back burner before turning to the refrigerator. The last time he'd looked, there'd been some ham in here. Maybe he'd make some sandwiches to go with the soup.

After the turmoil of the day, night came quietly to Crying River. The HazMat crew was finished,

Donny Mott had gone home to his wife, and traffic was flowing at a normal pace again.

It had taken Catherine a while to get ready for bed, and then she'd put off lying down. The more she delayed, the more certain Luke was that something was wrong. Her eyelids were drooping, her speech slurring from exhaustion, and yet she kept finding another reason to stay up. Finally Luke stopped her in the hall on her way from the kitchen.

"Catherine, you're asleep on your feet. Please, darlin', it's time to get you in bed."

"I just thought I'd watch the news before—"

"What's wrong?" he asked, then pulled her into his arms, cradling her head on his chest. "You have to trust someone. Please let it be me."

She sighed. It felt so good to be held—to know that this man was willing to stand between her and the world.

"I'm not sure," she finally said. "But I think I'm dreading tomorrow."

"You mean, going to church in Camarune?"

She looked up, her chin quivering slightly. "I keep remembering the feel of the bullet in my back and then seeing your face fading before my eyes. I didn't know what had happened, but I knew I was dying. I thought I'd never see you again."

"Hell," he muttered, and then picked her up and carried her to the bed.

The moment her head touched the pillow, she let out a soft moan.

"I'm so tired."

"Then sleep," Luke said. "I'll be right here beside you tonight, just like I'll be beside you tomorrow. And don't forget, Abram and his sons are coming, as well."

"You finally got in touch with them?" she asked.

"Yes. He called tonight while you were in the shower."

"I wonder what Lovie's going to say?"

"Who knows," Luke said. "But if it will clear up this mess, I'm willing to listen. Now close your eyes. I'll be here when you wake up."

"Promise?"

"Darlin', I would be here for you every morning for the rest of our lives if you would have me."

Her chin started to tremble. "Oh, Luke, are you proposing to me?"

"Are you going to say yes?"

"Probably...maybe...if this would all go away."

It wasn't what he'd wanted her to say, but he understood.

"Then I'd better see what I can do to make it happen," he said softly. "In the meantime, close your eyes."

Catherine moved a little closer, until her head

was resting against his chest. Slowly she began to relax.

Luke held her until she fell asleep. Then he crept out of bed, rechecked the locks and turned off the lights and TV. Minutes later, he crawled back into bed and pulled the covers over both of them. He moved a little closer to Catherine, then closed his eyes. The next time he opened them, Sunday morning had arrived.

Preacher Cauthorn was trying not to be angry on the Lord's morning, but it wasn't easy. Nellie had scorched the collar on his favorite white shirt, and now he was going to have to wear the old blue one, even though it was too tight under the arms and too short in the sleeves. He yanked it from the hanger and began buttoning it up, muttering beneath his breath as he began to dress for church.

Nellie, on the other hand, was in the living room, dressed and waiting. She picked up the phone and called Lovie to see if she wanted a ride to church. She let it ring several times, but there was no answer. Finally she hung up.

She was still in the dark as to where Lovie had gone the other day. She'd asked, purely as a matter of conversation, of course, but to her surprise, Lovie had told her it was none of her business. Insulted, Nellie had taken herself home without purchasing the milk she'd gone there to buy.

Now, here it was, almost nine o'clock on a Sunday morning, and Lovie wasn't answering her phone. Surely she hadn't gone missing again. Footsteps sounded in the hallway. She scurried away from the phone and quickly sat in her chair. Preacher was acting so strange these days, and if he saw her near the phone, he would assume the worst and accuse her of meddling again. He came into the room, stretching his clothes and frowning.

"That shirt looks a little snug," Nellie said. "Maybe I need to put you on a diet."

"This shirt was a little snug the day you bought it, which was more than five years ago, but thank you for noticing."

Nellie pursed her lips and arched her brows. So, it was going to be one of those days, was it?

"We've been invited to the Snellings' house for Sunday dinner," Nellie said.

Preacher groaned. "Not the Snellings again! You know I cannot abide that woman's cooking."

Nellie's lips pursed a little tighter. "That's not a very godly thing to say."

"God doesn't have anything to do with Frances Snellings' cooking. If he did, it wouldn't taste so vile."

Nellie sniffed. "Fine. If you don't want to go, then you're going to have to be the one to tell her we're not coming. However, I don't know what we'll have once we get home, because I assumed we would be dining out and didn't prepare anything ahead.''

''Never mind,'' Preacher muttered. ''We'll go this time, but in the future, don't accept any more invitations without talking to me first.''

They left in a huff, neither speaking to the other as they began the four-block trek to church. It was not an auspicious beginning to the day.

Lovie had been standing before the full-length mirror in her bedroom for more than fifteen minutes, eyeing her aging reflection. There'd been a time in her life when her belly had been flat and her legs firm and slim—when her breasts had pushed against the bodice of her clothing, rather than pointing the way to her thick, paunchy waist. Last night she'd considered cutting her hair and then decided against it. It was a little too late for that type of penance, so she'd wound it up in its usual knot and pinned it at the back of her head, instead. Her dress was old, but it suited the day. Since she was about to murder her reputation, it seemed fitting to be wearing black.

The phone rang in another part of the house, but she let it ring. The only thing she had to say this morning would be said in church.

Finally she turned away and went to get her purse from the dresser. On the way to the front door, she had a brief sensation of déjà vu. It took her a moment before she connected with the memory and when she did, she felt sick. The last time she'd been this scared had been the morning she'd awakened to find Emory's dead body hanging from the rafters of the garage.

As she opened the door, a brief moment of cowardice almost sent her back inside, and then she took a deep breath and walked out, firmly closing the door behind her.

The day was warm and sunny. A perfect day for a walk. As she stepped off the porch and headed for the sidewalk, she couldn't help thinking that she was walking to her own funeral.

Catherine's belly was in knots. Last night her sleep had been a series of nightmares. She'd awakened with a headache that was growing bigger by the hour. Added to that, the weight she'd lost made her clothes hang on her body, and nothing she had was proper to wear to church. Her hair was in tangles, and her incision was sore. Finally she sat down on a chair in front of Luke's dresser and started to cry.

Luke found her in tears and immediately took her into his arms.

"Catherine...darlin', what's wrong? Are you that scared? Because if you are, we can call this thing off. If Lovie has something she wants you to hear, she can come say it to your face."

"My clothes are all wrong, my hair is a mess,

and I don't know what hurts worse, my wound or my head.''

It was so exactly what he hadn't expected her to say that he had to stifle a smile.

"A pain pill will take care of your aches, and I'll gladly brush your hair for you, but I don't think I can do a thing about your clothes. However, I have to tell you, you look damn good to me. Besides, do we care what they think about your clothes?''

Catherine stopped. Luke was right. They already considered her in cahoots with the devil. Why should it matter what they thought about what she wore? She leaned her head against his shoulder as her tears began to dry.

"Thank you. I needed to be reminded of that."

"Hand me the hairbrush and relax. I'll have the tangles out shortly, and then we need to leave. We're supposed to meet Abram and his family at the south edge of town. I thought we should arrive together. A little show of force can't hurt.''

Catherine looked up into the mirror, meeting his gaze in the reflection, and then handed him the brush. He began drawing it through her hair in slow, steady strokes. She closed her eyes and shivered, remembering he made love in the very same way.

"That feels good," she said.

"Does it, baby?"

"Oh, yes."

"That's fine, just fine," he said softly. "I like to make you feel good."

She managed a laugh. "Oh, but you do...and you do it so well."

He grinned and then winked as he continued to brush.

She watched him, admiring the crispness of his white, short-sleeved shirt, the neat, black string tie and the black Western slacks he was wearing.

"I suppose it doesn't matter what I'm wearing," she said. "You look good enough for both of us."

His grin widened. "Keep talking, woman, and you'll find yourself back in bed with more on your plate than you can handle."

She laughed again, only this time, she felt it. "You're good for me, Luke DePriest."

His grin died as he laid down the brush. "I would be good *to* you as well, Catherine Fane...if you'd let me."

His obvious reference to last night's proposal ended their play. Suddenly it was back to the worries again.

"Luke?"

"Yes, darlin'?"

"Do you think a *show* of force will be enough, or will we need the real thing?"

"I don't know what to think," Luke said. "But trust me. Whatever happens, I've got it covered."

* * *

Preacher was in the middle of the opening prayer when he became aware of the sound of shuffling feet. He ended quickly with a resounding amen and then looked up with a smile on his face. It froze there.

Finally, Lovie thought, and stood to face the congregation. The sick feeling she'd had all morning was getting worse. *Lord, just help me get through this and I'll never ask anything of you again.*

She turned to Preacher.

"I'm sorry to interrupt services, but my special guests have arrived." Then she pointed to the people sitting on the two front rows. "As a favor to me, I'm asking if you people would mind moving back so that Catherine Fane and her family could sit?"

A horrified gasp rose from the congregation. After a questioning look at Preacher, who was still mute, they began clearing the rows as Lovie had asked. As they did, Lovie motioned for Catherine to come down.

She shrank back against Luke.

"Easy, darlin'. We're right here beside you."

Abram laid a hand on her shoulder. "No one's going to hurt you again. We won't let them."

His sons and their families echoed the promises. Now it was up to her.

Catherine looked to Luke, then clutched at his

hand. He led her forward, scanning both sides of the aisle with a cold, angry face as they went.

Preacher came to his senses just as the last of the visitors was seated. He looked wildly at Lovie and then up at the cross above the front door, praying for guidance, but when he started to speak, his welcome was too forced to be real.

"We welcome all here to the house of the Lord, and when you leave, we pray you take His spirit with you."

A faint amen came from somewhere in back.

"Now then, if you would turn to page—"

"Wait!" Lovie said.

Again all eyes turned to her. Whispers began drifting about the room, speculating as to whether the old woman had finally lost her mind.

Preacher stepped down from the pulpit and started toward Lovie. She waved him back.

"I invited these people here today, because in one way or another, they're all connected to Annie Fane."

A hiss of disapproval swept through the room as Lovie felt the ground melting beneath her feet.

"And," she continued, "because of that, they, above anyone else in this town, deserve to hear what I have to say." At that, she looked directly at Catherine, then stepped up to the altar, just as she'd done when she and Emory were wed. She took a deep breath and turned to face the congregation.

"When I was a young, foolish woman, I wanted more than life had chosen for me to have. I had a home and all the comforts a person could need, but I wanted more. I had a husband who, in his own way, tried to love me, but I wanted more." When she looked at Catherine again, her voice started to shake. "And I had the best friend a woman could have, and I wronged her—because I wanted more. I can no longer live with the guilt of what I've done, or the wrong I did to her. That woman's name was Annie Fane."

A profound silence had enveloped the room. Catherine was staring in disbelief, wondering how this was all going to end.

"Annie had a way with herbs. She grew them, and cooked with them, and sometimes even healed with them. She took nothing in trade, but gave from the goodness of her heart. And one night, my husband Emory came knocking on her door, begging her to come, claiming to her that I was dying."

A child whimpered in the back of the room and was quickly hushed. Lovie continued.

"With an extract of mistletoe, a good dose of common sense and her faith in the Lord, she kept me from bleeding to death. I should have been grateful, but in reality, I was scared out of my mind. At that point in my life, I would rather have died than face the truth of what I'd done, and in ignorance, Annie had saved me to face my own truth."

Catherine had scooted to the edge of the seat. Luke's hand was on her back, reminding her he was there, and Abram's knee was pressing against her thigh, honoring his promise to keep her close, but she couldn't stop staring at the old woman up front.

Lovie took a handkerchief from her pocket and dabbed at a line of sweat on her upper lip.

"That night I miscarried the only child to ever take root in my womb, and it was not my husband's."

A soft hiss of disapproval sifted through the silence. Lovie flinched, but kept on talking.

"Emory Cleese could not father children, and the fact of his condition was well known to some in those days. When he learned the reason for my hemorrhage, he lost his mind. Three days later, I found him hanging from the rafters in my garage."

Someone moaned, and another began to quietly sob, but Lovie kept her focus on Catherine's face.

"In a way, Emory's death set me free. Now there was no one to face with my guilt, except Annie. She was the only person left living who knew I'd lost a child. My next mistake was in not trusting the strength of Annie's friendship. Instead of confiding in her and asking her to keep my secret, I decided the best way to make sure she never told was to make sure she had no one to talk to. It was warped, and it was cruel, but I thought only of myself."

Catherine reached blindly for Luke's hand, taking comfort as he pulled her back beneath the shelter of his arm.

Lovie continued.

"Within the space of three months, I had broken three of God's holy commandments. I had committed adultery, borne false witness against a friend and killed my own child. And you know what? My lie worked like a charm. It was so easy. Everyone was willing to believe the worst about Annie. I never knew why. Maybe it was because she was so strong within herself that they wanted to see her fail, but I do know that I succeeded beyond my wildest dreams. Within weeks, she was both hated and feared."

Lovie swayed and grabbed onto the pulpit for strength. Preacher jumped to catch her, but she waved him away.

"Sit down, Preacher. Please."

He sat.

"I hadn't been satisfied to ruin my life, I had to ruin Annie's, as well. The years passed. Sometimes I could forget that Annie Fane even lived, and then someone would come into my store with some crazy tale about the witch and a curse that she'd cast. I can't tell you how many times I wanted to tell—to stop the evil from spreading. But the years had taken a toll on me, too. I was selfish and weak in spirit, and I wanted my neighbors' goodwill. So

I let the lie stand. Then the Blairs were killed on Pulpit Rock the same night Annie disappeared. No one knew what had happened, so they blamed it on her. Said it had happened because she'd cursed them somehow."

Lovie started to cry.

"I swear to you, her family, on whatever honor I have left, that if she'd stayed, I would have told. But she was gone, and I saw no need to put myself in a bad light when Annie wasn't around to save."

Lovie pointed at Catherine. "Then, like the proverbial bad penny, Annie did return. Only she didn't come back as I'd imagined. You cannot know my grief when I learned that she was dead. But that grief was nothing to the horror I felt when I realized that you people—people who had never even seen Annie Fane—were transferring your stupidity and your hate to Annie's kin. Again I faltered. Again I was weak. I kept waiting, trying to tell myself that when Catherine left, it would all go away. But like before, I waited too late and almost got her killed. I have never prayed so hard as I did for her recovery, and, Catherine, I'm telling you now, in front of God and everyone here, that I am sorry to the depths of my soul."

Then, for the first time, she looked out at the congregation, making eye contact with every face.

"And I'm telling all of you, in front of God and Annie Fane's kin, that the only evil ever practiced in this town came from me. Annie was not a witch, she was an angel. God forgive me for crucifying her.''

The silence within the room was frightening. Even the children had sensed the ominousness of the occasion and were unnaturally silent.

Lovie slumped, but her heart was free. She turned loose the podium and stepped down from the altar. She glanced at Catherine one last time and tried to smile, then dropped her gaze to the floor and started up the aisle.

The disapproval and disgust from the congregation were almost physical, but Lovie wouldn't look up—couldn't look up. Her days in Camarune were over.

"Lord have mercy," Abram Hollis said, and then put his arm around Polly and hugged her. His sons and their families were silent, but their expressions on the faces were those of disbelief.

Luke kept watching Catherine's face, waiting for a sign of her reaction. Other than a slight tremble to her chin and some tears in her eyes, he couldn't tell what she was thinking.

Suddenly someone in the back of the room called out the word "whore."

Catherine jerked as if she'd been slapped and then pulled herself to her feet, her eyes blazing.

"Stop!" she cried. "It stops right now!"

17

Catherine was so angry she was shaking. She pulled away from Luke and stumbled to the front of the church.

"This hate does not transfer from me to her. It stops right now, do you hear? Haven't you people learned anything from your mistakes? Few of you here ever set eyes on my grandmother, yet you swore she was a witch. None of you knew me, yet you hated me enough to want me dead. Now you're ready to cast another stone at one of your own. Lovie Cleese doesn't stand alone with this guilt. You were all ready to believe the worst."

Lovie had stopped in the middle of the aisle, her back to Catherine, her head bowed.

Rationally, Catherine knew that feeling anything from rage to hate would have been normal, but emotionally, it was sympathy that came first. Defeated by her own tender heart, she called out the old woman's name.

"Lovie."

Lovie jerked as if she'd been slapped, then lifted

her head and turned. The look on her face was one of acceptance. Whatever Catherine Fane had to say was nothing more than she deserved.

"In the end, you did the right thing, and I thank you. All of us thank you. But it's over."

Lovie was stunned. Did this mean she was forgiven, or was she hearing something she just wanted to hear?

Catherine pointed at the congregation. "Do you hear me? It's over."

Lovie's expression went from shock to hope. The longer she stood there, the straighter she stood. Finally she turned and walked out of the church, her head held high. The girl was right. It *was* over.

Catherine moved, only then realizing that Luke and Abram were right beside her. Suddenly her physical strength gave way. She reached for Luke, leaning against him as he encircled her with his arms.

"Home...take me home."

He took her out of the church. The entire Hollis family exited behind them as quietly as they'd entered, leaving Preacher Cauthorn and his congregation to stew in their own shame.

Catherine paused on the steps outside the church, silently watching the old woman in black who was walking up the street.

"You did a good thing in there," Abram said. "Annie would have been proud."

Catherine looked at him then, her eyes brimming with tears.

"It's a shame she wasn't with us today. She's the one who should have been present."

Luke put his hand on the back of Catherine's head, then gave her a hug.

"Now, darlin', who's to say she wasn't?"

"Amen," Abram said, then looked to his family. "We'll be going now. I expect you to stay in touch."

"I promise," Catherine said, and then watched as they loaded themselves into their vehicles and drove away.

Luke took her by the hand. "Are you ready?"

She nodded.

"Then let's get out of here. I have a sudden need for fresh air."

Catherine knew just what he meant. Despite the fact that Lovie had dispelled the myth fostering so much hate, a feeling of miasma still lingered. It would take more than one confession to alleviate the presence of the evil that had been here for so long.

She followed Luke to the car, still holding his hand. As she slid into her seat, the congregation inside the church began to sing.

"Listen to that, would you?" Luke said.

They were singing "Amazing Grace."

Catherine listened, following the first verse in her mind, then looked at Luke.

"Good choice, don't you think?"

He leaned down and kissed her. "I was real proud of you in there." Then he added, "Buckle up."

She grinned as he shut her in and then circled the car.

Luke slid behind the wheel. "Ready?"

She nodded.

He started to smile as he pulled out of the parking lot.

"You know what this means?"

"What?" she asked.

"That there's nothing standing between you and me now but a yes."

Catherine laughed, but that wasn't entirely true. There was still that little matter of her birth. Could—no, *should*—she marry a man like Luke without sharing that kind of secret? She didn't think so. Look what a mess keeping secrets had caused Lovie Cleese.

"You know how I feel about you, mister, but right now, one revelation a day is about all I can handle."

Luke grinned and then sighed. Again, it wasn't exactly what he'd wanted to hear, but it wasn't a no.

"Just wanted to stay top man on the dance card, darlin', that's all."

She laughed again, but all the way back to Crying River, her head was swimming with new fears. Once it dawned on everyone that her grandmother hadn't caused the Blairs' deaths at Pulpit Rock, someone might begin to wonder who had.

Catherine was elated. Life was once again moving in its normal rhythm. Two days ago she'd been pronounced completely healed and released from the doctor's care. Yesterday Luke had taken her to lunch and then to the local jeweler to try on rings. Just for the fun of it, he'd said. But his heart had been in his eyes as he'd watched her trying them on.

Last night Catherine had gone to sleep in his arms and awakened the same way. Everything inside of her said this was the man, but her conscience still wasn't clear. Before she took this man's ring and full possession of his heart, she had to tell him the truth. He was coming at noon to take her to Annie's cabin to retrieve her Jeep, but she wasn't going just for her vehicle. She was going to find Fancy's grave, and Luke was going to help her. He just didn't know it.

The hunter opened the door and then stood within the shadows of the cave, letting his eyes adjust to the light. It wasn't often he went out in the day, but he was pretty sure it was Monday, and he needed a new shirt. If he was right, every woman on this side of the mountain would be doing her wash, and every one with a husband would have clean shirts on the line, flapping in the wind.

He turned to pick up the carving he'd chosen and held it up to the light. About twelve inches tall, it was of an eagle in flight. One bird for one shirt. It would be a fair trade.

He slipped out of the cave and then paused, secure under the cover of the trees, scanning the area to make sure he was alone. He saw nothing but birds and the day-old footprints of a deer. Nodding to himself, he started his trek.

It wasn't until he'd come to the third farmhouse down that he saw clothes hanging on a clothesline. He stood for almost an hour, watching the residents of the house coming and going until he knew everyone's location.

A woman and young girl were outside in their garden picking beans. A teenage boy had slipped out the back door with a fishing pole in his hand about a quarter of an hour before his father came out, calling his name. The hunter waited, knowing the boy wouldn't answer. He had vague memories of once doing the same. Finally the man seemed to give up and went back inside, coming out the front door a little later. The hunter watched as the man got in his truck and drove away. The only dog he'd seen on the place had gone with the boy. It looked safe to go in.

As always, it was easy. He took the shirt that he wanted. Not the best. Not the worst. Just a plain blue chambray with snaps. Buttons had a tendency to come off, and he had no needle or thread.

He laid the eagle in the clothes basket beneath the line and then covered it with towels. He was heading for the trees when the sound of approaching voices stopped him. That would be the woman and girl, coming from the garden. He flattened himself against the side of the house and then stilled, waiting for them to go in the house.

To his dismay, they stopped outside. He heard something thump on the porch and assumed they'd put down the basket of beans they'd been picking. Then he heard water running and remembered an outside faucet on the side of the house. His mother had always washed the dust from her feet before going inside. He wondered if they did that, too. Patience was a virtue he'd been forced to practice, and so he waited. Soon he heard the little girl's voice.

"Mama, is Daddy going to bring me some firecrackers?"

"You know your daddy doesn't like those things. They make the chickens quit laying."

The little girl whined, "Fourth of July is no fun without fireworks."

"We'll see fireworks at the park in Camarune when we go to Aunt Myrtle's picnic."

The little girl's whine grew louder. "Why do we have to go to Aunt Myrtle's house every year for Fourth of July?"

"Because she can't come to ours," the woman said. "She takes care of Mr. Blair, and he doesn't like to be moved around."

"I don't like that old man," the little girl said. "He scares me."

"That's not a very Christian thing to say," the mother said. "It's not Jubal's fault he can't move."

"Why's he in that chair?" the little girl asked.

"He had a stroke years ago, and you ask too many questions. Let's get these beans in the house out of the sun. There's plenty to do before tomorrow's picnic."

The door slammed, and they were gone. It was what the hunter had been waiting for, but he couldn't remember what he'd been going to do. His skin had gone clammy, and he felt a strong urge to retch.

Jubal Blair. Jubal Blair.

The shirt that he'd taken was dangling from his hands as he blindly turned and walked away.

Jubal Blair. Jubal Blair.

He walked through the garden and into the tobacco field beside the house, a tall scarecrow of a man with a long, flowing beard. It was sheer luck that got him to the trees without being observed, but it was instinct that got him back to the cave.

The darkness sheltered him as he crawled onto the cot and curled in upon himself. His pupils had dilated, his body was trembling. Even though it was an even seventy-two degrees year-round inside the cave, sweat ran profusely down his face.

Jubal Blair. Jubal Blair.

It was like looking at a ghost, only the ghost wasn't there. Just the memory of a horror he'd spent half his life trying to forget. A low moan slipped out from between his clenched teeth, and then he started to wail. Softly at first, and then louder, until everything within a quarter-mile radius of the cave heard the gut-wrenching screams. Birds took to the air, and small animals took to their dens. But the hunter was past help. Everything he'd spent years trying to forget had, in one careless moment, come flooding back.

Jubal Blair. Jubal Blair.

Why wasn't he dead?

Time had no meaning for the hunter, and he wasn't aware of the moment when his thoughts turned around. One second he was blind to nothing but pain, and the next he was on the edge of his cot, swallowing rage.

The son of a bitch wasn't dead.

Just the thought made him shake. Everyone was dead, even him. Yet Jubal Blair lived on. He sat there in shock, staring down at his shoes, remembering…remembering….

Blood poured from his body in several places. He stopped more than once to put pressure on the wounds, but it didn't seem to help. Twice he passed out, and each time he came to, it was the sound of a baby's wail that pulled him back into this world. Fancy was dead. He remembered that. But the baby—their baby—was lost. Was that her cry he heard? Or had the dogs already carried her off and it was just the shriek of his own soul following Fancy to heaven?

Sometime during the night it began to rain. He felt the raindrops hammering upon his face and then, harder, upon his limbs. Blood mingled with the raindrops, turning the runoff beneath him into a pale pink stream. But he wouldn't give up that last breath until he knew what had happened to their child. Their baby was lost. He had to get well.

The hunter blinked and then drew a deep, shuddering breath. Jubal Blair was alive. Maybe that was why his search all these years had been in vain. Maybe Jubal had had the child all along.

He pulled himself up, stumbling to a small table

against a far wall. A piece of mirror had been propped in the middle of a small shelf. He lit a candle, holding it high above his head as he looked into the glass.

The features that met his gaze seemed muddied in the flickering light, but his eyes were distinct and had the look of hunted prey. Shock hit him then. No wonder he'd failed to find the baby. He hadn't been looking, he'd been hiding. But no more.

He set the candle on the shelf next to the mirror, then grabbed a pair of scissors from a drawer. With angry jerks, he began hacking at the long, wiry length of his hair, letting it fall about his feet on the floor. When it was just above his shoulders, he started on his beard. Twice the two entangled. Frustrated, he ponytailed his hair at the back of his neck with a narrow piece of leather, then continued his task.

Minutes passed. Painful minutes in which the man behind the whiskers began to emerge. The more he cut, the faster his heart began to pound. He knew that man. But it had been years since he'd given him a name. Finally the scissors gave way to a knife, and he stood, scraping at his face until there was nothing left to hide behind. The knife clattered as he dropped it on the table. He closed his eyes, gathering strength for the reunion about to unfold, then took a step back and looked up—straight into the eyes of Turner Blair.

But there was more yet to do. He needed his suitcase—the suitcase he'd packed on that night long ago. The one he'd dropped in the woods as he'd given chase to the dogs.

Frustration mounted as he began digging through piles, moving boxes aside, then stopping in quiet anger, trying to remember where it might have gone. Finally his gaze fell upon the space beneath his bed. Moments later he was down on his knees, stretching his arm as far as it would go. It was there! He pulled it out, grimacing in satisfaction as he set it on the bed.

Inside was the suit that he had planned to wear when he and Fancy wed. He shook it out, ignoring the musty scent and wrinkles, then began to strip, replacing his garments with those he'd just unpacked.

A short while later, he slipped into the suit coat, testing the sleeves for length. His shoulders were some wider, but his body was leaner. It would do. Then he put on his hat and walked out of the cave—ready to face Jubal Blair.

Luke was almost running when he came in the door.

"Catherine, where are you?"

She came out of the kitchen, drying her hands as she walked. When he picked her up and began swinging her around in his arms, she laughed.

"What's up? I've never seen you so excited."

"I'm not excited, I'm in love," Luke growled, and stole numerous kisses from the side of her neck.

Her heart skipped a beat. "Oh, Luke, so am I...so am I."

He stopped, his playfulness turning to need. "Are you going to marry me, darlin'? I would sure like to know."

"You ask me again tomorrow and the answer is yes."

Surprised, he put her down, then cupped her face with his hands.

"Why then? Why not now?"

"Because there's something about me you still don't know, and I won't go into a marriage without total truth."

He started to argue, then stopped. "Fair enough. But I can tell you right now, there's not a damn thing you can tell me that will make me change my mind."

"I know," Catherine said. "I really do. But please, trust me to do this my way."

Luke sighed. "When you put it that way, how can I refuse you?"

She grinned, then changed the subject. "So, are we still going to get my Jeep?"

"You sure you're up to driving it back by yourself?"

"Yes, yes, a thousand times yes. I'm me again. Let me prove it."

"Then grab your things and let's go. We'll pick up some sandwiches on the way."

A couple of minutes later, Catherine came out of Luke's house with her purse and Lovie's vase.

"What are you going to do with that?" he asked, as she sat down and began buckling up.

"Return it."

He glanced at her, trying to read her body language, then headed for the highway. It was impossible to tell what she was feeling about seeing the old woman again.

"I could do it for you on my way back through town," he offered.

"No, I'll do it." Then she smiled. "But thanks."

Soon they were on the outskirts of Camarune. As they drove into town, Maynard waved at them from the pump where he was fueling someone's car. They waved back.

"He helped save your life, did you know that?" Luke said.

Catherine looked startled. "No! How?"

"Right after George Henry shot you, he came out of nowhere and wrestled him to the ground. Things might have turned out a lot different if he hadn't been there to help me."

Catherine was quiet for a moment as they continued through town.

"I'll have to thank him for that."

Luke nodded. "That would be good."

Another length of silence grew between them, but it was a comfortable quiet. Catherine kept thinking of what she would do when they got to the cabin.

Maybe she would just blurt the whole thing out, like, "Gee, Luke, I've been meaning to tell you about my parents. They were murdered, and I think my mother is buried in Annie's backyard." Or maybe something more specific, like, "Oh, by the way, Jubal Blair is my grandfather, and he's the man responsible for the deaths at Pulpit Rock." Any way she said it, it was going to be a shock.

It wasn't as if she was afraid he wouldn't love her anymore, because none of that was her fault. But what was this news going to do to the uneasy peace in Camarune? Besides Jubal, how many people were still living who would be directly affected by the news? Would this put her right back in the hot seat with people who'd just decided to give her a second chance?

"We're almost there," Luke said.

Catherine's anxiety grew as she looked out the window. The looming presence of Pulpit Rock was on her right. That meant Annie's cabin was just up the road and around the curve. A few minutes more and the rest of the story would unfold.

"Everything looks okay," Luke said, as he

pulled up and parked. "I'll check the cabin while you see if your Jeep will start. It's been sitting quite a while. We may have to jump it."

That suited Catherine just fine. It delayed the moment when she would have to confess. She headed for her car as Luke went inside the cabin. After one failed try, the engine came to life. She left it idling and got out, intent on following Luke inside. Just as she started up the steps, she heard the radio in his patrol car begin to squawk.

"Luke! Luke!" she yelled.

He came out on the run. "What's wrong?"

"Dispatch is trying to reach you."

He bolted toward the car.

Catherine went on into the cabin. It was strange, but, in a way, it felt a little like coming home. But this wasn't a day for reminiscing. There were more important things to do. A few moments later, she came out with Annie's keepsake box and the rest of her journals, carefully placing them on the floorboard of her Jeep. Thinking Luke would follow, she started toward the backyard, when he yelled at her to wait.

She turned.

"Sorry, darlin', but duty calls," he said, as he caught up. "Are you ready to leave?"

Catherine was disappointed, but, in a way, also relieved. If he couldn't stay, then she didn't have to spill her secrets just yet.

"Almost," she said. "I was just going out back to check on some stuff."

He hesitated, obviously not wanting to leave her alone.

"Go on," Catherine said. "I'll be right behind you."

"I've got to take a report at a farm on the way down. There's been another robbery."

Curious about the man she'd seen in the woods, she had to ask, "What did he take?"

Luke almost grinned, then decided it wouldn't be proper, considering the fact that he was supposed to arrest this man if they ever caught him.

"Traded a shirt for a foot-high carving of an eagle, I'm told."

Catherine sniffed. "Sounds like they got the better end of the deal, if you ask me," she said, then added before he could argue, "And I've got to return Lovie's vase."

"Then I'll meet you at Maynard's and follow you home."

She nodded. "I love you. Be safe."

Luke paused, his mind suddenly straying. The plain yellow sundress she was wearing was loose on her body, more for comfort than for style, and with her face in shadow and the sunlight caught in her hair, she looked timeless. He was so scared about her hesitation to say yes to his constant proposals, and it had been so damned long since he'd been able to love her—really love her.

"Luke?"

He took her in his arms, hesitating but a moment above her mouth before he lowered his head.

The kiss was hard and hungry, and Catherine clung to him, feeling his desperation and his need.

"Tonight," she whispered, when he finally let her go.

"God help me to wait that long," Luke said, and then frowned. "Damn, I hate to go."

She smiled. "See you down in the valley."

"Hurry," Luke said, and gave her a last quick kiss before he headed for the car.

She waved until he was out of sight, then walked toward Annie's backyard. The directions to where Fancy was buried were etched in her mind. Right beneath a black walnut tree and north of Billy's grave.

Her heart was thumping erratically as she cornered the house, only to realize as she stared across the yard that, unless she could see the nuts they dropped, she wouldn't know a black walnut tree from an oak.

"Lord," she muttered, then took a deep breath and started toward Billy's grave. There were other directions, but what had they been? Was it ten yards north of Billy's grave, or was it twenty—no, fifty?

She stopped at the end of Billy's headstone, then

looked to the north. Almost immediately, her gaze focused on a tall, stately tree, separated from the others around it by several feet. She began to walk, staring intently at the ground and bushes beneath, and reminding herself that nearly thirty years had passed. If Annie had left any kind of marker, it would probably be long gone.

She circled the tree, then circled it again, shoving aside the branches of the scrub brush growing beneath, but saw nothing. She glanced at her watch, surprised that fifteen minutes had already passed. Her Jeep was still running, and the last thing she wanted was to show up late in Camarune and frighten Luke into thinking she'd come to some harm. As much as she hated to admit it, she was going to have to come back.

As she turned to go, she caught a glimpse of something white. Poking it with her toe didn't yield any clue, so she bunched her skirt around her waist, kneeling for a closer look. It was only a bit of a stone protruding from the ground.

She flattened her hands against the grass to push herself up, and as she did, she felt another stone just below the surface of the grass. Less than a foot away, she found another, then another, all in a row, all but invisible to the human eye. Her heart skipped a beat. Was this it? Had Annie marked Fancy's grave with a circle of stones?

She moved back to the first stone she'd seen and

traced the same path, only in the opposite direction. Within seconds, she'd found a second stone there, then another, and another. She stood abruptly and began kicking the grass away from those that were buried. When she was through, she stepped back, eyeing the pattern they made and then froze. Now, for the first time in her life, she was as close to her mother as she could ever be.

Without warning, sobs tore up her throat.

"Damn you, Jubal Blair. Damn you for taking her away."

She came down the mountain with tears still in her eyes, but her heart was at rest. Certain that she'd found what her Grannie had wanted her to find, she was ready to move on with her life. Telling Luke would come easy, and after that, everything else would have to work itself out.

Her thoughts began to wander, and only after she realized she was coming into town did she return her attention to her driving.

As she turned down the main street, she saw a man come out of Maynard's station, then cross in front of her car. She slowed to let him pass, absently noting that while he was tall and straight, he walked with a marked limp. She kept having the feeling she'd seen him before. His hair was dark and long, but tied neatly at the back of his head. Although the suit he was wearing looked too hot for the day, he didn't seem disturbed by the fact. As she pulled up to the grocery store, curiosity sent her to the rearview mirror for one last look, but he had disappeared from sight.

Someone nodded to her as they passed on the street, then hurried on their way. For Catherine, it was a case of too friendly, too late. Bracing herself for the confrontation, she picked up Lovie's vase and got out of the car.

At the jingle, Lovie looked up. Even though she saw nothing but the woman's silhouette, she knew who it was.

"I came to return your vase," Catherine said, and set it on the counter by the cash register.

Lovie smoothed at her hair, then swallowed nervously before moving around the counter.

"I meant for you to keep it," she muttered.

"I didn't know," Catherine said, and started to leave. But the pain in Lovie's eyes reminded her too much of the pain she'd seen in Annie's during her last days. She shrugged, then pointed toward the vase. "Maybe I could have a refill sometime?"

Lovie pressed her fingers against her lips to steady the tremble, then took out a handkerchief and dabbed at her eyes.

"My roses are coming on again," she offered.

Catherine sighed, then almost smiled. "Roses are my favorite flower."

"Mine, too," Lovie said, and then looked away.

"I'd better go," Catherine said.

Lovie took a step forward, then stopped. "Will you wait?"

Catherine turned. "Why?"

"I have something that, by rights, should belong to you."

When Catherine hesitated, she added, "Please?"

"Well...okay," Catherine said.

She hurried into the back room, coming back a few moments later carrying a picture frame. She handed it to Catherine.

"It's Annie and Billy on their wedding day. I took the picture with my camera. When I had it developed, I kept a copy for myself."

Catherine looked, and a wave of sadness swept over her. Those sweet, smiling faces. They were so young, so happy—and so unaware of what fate had in store.

"I thank you," Catherine said.

Lovie shook her head. "It's I who should be thanking you. If there's ever anything I can do to—"

Before she could finish, Nellie Cauthorn burst into the store. Ever since Lovie's revelation in church, Preacher had been making her buy groceries in Crying River. But she had news of gigantic proportions, and Lovie had always been her best friend. God forgive her for even thinking it, but

Preacher be damned. She had to tell someone the news.

"Lovie! Lovie! In a million years you won't guess who—oh…afternoon Miss Fane, I hope you're well…. Lovie, you won't guess who just came to town."

Lovie was so startled by Nellie's appearance that she couldn't think of anything to say except, "Who?"

"Turner Blair!"

"Who?"

"Turner Blair!" Nellie repeated. "Can you believe it? I got it straight from Harold Watts, who was just getting gas at Maynard's. He said he knew him on sight. Said Turner was asking if they knew where he could find his daddy!"

Catherine gasped, then let out a moan.

Both women turned to stare. "Are you all right?" Lovie asked.

Catherine grabbed Nellie's arms, all but shaking an answer from her.

"Isn't Turner Blair dead?"

"Oh, no," Lovie said. "He wasn't with the others that night on Pulpit Rock. He'd left a note at the house. As I recall, something about leaving for a new job and getting in touch. But to my knowledge, he never contacted anybody. Poor man, imagine, coming back to find his daddy like that and his brothers all dead."

Catherine started to shake. She couldn't even focus on the fact that the man she'd just seen was her father, or that he was alive. Knowing what she did, there was only one reason Turner Blair would be looking for his father—to finish what he'd started that night at Pulpit Rock.

Catherine started to shake. "Oh, my God! Oh, my God! He's got to be stopped."

"What are you talking about?" Nellie cried.

"Lovie, call the sheriff's department. Tell them to radio Luke and get him to Myrtle Ross's house. Tell them it's a matter of life and death!"

Lovie blanched. "What are you talking about, girl?"

"Just do it!" Catherine screamed, and ran out the door.

Nellie was stunned, her mouth agape. "That woman might not be a witch, but she's certifiable, I suspect."

Lovie slapped her. "Don't ever use that word in my presence again," she cried, and then headed for the phone.

Nellie was so shocked she forgot to cry. "What are you doing?"

"What I was told," Lovie snapped. "Now either be quiet or get out. I'm going to use the phone."

18

Hot air swirled around Jubal's face as he sat on Myrtle's porch, watching the world go by. Sweat hung above his eyebrows in wet suspense, taunting him by the fact that when they dripped, the briny drops would inevitably burn his eyes.

Down the street, the steady pop, pop, pop of a string of firecrackers was a promise of the day to come. Between the impending holiday and Myrtle's persistent need to furnish her family with a picnic, tomorrow would be a day of torment for him.

His fingers curled spastically around the cane on the arm of his wheelchair, and he began to thump it upon the porch. He was hot, he was thirsty, and a goddamned prisoner to the sweat and the flies.

"I'm coming, I'm coming!" Myrtle yelled.

He paused, giving her a few seconds to appear, after which he would resume his demand.

"What do you want?" Myrtle asked.

He mimicked the need to drink, and then tossed his head toward the door.

"Oh, you're thirsty? It is a little hot out here,"

she said, and then swiped his face with the tail of
her apron. "I'll get you something to drink."

Jubal snorted beneath his breath, then grimaced.
She'd wiped the sweat off, all right, but if he wasn't
mistaken, had left some pork grease in its place,
compliments of the food she was preparing for tomorrow's big to-do.

Another round of firecrackers went off up the
street, followed by a series of wild, childish shrieks.
He looked, half expecting to see some kid running
with his clothes set on fire. But the only person he
saw was a tall man in black, coming down the
street.

For lack of anything else to do, he began to stare,
taking note that the man dragged one leg and that
his clothes didn't fit. A bee flew by his nose, and
he snorted, afraid the damned thing would go up it,
instead. When it buzzed on, he relaxed.

The man was closer now. Jubal could see shadows of his features beneath that wide-brimmed,
floppy hat. If he could have, he would have
smirked. He couldn't remember the last time he'd
seen someone dressed like that—a long black coat,
hanging halfway to his knees, black trousers that
made those long legs look even longer. Then his
gut knotted. His boys had owned suits like that
once. They'd worn them as pallbearers when they'd
carried their mother to her grave. The memory was
painful, and he wanted to look away, yet he found

himself matching his breaths to the stride of the man's steps.

Somewhere in his observation, Jubal realized that the man was staring back at him. The tenacity of the stare at first made him mad. Why, he thought, did people always feel the need to stare at cripples? But the man kept coming closer, and Jubal's anger turned to anxiety, and then to a growing fear. Where was Myrtle? She needed to take him away.

He thumped the porch.

The man kept coming.

He thumped again.

Then the man was there, standing before him with a look in his eyes Jubal had spent twenty-seven years trying to forget.

His mind stopped. Was he dead? He must be, because this was hell.

"Daddy?"

Jubal grunted.

"I killed you. Why aren't you dead?"

Jubal's eyes rolled back in his head, and he began beating the porch with the cane, trying to make the spirit go away.

Turner was in shock. He wouldn't have believed this unless he'd seen it himself, but it was true. Then he thought to himself, he should have known. People had been trying for centuries to kill the devil. He had been naive to believe he had accomplished something that even God couldn't do.

"What did you do with my child?" Turner asked.

Jubal's thumps became harder, wilder. Suddenly the cane flew from his hand, landing with a thump near Turner's feet.

Turner stared at it, then picked it up before moving closer to the man who'd given him life.

"I'm asking you again, and I want an answer. What did you do with my child?"

"Give me that cane!" Myrtle cried, as she came flying through the door.

Indignant on Jubal's behalf, she started to grab it from the stranger when she looked at his face. The glass of water she'd been holding slipped through her fingers, shattering at her feet.

"Oh...oh, my," she gasped, and pressed her hands to her cheeks. "Turner? Turner Blair. Is that you?"

Turner looked at her then, and the expression on his face nearly stopped her heart. Overcome by a sudden urge to pee, Myrtle took a step back.

"Get out," he said softly.

She threw up her hands and ran, screaming as she went that she was going to call the police.

Turner took the cane and pressed it across Jubal's throat.

"I'll ask you one last time, old man, and then I'm going to break your sorry neck. What did you do with my child?"

* * *

He was already on the porch when Catherine reached the corner of Bleeker Street. In the distance, she could hear the faint squall of a siren. It could only be Luke. Thank God Lovie had done as she asked.

Her legs were shaking, her heart pounding in her chest, and the muscles in her back were starting to spasm. Obviously she wasn't as fit as she'd imagined. Then Myrtle screamed.

"God give me strength," Catherine said, and bolted across the street.

She was screaming Turner's name as she ran up the steps, but the man seemed deaf to everything except Jubal. From the corner of her eye, she could see Luke jumping out of the patrol car and people running out of their houses, but she couldn't wait. In another second he would break Jubal's neck. She thrust herself between them as Luke was shouting out her name.

"Stop!" Catherine screamed, pulling at Turner's arms until he was forced to let go of the cane. "He doesn't have your child. He never did. Fancy gave her to Annie Fane!"

In the back of her mind, she heard Myrtle gasp. By tomorrow, it would be all over town. But it didn't matter. Nothing could matter but this.

Turner spun, grabbing Catherine by both arms

and almost shaking her. He hadn't heard anything she'd said until she'd shouted Fancy's name.

"Don't say her name. Don't you ever say her name."

Suddenly Luke was between them, yanking Turner's arm behind his back and grabbing for the other. His terror for Catherine's welfare was second only to his rage at the man who'd tried to harm her.

"Wait!" Catherine begged. "Don't do this!" she cried. "Let me explain."

"He tried to—"

"This man is Turner Blair." Just saying the words made her cry. If only she'd known. He'd been alive, after all.

Luke froze. Turner Blair? Jubal's missing son? There was a moment of total silence as everyone stared at Turner.

But Turner was doing a little looking of his own. This was the woman from the cabin. Before, he'd only seen her in the dark, or from a distance, but he recognized her now, and what struck him as most unusual was that he was looking at a woman who wore his mother's face. He took a step toward her, but Luke firmly pushed him back.

"Stay where you are or I'll haul your ass to jail and sort this out behind bars."

Turner stopped, although the man's threat didn't scare him. He'd been in a prison all his life. And even though he was fascinated with the woman, he had yet to make the connection between them.

Catherine couldn't quit looking at the man in the hat—at his strong, angular face and black hair, and that wide mouth, so like her own.

Luke was getting nervous. He kept remembering a bullet coming out of nowhere and Catherine falling on her face in front of him.

"I want you out of here right now," he said softly.

"No, you don't understand."

"Then make me."

She looked at Turner then, needing to see his face when she finally spoke the words.

"He's my father," she said softly, unaware that Turner didn't hear her. She pointed to Jubal. "And *that*, I'm sorry to say, is my grandfather."

Jubal glared, trading mutual hate.

Turner frowned. Jubal's grandchild? But who? His brothers had all had sons, except for John's eldest, and she'd had long red hair.

"I thought your parents were dead," Luke said.

"So did I." Then she looked at Jubal, her stare hardening. "I wasn't the only one suffering under that misconception, was I, Grandfather?"

The look of rage on Jubal's face was Turner's final truth. He pointed at Catherine.

"You're not Johnny's child. She had long red hair."

Catherine laid her hand on Turner's arm.

"No, I'm not Johnny's girl...I'm yours...yours and Fancy's."

A murmur ran through the crowd as the news was passed along, but Catherine was past caring what they knew. She waited, watching Turner's face. She didn't know that his head was swirling—afraid to hope, afraid to care.

Turner's dark eyes shimmered with a sudden film of tears.

"My baby?"

Catherine nodded.

"Your momma died," he said suddenly, his hungry gaze raking every feature on her face. "My father ran her to the ground with his dogs and killed her."

The despair in his voice broke her heart. "I know. Annie told me."

"Jesus Christ," Luke whispered, only then realizing what was coming undone. Without another word, he moved, leaving nothing but space between Turner and his child.

Turner laid his hand on the crown of her head, and then suddenly yanked it away, uncomfortable with the connection.

"I heard you cry. I looked everywhere for you, but you were lost."

"I wasn't lost. Fancy gave me to Annie before she died."

He grunted, and then his eyes filled with tears. "I should have been there. If I'd been where I promised, none of this would have happened."

"You're here now," Catherine said.

"I won't lose you again?"

Tears suddenly blurred her vision of the dark man's face.

"No, Daddy, you won't lose me again."

He nodded, too moved to speak.

"Will you walk with me?" Catherine asked. "There's a lot I think you should know."

He hesitated, then nodded, and took her by the hand, as he would have a child.

"Wait," Luke said.

Catherine touched Luke's arm, and then his face, her eyes pleading with him to understand. "We won't go far."

Luke struggled with his fears for her, and then finally relented, trying to make her smile.

"Now are you going to say yes?"

She smiled through tears. "Yes, I'm saying yes."

He looked a little startled. "Is that my yes?"

"Yes, my love, yes. That was your yes."

"Then go have that talk with your daddy, and while you're at it, tell him he'd better get ready to give you away."

Catherine looked at Luke, then at Turner, and knew that her heart was complete.

"You have your mother's eyes," Turner said suddenly. "But you have my mother's face."

"Tell me more," Catherine said.

And so he did, beginning as they walked away.

Luke stood, watching them go, and as he did, his gaze fell on a bare patch of earth through which Turner had just walked. He moved closer, then knelt. He knew that footprint—and the notch in the sole. He'd been chasing it all over the mountain for too many years.

He stood abruptly, his first urge to shout for them to stop. And then he thought of the hell that the man had been through and the joy he could see in him now. For a long, quiet moment he stared down at the print, then calmly plowed through it with the toe of his boot. As he moved toward the crowd, he was smiling.

___ Epilogue ___

A year had come and gone since the Fourth of July revelation. Jubal had gotten out of his troubles by dying the same night the lies had come undone. He'd spent his last conscious thought cursing the only One who could have saved his mortal soul. The gates of hell were open wide when he fell in.

As Luke predicted, Turner had given Catherine away at their wedding, and soon afterward, Catherine had moved Turner into Annie's cabin. The shelves that had once been lined with books now held his carvings in all stages of development.

Dancy Hollis, who had never cared for herbs in the same manner as his brothers, had, quite by accident, become an agent for Turner's work. With a growing demand for the pieces, it was ironic that the hunter who'd lived by skill and wits alone was becoming a wealthy man.

It took months for the people on the mountain to realize that the thefts had stopped. Relief that it was over stifled their disappointment in his not having been caught. And since there was little chance that they would frequent the Santa Fe galleries where Turner's work was displayed, it was unlikely that the connection would ever be made between the thief and what Turner was selling.

Six weeks earlier, Catherine had given birth to her first child—a little girl with round blue eyes and a head full of curly blond hair. She was just a bit of a thing, like a small, china doll, and they'd given her the name of Annie.

Today little Annie was taking her first trip out of Crying River. She would be traveling up the mountain above Camarune to her grandfather's house. It promised to be a fine day.

Luke DePriest was in love all over again. Between each load he took to their car, he had to stop by Annie's crib. He smiled as he looked down, thinking to himself that she looked a bit like a yellow caterpillar, wrapped tightly in her butter-colored blanket, with nothing visible but that little face and some wisps of curly hair. It was a bit frightening to know that one day she would be transformed into a young woman.

"Is everything loaded?" Catherine asked.

Luke jumped. Caught again, he thought, and then grinned.

"Everything but my two best girls," he said, and hugged her.

Catherine sighed, then relaxed, molding her body to his as he held her close.

"Are you up to this?" he asked.

She nodded. "It will be good to get out of the house. Besides, I'm sure it's beautiful at the cabin this time of year."

"One thing's for certain, it will be cooler," Luke said, and kissed a favorite spot below her ear.

"Why?" Catherine drawled. "Are you hot?"

"As a two-dollar pistol."

"Maybe you should turn up the air-conditioning."

He smirked. "The only thing I need to turn up...or rather, on...is you. However, until your checkup next week, that isn't happening, so don't remind me, okay?"

"You aren't the only one who's missing...uh... stuff."

His smirk spread. "Stuff? Stuff? You're calling my best efforts 'stuff'?"

"Your best efforts are the 'stuff' of which dreams are made, my love." Then she pointed at Annie, who was starting to squirm. "She's a miracle, Luke. She's sealed our love and healed my father's heart."

Luke kissed her then, tasting toothpaste and peppermint mouthwash and the essence that was his Catherine. Then Annie started to squeak.

"Time to go, little girl," Catherine said, smiling as Luke picked her up.

A short while later, they were on their way.

As they drove into Camarune, Luke took a turn down Main Street, instead of driving straight through.

"Where are we going?" Catherine asked.

Luke grinned. "Just a little side trip. You'll see." Then he pointed.

She looked. "What in the—" Her mouth dropped. A great long banner had been draped across the front of Lovie's sign. Instead of Cleese's Grocery, it read, Welcome Home Annie.

Catherine's lower lip trembled. "How did you know?"

"She called me yesterday, asking when we might be coming through. I told her about today. She asked us to stop by, that she had a surprise."

"This was a good one."

Luke shook his head. "Oh, I don't think this is all of it." He parked, then honked. Moments later, Lovie came out waving and grinning.

"Let me look at her," she cried, peering toward the infant seat in the back of the car.

Catherine reached over the seat and lifted off the blanket that was shading Annie's eyes.

For a long silent moment, Lovie stared.

Catherine felt sorry for the old woman, knowing

that she lived with the ghost of her own child every day.

Finally Lovie looked up. "Isn't she a pretty little thing?"

"You said the magic words to Daddy, that's for sure," Luke teased.

"Is she a good baby?" Lovie asked.

"Yes, ma'am, she is," Catherine said.

Lovie nodded approvingly. "I know you're on your way to see Turner, but I have something for you. Wait here. I'll be right back."

They smiled at each other as she scurried into the store and then came back again, carrying a small white book in her hands.

"Here," she said, thrusting it through the open window and into Catherine's hands.

"Oh, Lovie, this is a wonderful gift," Catherine said. "Her first Bible. Look, Luke, it even has her name embossed in gold on the front of the cover."

"There's something for her inside of it, too. For college someday, or maybe for a trip. I think everyone should see a little of the world while they're young."

Catherine opened the cover. A folded piece of paper fell out in her lap. Still smiling, she opened it up, briefly scanning the words. Then she suddenly stopped, her eyes widening, then filling with tears.

"Lovie...no...you can't do this."

The old woman's face was alight from within.

"It's mine. I can do with it as I choose. I'm the only one left in my family, you know." Then her chin began to quiver. "I destroyed everything that Annie Fane held dear. Her good name—her home—her life. It seems fitting that her namesake should have all that's mine when I'm gone."

Catherine handed the paper to Luke, too moved to speak, but Luke was already getting the gist of what his child had received. Lovie had made Annie her heir. He gave it a quick read, then leaned across Catherine's lap far enough that he could see Lovie's face.

"You sure you want to do this?" he asked.

A single tear slid down her cheek. "It's already done. And it's given me the first good sleep I've had in years. Don't deny her the gift or me the right to give it...please."

Luke glanced at Catherine. All she could do was nod.

"Then we thank you, Lovie, and Annie thanks you, too."

Lovie sighed, and it was as if she'd been holding her breath, waiting for that yes. With a last long, lingering look at the baby, she stepped up on the curb and went back in the store.

Luke looked at Catherine. "This is quite a gift. You know that, don't you?"

"What do you mean?"

"Lovie doesn't just own her house and the store.

She owns most of Camarune. The café, the Laundromat, the pharmacy, even Maynard's station, are some of her rental properties.''

Catherine was stunned. She looked toward the store. Inside, Lovie was at the counter, bagging a customer's groceries; then she looked over her shoulder to the baby asleep in the back seat.

"Life is something, isn't it, Luke?"

"How do you mean, darlin'?"

"We don't always know it, but there's a single, invisible thread that ties all of us together. Sometimes that thread gets broken, but if you go back and pick up the loose ends, there's always the chance to fix it. All you have to do is know how to tie a good knot."

Luke reached for her hand, then lifted it to his lips. "Life is something, all right, but so are you."

"Luke, will you promise me something?"

"Anything."

"Let's not let the thread get too thin."

"It's a promise," he whispered.

"Seal it with a kiss?"

He grinned, then leaned across the seat and gave it his best.

They were silent for a while as their journey continued, each pondering the magnitude of Lovie Cleese's gift. But by the time they neared the cabin, Catherine's spirits were on the rise. Her relationship with Turner was still growing, but she'd learned to appreciate and love his gentle nature.

"There's Daddy," she said, smiling and waving at the man who was sitting on the porch.

"I'll bet he's been sitting there since dawn, waiting for you to show," Luke said as he parked.

Catherine looked at Luke and then smiled. "You're probably right."

"Why don't you run on up and give him that kiss he's been waiting for? I'll get Annie, and we'll get the rest of her things later."

"You sure?"

Luke nodded, then winked. "I'm sure, darlin'. You've got enough love for all of us. Go give your daddy his share."

Her step was light as she got out of the car. Everywhere she looked, she marveled at the things Turner was growing. Flowers, both tame and wild, grew with thick abandon, and in the far corner of the yard, a patch of tomatoes flourished. He had added a railing around the porch, and up one side, new tendrils of a climbing rose were stretching to connect.

Her heart still hurt for the silent look of wonder that always came upon his face when he saw her. She could only imagine the hell that had driven him to search for her all those years.

"Hi, Daddy...we're home!"

"I've been waiting," he said.

Catherine wrapped her arms around him and laid her face against his chest.

"I know, Daddy...I know."

Late that night, high up on the mountain and long after Catherine and Luke were home in bed, a gentle rain began to fall. Soft and warm upon the ground, it quickened hidden creeks and washed the mountain air clean, while watering everything from Turner's flowers to the dark, barren earth beneath Pulpit Rock.

And beneath that barren ground, a tiny seed began to unfurl, sending out feelers that would become roots, as well as a frail, white shoot to pierce the earth, in search of mother sun.